THREE DAUGHTERS

Anna Mitgutsch

Translated from the German by Lisel Mueller

A HELEN AND KURT WOLFF BOOK
HARCOURT BRACE JOVANOVICH, PUBLISHERS
San Diego   New York   London

Three Daughters

HBJ

Originally published in German under the title *Die Züchtigung*

Library of Congress Cataloging-in-Publication Data
Mitgutsch, Waltraud.
Three Daughters
I. Title.
PT2673.I77Z45413   1987   833'.914   86-19554
ISBN 0-15-175298-2

Designed by Francesca M. Smith

Printed in the United States of America
First edition
A B C D E

THREE DAUGHTERS

"Was your mother like you?" my twelve-year-old daughter asks, leaning against the bathroom door and watching me comb my hair. The question jumps at me out of many years of silence. I let my parted hair fall over my eyes. "No," I say, "no, your grandmother was completely different." "Different in what way?" "Think of the opposite." She hesitates, looks at me quizzically. How can she imagine the opposite, when

I am a mystery to her? A mystery and yet something she takes for granted. Like my mother to me, even now.

After her death other people had to explain her to me. Her face sharp, severe, unapproachable through the coffin window. "Mama," I said, thinking she was bound to open her eyes, at least for me. She had begun to smell; her body had been on view for three days. At home I put her photograph in a frame: my mother with her two-year-old daughter, erect, her hair piled high; there she sits, unapproachable. Her strong hands grip my tiny arms like the talons of a bird. Don't look so severe; I need you, I said to the photograph. I couldn't bear her gaze for very long; I put the picture back with the others. She was an unhappy woman, the mourners said, disappointed in life; she didn't trust anybody. "No one liked her," the woman my father married a year later said contemptuously. "She couldn't get along with anybody." I remember how she came home from the grocery store trembling: the doctor's wife, with her everlasting "if you please," had been there again, so of course people like my mother had had to wait. Thirty years' worth of humiliation; I shared them as if they had been inflicted on me, I, the eight-year-old, who lay helpless on the sofa while she took out her accumulated hatred on me, again and again, until I cried with pain and rage. Later I hated her for that; then I forgot her. After ten years I said Thank God she died so young; I would not have flourished under that gaze.

When my child and I vacation in our summer home, the house I grew up in for seventeen years, until I left it and did not come back for five, I sit in her place between the kitchen and the dining table. I handle her dishes and sleep in her bed. I've given away her clothes and removed the saints' pictures and the container of holy water from the wall, but above my bed there is still the drawing I made for her as a present at her last Christmas: a young girl, in profile, looking longingly through a lancet window into an open landscape. The bookcase holds the same photograph as the one she had chosen for her grave picture—it is inserted into her stone—taken when she was twenty-four, with a straight back and heavy, piled-up hair, her delicate face haughty and vulnerable. It isn't the face of a young woman; this face has assumed an irrevocable position toward life. For this face there are no surprises left: You have hurt me; you will hurt me again; I will not leave myself open to your attacks. It was the first year of her marriage, the first year after the war; two years later she became my mother. That's the picture flashing into my head when I think *Mother*: a twenty-four-year-old dressed in the style of the postwar period, with a stiff, unapproachable back. Later on she refused to be photographed.

I didn't think of her again until I was pregnant. At that time she had been dead for many years. I pushed my belly through supermarkets and lusted for head cheese, homemade head cheese. I woke up with the smell of sauerbraten in my nose; I could taste her bittersweet, jellied chocolate pudding between my tongue and the roof of my mouth. My mother came back into my life as food for which I was homesick. When I returned with my new baby to the strange, hot apartment and the baby's father left me, I sat beside the crying infant weeping and calling for her. I wanted to return to her arms; I cried for the love I was denying my own child; I wanted to be cradled, be a tiny thing in her lap, and never have to return to reality. Imprisoned in a small suburban apartment with diapers, a squalling child, dirty dishes, and the feeling that I had been dropped and forgotten by life, I began to understand her. "Mama," I screamed when I threw myself on the carpet behind the locked door, when I smashed the mirror and rammed my head against the wall. "You belong in a mental hospital; you're crazy," said the man whom I had trusted with my life, and I heard my father say, "She wasn't right in the head; she was off her rocker; she should have been institutionalized." I heard my mother yell, "You don't love me, you bastard," her face distorted and bloated as she went into the kitchen to break dishes, systematically, without speaking.

I found her tracks when I took my two-year-old daughter to that old house near the Danube, which I had left at nineteen. I found the carpet beater hanging by the door in the laundry room; it had been hanging there, like her blue denim apron, untouched beneath the attic stairs for twelve years: part of home, part of me, of my childhood, of the fear of life she had passed on to me, beaten into me. I held it in my hand and the old terror came back, terror of the blows, the threats, the impending beating. I held it in my hand and for the first time saw it as a material object, the way she must have seen it: a fat, curved rubber sausage, wound around with an iron spiral, an instrument of torture. I held my child in one arm, the carpet beater in the other.

I was so little when she began to beat me. "We never had a defiant stage in our house," she used to tell the relatives proudly. "You've got to nip that in the bud, at the first no, the first foot-stamping." I listened and was proud to be a well-raised child, a battered child. *Please please Mama, I'll do anything you ask, but please please don't this time, just this one time.* I ran outside and asked strangers to help me; I screamed for my father; I scooted across the gravel walk on my knees and clutched at her legs. It did no good; she beat me. "Never beat a child when you are angry," she told her younger sisters. "Just wait, in two hours when I get back you're going to get it; I'll beat the living daylights out of you." *Dear God, make her die,* I would pray on my knees. How often have I wished for her death, and then it came too soon. I was the best-behaved child in the family: Keep your mouth shut; don't talk when grownups talk; play quietly by yourself; don't bother anybody. "Don't lean against me. Can't you sit by yourself?

Having to lean means you are weak." She permitted herself
no weaknesses. I didn't dare hate her. I couldn't afford to hate
her; she was the only person who loved me. Thank you, Mama,
I had to say when she sat down, exhausted and breathing
heavily, after giving me a beating. Sometimes she collapsed
full-length on the floor and I was scared for her, hoping she
had not fainted from the hard work of punishing me; I felt
guilty for causing her so much grief. Afterward I had red welts
on my legs and hips; they became bloodshot, then blue and
green, and she wrote me an excuse from gym so no one would
ask questions. There were many reasons for being punished:
answering a command with *no* or *why*, coming home from
school half an hour late, giggling with other kids in church,
writing below the line in penmanship and mixing up "f" and
"k," getting a reprimand from a teacher or a C grade.

When I was fourteen I was beaten for the last time. We
became best friends; I told her nothing, she told me everything.
I was well trained; my responses were spontaneous and met
with her expectations: "I don't need a bicycle; it's too dangerous." "Everyone in my class is going to the dance; that's too
juvenile for me." "My friend Eva has a boyfriend; she let him
kiss her, how disgusting."

When she was dead I didn't want to go on living. I sat by
the window in my underwear; snow fell on my legs, but I
didn't catch pneumonia. I felt like a cripple without crutches
who doesn't want to learn how to walk. I kept the severe hairdo
she had chosen for me, wore the calf-length skirts she had
bought me, went in mourning for a year even though I looked
bad in black, and could not find any sense in my life. My
mother sacrificed herself for me, I said, my mother was everything to me, the only person who loved me, who understood
me; I could discuss anything with her. And now she is dead
and I am alone in the world. I sat on her grave weeping and
writing her letters. "If you leave me, I'm going to die," she

had said to me. I went to another town to study at the university; six months later she was dead. *I am responsible for her death*, I wrote in my diary.

Later, when I was a different person and discovered the world, I began to hate her. When I couldn't live without adventures any more, I began to despise her. I became everything that would have outraged her. I slept with every man who wanted me and a lot who didn't. I hitchhiked across two continents and went for three months without bathing. I gave up my career for a man, and gave that man up for another one, just so I could leave him, too. "You are a gypsy like your grandmother, the old witch," I heard my mother say, and suddenly I stopped hating her and forgot her; she no longer had a place in my life. But the fate of mothers lives on in their daughters. One day your mother appears and says, "All right, my daughter, you are old enough; now I'm going to show you my life." I screamed, "You don't love me, you bastard," and saw the bloated face of my mother, saw with horrified eyes how she spat in my father's face; but it was the man I lived with who wiped off the saliva and slapped my face. "I'm not a housewife; I don't want to be a housewife; I'm too good to turn into a moron," I screamed and swept glasses and dishes off the table. "Only a spineless, moronic dumbbell is going to be a good housewife," my mother had said to a young neighbor, who wanted to combine home and career. I tossed my crying baby into her crib, shut the door, and threw against the wall whatever came to hand. Then my first memory came back to me. I am lying in my buggy; it is night; only a night light is on; the buggy is rolling, faster and faster; a bang, another bang; I am on the floor, yelling at the top of my lungs; a hand grabs me, throws me back into the buggy; I hold my breath, panic-stricken; the buggy stands still. Before long I will beat my child, I thought in horror. When I began to rage, when I suspected being spied on and put down by everybody, when

I began to imagine ingenious plots to kill me, I was saved by the wide-open eyes of my mother: They're coming to get me; run, child, before they get you, too. I ran. I packed the two suitcases I had come with; I took my daughter. "You are not going to get me, none of you," I said to my husband, and filed for divorce when I had found a job and a two-room apartment.

My daughter is framed by the bathroom door. She has my mother's chestnut-red hair, her amber-colored eyes, her high forehead with the perfect hairline. She is waiting for an answer. I comb my hair back, check my eye makeup. "Your grandmother had a hard life and no choices. Times were different." There is no right way of saying it. "Look, I rebelled against my mother and her life, and you will rebel against me someday." "And then I'll become like my grandmother?" "Hardly," I say and laugh. Then I say, "Maybe." There are no guarantees, I think; she will be a woman; she will love a man and want to possess him forever; she will marry, perhaps have children, and will she have the strength to save herself?

☐

A little girl is sitting on the broad, uneven steps of the farmhouse. There are crusts of snow on the farmyard walls; above the square they make, the sky is high and blue. A farm hand holding a shovel comes from the barn; cow manure falls soft and steaming on the frozen manure pile. The child is holding a piece of bread and licking the sugar spread on the butter. Chickens scratch in the frozen ground, come tripping up the steps; a hen extends its head and pecks into the bread. The child drops the bread and starts to cry. A maid emerges from the dark hall, carrying a little girl not much bigger than the one on the steps. She grabs the younger child, pulls her back into the hall, puts the other child down, and walks slowly across the yard, hips swinging. The farm hand stands by the barn door, leaning on the manure shovel and grinning. The older girl runs inside the big room; the little one crawls back out on the steps, sucks her thumb, and watches the chickens.

Not until late afternoon, when the nine-month-old Marie starts to scream with hunger, does the girl hired for the barn chores take pity on her; between feeding the hogs and milking, she carries the child into the house. "The baby is like an icicle," she says reproachfully in the direction of the stove, where the children's maid is occupied. "I can't be everyplace at the same time," she sasses back. "Two kids, cook, make beds, wash dishes, sweep; I'm running my feet off." "At least you've got a warm room," the barn girl says and blows on her red, swollen fingers before she takes out the milk pails. "How would you like to have to chop wood all day?" The girl at the stove, herself not yet twenty, picks up the crying bundle and puts it on the table. The diaper is frozen stiff. No mess at least, she thinks.

When Marie's mother came home from the hospital two weeks later, the child's legs were paralyzed. The mother was weak, having just undergone her first mastectomy. Chores had piled up; Fanni, the older child, clung to her skirt day and night. In her absence her husband had found comfort else-where, and he continued to stay out all night. Little Marie lay in her bed whimpering; gasping, she fought for air, and her face turned blue. Her mother picked her up, spooned some cooked cereal into her mouth, and sat her on the floor, but the child fell sideways. She was as helpless as a newborn. Spring arrived and the doctor was sent for: soon the work in the fields would start, and here they were having trouble with the child. An unlucky child, Friday's child, her mother thought, helpless and bitter as she looked down on the tuft of red hair and the doughy face. An unwanted child. Born nine months after the first.

"Nothing doing for six weeks," the midwife had said to the

farmer when she passed him with the bloody rags on the way
to the stove. But he fell on his wife the very next night. "You
are hurting me," she moaned. "Shut up," he said; "do you
want me to find somebody else? All I have to do is snap my
fingers." She said nothing and gritted her teeth; it would be
over with in a minute. He was twelve years younger than she,
the handsomest man in the village. Walking in front of him,
the women started to sway when they felt his eyes on their
backs. "You beast," she spat through her teeth, but he didn't
hear; he rolled over on his side and turned his back to her.
She sat up; the pain was furious, and she jammed two diapers
between her legs. The baby had been large, and the tears had
to heal by themselves; yet he, the euphoric father, shot his
seed into her torn womb night after night. Nothing can happen
as long as you're nursing, that's what they said. But it did
happen. Nine months later Marie was born. Another girl. The
farmer walked out disappointed; surely she could have come
up with a son and heir the second time. This time when he
climbed on top of her she fought him off. "You pig, I'm not
a breeding machine." He got up and kicked the basket with
the sleeping baby contemptuously: what's a wife for? "Watch
out, tonight I'm going to make you a boy," he said to the
saloonkeeper's daughter, when he unbuttoned his shirt and let
down his pants in her bedroom. She pulled her nightgown
over her head and giggled. "You're not going to make me a
thing, you horny billygoat you," she said laughing.

The doctor prescribed ointments for massaging into the
skin. Twice a day, half an hour each time—who had time for
that? Cooking, milking, mowing, cleaning out the barn; those
things came first. Livestock needs to be fed and milked; those
animals bellow louder than a hungry child. The incision in
her breast was not healing properly; the doctor advised more
rest. How? she wanted to know. He shrugged his shoulders.
"It's not polio," the doctor said. "I'm at my wits' end. What

you need now is a miracle." Marie was sixteen months old and still paralyzed. Her large eyes followed the shadow-play of leaves outside the window; sometimes she reached for them. And she could hold the bottle with the diluted cereal herself. Her small bottom was red and sore from lying in wet, dirty diapers day after day. What you need now is a miracle, the doctor had said. "Other people have children so they have help with the work and can take it a little easier in their old age," the farmer said when his wife dunked the little lame legs into the wooden bucket in order to wash off the scabs and crusted dirt.

On the following Saturday she tied the child to her back with a large woolen shawl and wrapped up some bacon and half a loaf of bread as if she were going out to mow grass in the forest meadows, but she did not turn in at the lanes that led to the woods. She stayed on the paved road, looking neither left nor right. Passing through the villages, she made the sign of the cross at the roadside markers with the holy pictures and quickly said a Jesus and Mary, have mercy on us sinners. When the sun was high and there was not a bit of shade anywhere, she pulled a corner of the shawl over her child's head, broke off a piece of bread, and gave it to her to chew on. By noon the woman was at the border. The customs official asked her where she was going (at that time you didn't need a passport to cross the border). "Altötting," she said and walked around the gate. In the late afternoon, when she knelt before the wonder-working madonna, she was too exhausted to pray. The child was asleep against her back; her sore feet pulsed with pain. She dropped off, pulled herself erect, phrased her supplication in formulas of prayer over which she fell asleep again. Before she left she lit a candle at the altar. The night was clear and cool; she shivered; the child was crying. She tied Marie to her chest and put her arms around the whimpering bundle. In the morning, when the gray, leaden landscape took on color again and a clear white light stretched across the housetops, even before the sun rose above the edges of the fields, she was back in the village. She wrapped rags around her sore feet, forced them into the rubber boots, and set off, with her scythe and pushcart, to mow grass.

When Marie was eighteen months old she began to crawl again. At two she stood on her slightly stunted legs and stretched her arms through the rails of her crib. At that time her mother was pregnant again. When Marie toddled out into the yard for the first time, fell down, got up again, and regarded the world with big, astonished eyes—the chickens and pigeons fighting over the corn, the cats sleepily licking their fur in the sun, the blue square of the sky, the steaming manure pile— no one was around to say a miracle had happened. Marie's mother was in labor. Hours later, when the groaning and the brief screams had stopped and given way to the thin squalling of the newborn, the farmer stuck his head in the door. "Well, what is it?" "A son," the midwife said, and the wife was radiant. "This calls for a celebration," the farmer said and went off to the tavern. "A round on me," he called to the proprietor when he got to the smoke-filled room; "I have a son and heir." The farmers clapped him on the back, beer foam around their lips, saying, A good-looking guy like him is bound to be lucky in love. The proprietor's daughter laughed and rubbed her breasts against his shoulder.

□

And so goes the tale of woe of her childhood, which I heard so often on the sofa after lunch, an aid to digestion that has caused me to be sick after every meal ever since. The story was meant to win me over, to teach me to love her because she had not been loved by anyone else and no one had taken the trouble to understand her or even to listen to her. Who should understand if not her daughter, at the mercy of her and her stories, defenseless before an ongoing assault that came down on her like physical punishment, every day, part of the daily routine, and was designed to teach her to distrust people, to hate people, all but the one who inflicted the pain, which must be passed on so that hatred would be kept alive? And I have never asked anyone who was there at the time, Was it true, was it really like that? So terrible, so joyless, so cruel? I believed everything she said and I wept for her, for her stolen childhood, her missing youth, and she looked at me and said, "You see how lucky you are, how happy you should be." I was outraged at her father, who had beaten her. It never occurred to me to make a connection between his belt and her carpet beater, between the brutal, unjust blows she had received and the just punishment she dealt out to me so that I would become a respectable person.

□

Warm the bottle, change Franzl, sweep, wash the dishes, lunch is in the oven. Hurried instructions left by her mother, who has had to return to the fields. The hayrack was ready outside the door, the farmer went "Gee," the oxen started off, and her mother had to jump on the moving wagon. She would not be home until evening. Six-year-old Marie threw her satchel on the bench that ran around the table almost from wall to wall, and opened the oven door. Pieces of fatty pork and dumplings were swimming in grease; turnips and potatoes were waiting in two pots on top of the stove; everything was already cold. The baby was wailing in his crib; she dunked a scrap of cloth into the sugar solution by the stove and shoved it in his mouth. The water in the container above the stove was still warm. She had to stand on a chair to place the baby bottle in the water. Heini, the son and heir, was sitting on the floor, his face dirty, pushing a stool back and forth and calling, "Gee haw, gee haw."

"Where is Fanni?" Marie asked the four-year-old. He didn't answer. She took the broom and scared her brother up from the floor and the cat from under the table. "Get out of the way so I can sweep." Her brother pinched her calves and laughed when she didn't catch him. The baby started to squall again and she took the bottle out of the water; his greedy little hands were waiting. A large, darkly iridescent fly hummed and hit the windowpane. The door opened and Fanni came dancing in and threw her satchel down; she had a roll in her hand. "Where have you been all this time?" Marie asked as she gathered up the dirty tablecloth. "None of your business," Fanni said with her mouth full. Marie spun around. "Where did you get that roll? Let me have a bite." Fanni grinned and held the roll high over their heads. "Buy your own." "With what?" "With half a kreuzer." "Where did you get that?" "From Mother, for carrying wood." "I get stuck with the work and you get the money!" Blind with rage, Marie lunged at her older sister. "You rotten, sneaky skunk!" She scratched Fanni, Fanni bit her, and when they wound up wrestling on the floor, the roll disappeared under the bench by the stove. Heini picked it up and quickly deposited it inside his pants. The girls stopped fighting. While they looked for the roll, Heini gingerly edged himself out the door.

Every week after the Saturday bath, before the milking and feeding, comes the delousing. In summer it takes place next to the manure pile. Their mother has a fine-toothed steel comb, which digs into the scalp and pulls mercilessly at the matted hair; whole bunches come out. The lice are crushed between thumb and forefinger; they make a cracking sound. Fanni has silky dark-brown hair which falls in waves down her back. Marie's is like a cap of rusty florist's wire. "Carrot-top, carrot-top," the boys yell after her on the village street. "Ouch!" Marie screams when her mother goes to work with the comb. Bunches of hair join the lice on the manure pile.

"You've got plenty of hair," her mother says; "a few bunches don't make any difference."

There are bedbugs in the beds and fleas in the clothes. "Don't you dare scratch in church," their mother admonishes them; "I would die of embarrassment." During the consecration, before the bells start to ring, Marie feels a louse crawling slowly across her freshly washed neck. She pulls it off quickly and looks at the insect with satisfaction as it struggles between her thumb and forefinger. It's so quiet that the cracking sound is audible when she crushes its shell. The girls in her pew start to giggle, then burst out laughing; the ones in the next pew have started giggling, too. The priest intones the *Agnus Dei* and lifts the host; his disapproving glance rests on the giggling girls. Marie's face is as red as her hair.

After Mass, her mother grabs her by the arm and pulls her along, across the market square, up the long road to the village, not saying a word. "Just wait until your father shows up," she says when she pushes Marie through the gate into the farmyard. Marie hides in the hayloft. Around noon, when she is hungry enough to go into the big room, her father is sitting at the table. Before she can get away, he has removed his belt. Not a word has been spoken. They all drop their forks and look on with a mixture of pleasure and horror as the leather strap whacks down on her bare thighs, calves, arms, again and again, until her head hits the edge of the stove and she falls down. Her mother grabs her by the arm and drags her off to the bedroom and into bed. The others go on eating silently. This isn't the first time punishment has been turned over to their father. He rarely uses his bare hands; his blows always leave marks: a bloody nose, bruises, black swollen eyes, sometimes a loose tooth. The punishment is always just and deserved. He who loves his child chastises it.

All the girls in school have at least two pairs of shoes: low shoes for summer, lace-up boots for winter. Fanni and Marie have three pairs between them, two pairs of lace-ups and one pair of patent-leather shoes with gleaming buckles. Fanni gets to wear the patent-leather shoes, she is the pretty one; people stop to look at her and say, What a neat little girl. People had stopped to look at her when she was still in her baby buggy: the spitting image of her dad, they said, and that was a compliment. Fanni has a light-blue silk bow in her dark hair, and laughing dark-gray eyes. Black patent-leather shoes are a natural for her. She takes care of her things, never gets dirty; her underwear stays white longer, her pinafores stay pressed. Marie runs around like a boy, lousy and dirty, with skinned knees, no personal pride; nothing prepossessing in this child; she is always serious; she has a sharp, freckled face with reproachful, mistrustful eyes and an untamable red mane. Any attempt to tame this mane with ribbons and bows is bound to fail. Nor can Marie wear Fanni's outgrown clothes: even though Fanni is older, Marie is taller, her bones are larger and her shoulders wider than those of her dainty sister.

Since Fanni had to repeat second grade, they are in the same classroom. Marie, being a top student, sits in the front row; Fanni reads notes from the boys under her desk and giggles. Marie doesn't raise her hand, but when she knows the answer she glows, and during the winter she knows all the answers. In summer, during the harvest, she often has to stay home and help out; there's no time for homework. She has to turn the hay and rake it together, gather up field stones, and look after the little ones. There are still little ones at home. When she turns nine, the youngest is five months, and her mother has had to go back to the hospital. This time they are removing her other breast and her uterus. A tumor supposedly; the doctors won't talk, her father says. Seven kids, it's time to put a stop to it. He is embarrassed when he goes to church with his family: they're like a set of organ pipes, and him only thirty-two and still the handsomest man in the village. There are few unmarried women who haven't been to bed with him, not to mention several married ones, and he has a number of illegitimate children, including some who look like him, but he denies everything, and a paternity suit only makes the girl look ridiculous.

It's time for the harvest and their mother is in the hospital. She wanted to wait until fall, but the pain had become unbearable, and then she had a hemorrhage. The doctor wasted no time taking her to the hospital. The farmer was swearing, "Bitches, damn them, nothing but trouble." Fanni and Marie washed the bloody sheets and wiped the blood off the floor. Both were distraught, convinced their mother would die on her way to the hospital. Do people have that much blood? The younger ones stood around crying; only two-year-old Angela sat on the windowsill and stared open-mouthed at the doctor's disappearing car. There weren't many cars on the village street. Whenever one drove past they all ran to the windows and looked until it had turned the corner.

The farmer hired another hand for the harvest, but the housework and child-care chores fell on the two oldest girls. Fanni did the cooking and took care of the younger children; Marie had to do the hardest work. Milking, feeding the pigs, mowing grass—that's woman's work; no man would dirty his hands with such chores. The nine-year-old girl had to get up every morning at four. "Up, you lazy bums," their father would call out in front of their door and kick against it with his wooden shoe. If she wasn't in the barn in five minutes, she could expect curses, kicks, and slaps. "Here's where you sit," her father said the first day as he pushed a stool under the cow's belly; "this is how it works." The milk poured into the pail in a thin, even stream. She had to milk eleven cows every morning, half asleep, on an empty stomach. But her hands were too small; she didn't have enough strength to empty the udders completely. Her fingers cramped and would not cooperate.

When a cow had been milked, the farmer came and swore. "Can't you see that she's still full?" He gave Marie a kick that sent her reeling into the cow dung. She said nothing, choked down her tears: best not to open her mouth if she wanted to avoid more of the same. Once, when she couldn't control her crying and ran back toward the house, he dragged her back to the barn by her braids and thrashed her with the wagon tongue until she stopped moving. The cows kicked up their hind legs: they weren't used to her hands. "Are you still here?" her father shouted half an hour later. He pushed her out of the barn. "Go mow the grass, you lazy slob; they're never going to make a farm woman out of you!"

"Beggars is what you're all going to be, beggars," said her grandfather, who was, for the most part, an unseen presence in his retiree's room. Her mother brought him his food. On Sundays he walked to communion like a patriarch, while people stood aside respectfully. He was still tall, erect, majestic, an imperial farmer. The wealthiest farmer in the district, he looked no one in the face, stopped to talk to no one. The young farmers took off their hats when they approached him. He glanced down on them briefly from his height, saying, "Not right now," and walked on. His son-in-law hated him and tried to imitate him. With his daughter he had hardly exchanged a word over a period of forty years. "I put your food on the table, Father," she would say timidly, her hand firmly on the door handle, just before she shut the door inaudibly. Usually he didn't bother to turn around. He came to christenings and weddings, and his silent, disdainful presence was an honor. He had never played with the children; they were only allowed to make brief visits to his low, smoky room, where they stood, timid and respectful. "Beggars is what you're going to be." He hated their solemn-eyed, humble timidity; there wasn't a one who would meet his gaze with his kind of arrogance and self-assurance. But Marie admired him because one morning he had stepped outside his door just when the farmer booted her out of the barn, and had called across the yard in his supercilious, nasal voice, "Abusing people won't make a farmer out of you, you fortune hunter!" He was the only one who could stand up to the farmer and silence him with a look. From then on her father stopped beating her in the yard: he waited for her by the haystack in the meadow; he thrashed her inside the house from one corner to another, but the square between pigpen, cattle barn, and the front steps of the house, visible from the old man's window, became a haven for her.

After a month her mother came home from the hospital, thin and pale. She was wearing a bandage around her breast, which the doctor had to change once a week. On a fine work-day each week she would have to drop everything and walk the half-hour to the closest market square where the doctor was on duty. "Highfalutin fuss," the farmer scoffed, grumbling about being left with the work. Marie was milking only six cows now, but these remained her responsibility and she still had to get up at four in the morning. She shared the grass mowing with her mother, but if she stopped, barefoot in the wet grass, to turn her face to the rising sun, her mother would nag, "Stop staring and start working, or I'll tell your father."

Four weeks later Marie was back in school, ready to drop from fatigue, glad to be able to sit down and have no one shout at her or threaten her with beatings, but by now she didn't understand the work on the blackboard. She couldn't keep up and was too tired to concentrate. When she was called on, she stood up and, because she didn't know the answer, had to remain standing, red-faced, while everything around her became more and more unreal. She had to do her home-work secretly, on the windowsill, by the last glimmer of day-light, after she had milked her six cows and lugged the milk pails to the place where the dairy van picked them up. If her father caught her doing homework, he would slap her face

with the notebook: "A waste of time. Who needs an educated
farm girl." He bragged that he had never got beyond second
grade. He could barely write his name, but when it came to
selling cows and trading land, and to card playing, no one got
the better of him.

The lovelessness and humiliations of her childhood gave way
to the loneliness and bottomless self-loathing of her adolescence. She grew rapidly and her large bones made her appear
strong. Soon she didn't need new clothes; she wore her mother's hand-me-down jackets and skirts, taken in by the village
seamstress. The black patent-leather shoes were passed on to
the next of the five sisters, and Fanni was given new ones.
When her mother bought the new shoes and a blue taffeta
dress for her pretty, oldest daughter, Marie cut her heavy lace-
ups down to ankle height. She sat on the windowsill, letting
her left foot with the cut-off shoe dangle proudly down the
wall. As the younger children watched in admiration, she went
to work on the second shoe with the bread knife. At that
moment her mother appeared, unnoticed by the breathless
group; she saw Marie's leg, the shoe with the uneven, ragged
edge, and screamed, "Just wait until your father finds out."
She lost no time finding him, tattled on her daughter as if she
were a rival sister, and rubbed her hands on her apron when
he dragged Marie from the window by her thick red braids
and came down on her with his fists and feet until blood ran
from her nose and mouth. Then he went back to work. "Wash
your face," her mother said; "you look terrible."
    After that, nothing could mitigate the hatred between mother
and daughter. Her mother would call her an ungrateful beast
when Marie, eyes filled with contempt, would allow her every
movement to show how much she despised her. She showed
it in small, deliberate gestures: setting the table and forget-
ting her mother's plate; slamming the door in her face; walk-

ing by whistling and swinging her arms while the pig slops ran down over her mother's feet from the overfilled bucket. "Gratitude for what?" Marie asked defiantly. "For being alive." "I wasn't asked," Marie countered. "You could just as well have dumped me down the toilet." Then came her mother's tears, and the endless sobbing, and in between, chokingly, the story of Marie's paralysis and the pilgrimage to Altötting, and how she was responsible for Marie's straight legs and that Marie had more reason to be grateful than all the other children; Marie sneaked out the door and hated herself for nevertheless hating her mother.

When, one morning, Marie came to her with terrified eyes and blood on her nightgown, believing something monstrous was happening to her, some undeserved, shameful ordeal, her mother laughed and turned away. Marie had to cope by herself— stuff rags between her legs and get on her knees and pray to the Blessed Virgin to take this dreadful curse from her. It was Fanni, who knew the score, all about having and making babies, who finally enlightened her, and when Fanni started menstruating, six months later, sanitary pads were suddenly available.

One hot August evening, Marie, dusty from working in the fields, pulled off her blouse at the well beside the house and let the cold water run over her skin. Her mother yanked her into the house, slapped her, and screamed that she was a shameless, goddamned whore.

Shame was the only emotion the thirteen-year-old girl associated with her body, and the more female it became, the greater the shame. When Fanni wanted to tell her about her encounters with boys in the kitchen garden and her evening discoveries behind the grain shocks, Marie said, "You ought to be ashamed of yourself," and made a disgusted face. The sixth commandment was never a problem for her at confession.

When Marie was fourteen, the farmer let the foreman go.
Marie could replace him: she was as strong as a man, and she was graduating from school. She regarded the last day of school as the beginning of a death sentence. She had wanted to be a teacher in a convent school; she still wanted that. Because of this dream, she had secretly done her homework and borrowed workbooks when she had to miss a day of school. Her final grades were all A's. On Sundays she walked around the eight-grade school and felt cast out. Now there was no place where she could prove that she, too, had some worth—more, in fact, than the other farm children, almost as much as the town children, who always had time to study. Now there was no chance to escape after the milking and mowing until she fell into bed at night, dead tired. Milking, mowing grass, having cream soup with pieces of bread in it for breakfast, turning hay, cleaning out the manure, taking it to the manure pile, having cooked pork with dumplings and carrots for lunch, feeding the livestock, carrying wood, pitching hay into the wagon and unloading it in the hot, sticky barn, milking, separating the milk and lugging the pails to the village stand, having bacon, cottage cheese, and bread with cream soup for supper—this was to be her life, day after day, from now on until a man would take her away to another farm and the same thing would start all over under the thumb of her mother-in-law.

She didn't want to marry; she was repelled by men, repelled by what the adults did secretly in the haylofts, between the rows of potatoes, and in bed, and she didn't want to know about it or ever have anything to do with it. Sometimes on Sundays Fanni went out wearing her best clothes and didn't sneak back to the girls' room until after midnight; nevertheless she was detected because her younger sister Heidi woke up when she crawled into her side of the bed. On such Sundays Marie went to bed right after lunch, stared through the window at the sky, watched the pigeons that alighted briefly on the windowsill to bill and coo, and then fell into a deep, dreamless sleep, from which she would wake up sick to her stomach when dark was beginning to fall. The urge to vomit often rose so quickly that she didn't make it when she ran across the yard to the outhouse and let herself fall to her knees, too weak to stand up. Afterward she would see stars, but when the animals began to bellow and rattle their chains, she sat under a cow's belly and, pressing her reeling head against the warm flank, emptied the udders with the strong, mechanical movements of her hands.

Marie had never been close to her brothers and sisters. When she was younger, she had to change, feed, and carry around whichever child happened to be the baby at the time. Dirty diapers and the sickly-sweet smell of nursing infants brought on revulsion and anger. Once the younger ones were out of diapers and old enough to fetch their prepared meals, she stopped taking notice of them, even when they clung to her skirt howling because of skinned knees or broken teeth. "Go find your mother," she would say. She hated the boys the most; they were two and three years younger than she and had learned quickly that they could torment their older sister and receive their mother's approval for such behavior. To do something to Marie, bug Marie, this became their greatest pleasure, and they didn't even have to worry about getting punished. Once Marie thrashed her brothers, but she herself was whipped afterward, while the boys looked on with special satisfaction. How could she beat her younger, weaker siblings! The older they got, the more refined their torments became. When she was thirteen, a bunch of ten- to fifteen-year-olds tied her to a tree and forced her to watch as they slowly tortured her favorite cat, Schorsch. Schorsch got away. With empty, bleeding eye sockets and a hacked-off tail he came back, after she had been

untied and sat crying in the meadow near the house at night.
She lay down in the barn with him, but in the morning he was dead. She put a curse on her brother Heini: "May the same thing happen to you; may you lie in the dirt and die, with no one to help you." Nine years later she remembered her curse, when she received the news from the Russian front that he had died in the line of duty in the field hospital at Worsk, of dysentery and typhoid fever.

Her envy of Fanni was as intense as her hatred of her brothers. Fanni, whom she considered to be the same age, had always been favored, not only by their parents but by life itself. Everyone liked her. She was in the same classroom as Marie; she didn't do a lick of homework, didn't even bother to copy down the assignments, and yet was the teacher's favorite. He even took her along on his motorcycle outings. What she didn't tell anyone was that she lost her virginity on one of these outings. At sixteen she was voted queen of the local church fair. "Hard to believe those two are sisters—like day and night," people said, and Marie turned as red as her hair and ran off with her fists clenched.

Sunday always gave Fanni another opportunity to show off her beauty in front of the church; for Marie it was like running the gauntlet, and after a while she only went to early Mass, when it was still dark and no one saw her except a few half-blind old women and worn-out farmers' wives who considered going to church a chore and wanted to get it over with. Fanni, the beautiful sister, whose new dresses emphasized her figure, who had time to do her hair in the morning, who would put a snowy-white kerchief around her freshly waved hair and walk out to the fields for an hour or two to flirt with her father and the hired man: it was this sister, whose dark, ugly foil she was for thirty years so that Fanni might shine all the more brightly, who shaped Marie's sense of herself as a woman, more than the cruelties of her brothers and her father. Fanni was the other, the scoffing mirror, which said, Do what you will, you'll never be like me, you'll never make it. And so the decision: I'll destroy you and all women and the woman inside me.

Among her younger sisters only Rosi aroused her envy and resentment—Rosi the delicate one, who was too weak to work and whose weaknesses did not count against her; Rosi the schnitzel eater, for whom their mother fixed special treats. When Marie came home from school, she would open the oven door and spit on Rosi's schnitzel before eating what was left over from lunch for herself and the others. Once she dipped her spoon in Rosi's rice pudding, so full of raisins. As she was lifting the spoon to her lips, it flew across the room; her cheek was burning. "Thought you'd steal your poor sister's food, you spiteful little witch," her mother said. When Rosi graduated from grade school, Marie was seventeen. Rosi was the only one who was permitted to move out and go into training at a dressmaker's. The excuse was that Rosi was not strong enough for farm work.

A well-fed girl who inclined toward plumpness, Rosi had reddish-blonde hair and a haughty smile, and when she came home in a new dress she had made and everyone admired it, Marie felt the material and asked, "Will you make me a blouse if I give you the money for the material?" "That's all I need, to make clothes for all of you," Rosi answered, annoyed. That evening she found her new dress lying on her bed, cut into strips. She went to her father, who beat Marie with a shovel so that she couldn't walk for a week and everyone thought one foot was broken. "This time he's taken care of her for good, devil that she is," Rosi said gleefully, but Marie got up on her bruised, swollen leg again. She looked at no one when she and the others ate cream soup from the big soup bowl; she did not look at her father as he barked orders at her; her eyes, defiant and disdainful, stared off into the distance, where she would not encounter scoffing, hostile, or offended glances.

The one sister to whom she felt any closeness was Angela, an unprepossessing child with a thin, old-looking mouth and stringy blonde braids. Until Marie got married, she and Angela shared a bed. Fanni and Heidi slept in the other bed that stood in the girls' room. Rosi-the-delicate-one slept in a bed by herself until she left for her training and Fanni and Heidi each got a bed of her own. When the young fellows from the village climbed into their window at night—and they usually came to court Fanni—they had to put up with Marie's sharp tongue and jeering remarks; often the brisk repartee went on half the night and Marie was enjoying herself. But in the daytime no one turned around to look at her, no one went out of his way to speak to her; she looked straight ahead and her mouth took on a severe, bitter look. At eighteen she was an old maid.

□

Later I got to know them, these sisters. In fact, I knew them when I was being told these stories, and I didn't always find it easy to keep up the mandatory hatred, the requisite thirst for revenge. There was Aunt Fanni, who was always humbly telling us how dumb she was and who admired my mother in a childishly envious way. "Another new scarf, let me feel," she would say reverently and touch the material with her work-roughened hands. Yes, she was pretty when I was small, but certainly no beauty queen—a lot like my mother, actually, in her looks and gestures, but not so well dressed and less arrogant. Sometimes I wished Aunt Fanni was my mother. She was the first, the only, person to whom I confessed my great unrequited love when I was sixteen. We sat side by side on the cold stove in our nightgowns; only a dim lamp was left burning above the dining table and she was shivering, but she listened to me as I told her, with my face flushed, what he looked like and how he sometimes almost took notice of me, and I knew that she understood. And when I walked into the big room in my black mourning clothes and could not take another step, she knew exactly what to do to release me from my immobility and speechless grief. That night I ran into the room distraught and screaming; my mother had come to my bedside, to the big double bed of her wedding night, exactly twenty-four hours after her death. Fanni took me into her bed and asked no questions; she held me until I fell asleep toward dawn.

Later, when I retold my mother's stories with small question marks after them, they would laugh: Oh yes, Rosi the schnitzel eater, one of Marie's coinages, of course; oh yes, our mother was good to us. Marie? Well, it's true the two never cared much for each other; Marie was always unruly and impertinent and used to hurt our mother, who after all was responsible for Marie's straight legs. We had a ball as kids, you can imagine, five girls so close in age, and especially when Marie was around. We used to laugh ourselves sick—what a big mouth, and boy, was she smart; you get that from her, you're smart and a big talker. She could think of *more* wisecracks and get *more* ideas. The harvest helpers always asked for her to be there: "When Marie is working we have a party, the day goes by twice as fast." Maybe our father did beat her now and then—he did that to all of us—but Marie was strong, nothing could faze her, she was always on top of things and full of fun. A joyless childhood? Come on, where do you get that? It was great, and there was always something going on, and if we got into trouble Marie was in on it—she wouldn't miss any opportunity for mischief. Did you hear about the cut-off shoe and how she dyed her hair black with shoe polish? Yes, and how our father beat her within an inch of her life. Well, you have to admit those were pretty wild pranks. And "within an inch of her life" is an exaggeration.

The memories coincide: everything is correct and everything is wrong, experienced wrong, remembered wrong. My aunts did not batter their children: "A slap in the face now and then when I was particularly bad," my cousin said, "and then I yelled at the top of my lungs, but it really didn't bother me much, and I never had the feeling she cared less for me just because her hand slipped now and then." Did you know, I said loudly to the assembled relatives, that my mother used to beat me until she raised bloody welts? "Oh, hush, your mother was a woman above reproach who wanted nothing but the best for you, she was the most intelligent and ambitious of all of us. You can't say things like that; leave the dead in peace. And if she did, it was deserved; you were always a difficult child and caused your mother a lot of grief." I keep my mouth shut and stop trying to understand.

☐

When Hitler marched into Austria my mother was sixteen. There was only one radio in the whole village, owned by a neighbor who put his transfigured face close to the green eye in its center and whispered in awe, "The Führer is speaking." You could hear his speech and you could hear the roar of the crowd gone wild in the Heldenplatz, but more than anything you heard the hissing and clacking of static in the radio. Even so, the Gestapo picked up old Hermann a year before the end of the war. Someone who had a dispute with him, of some years' standing, over a piece of property must have turned him in, claiming he listened to foreign broadcasts.

On election day the farmers were herded into the community house; to remain absent was a punishable crime. Everybody knew everybody, and a brown-shirted, uniformed man stood behind each voter and marked with his index finger the spot where the "x" was to go. A few Sundays later the swastika was waving from the eaves of the community house, and old Professor Binder had to apologize publicly for having called Ernst Hoheneder, who now stood before him in black boots and with a skull on his cap, a brownshirt scoundrel. The

parish priest, who reportedly said Hitler was the greatest criminal of the century, had been picked up several days earlier;
he had also pushed the finger off the ballot and written NO
across it. He and the professor were the only ones in the
community who were aware of what the takeover meant; for
the others it was like a suspense film.

All Marie knew about politics was that it was men's business. The terror and fear that spread even to remote villages,
first as twinges of disquiet, later as horror and despair—this
fear was a source of titillation for her, since for once it wasn't
her head on the block. This time it was someone else's turn;
perhaps everyone's turn would come, but if you crawled into
the woodwork and attracted no attention, other people's turns
would come first for a change.

At sixteen she went dancing a few times, since Fanni had
a steady boyfriend, the only son of a wealthy farmer, who
could serve as a chaperon for Marie, too. Marie had new
buckle shoes and a dirndl dress and she liked to dance, even
though she rarely had a partner and Fanni's boyfriend had to
help out. He usually sat at the bar, watching his future wife
as she flitted from one arm to another. And Fanni had no
reason to be jealous of Marie. One evening he brought along
a friend from his village, Lois. Tall, broad-shouldered, blond,
dashing, and quick-witted, Lois danced with Marie nearly all
evening. After the dance he walked her to her gate, but somewhere between the two villages he had put his arm around
her on the moonlit road and at the gate he kissed her. The
following day Marie was walking on air. She looked at herself
in the mirror several times and found time to do her hair in
the morning. She heard neither her mother's scolding nor her
father's cursing; she sang all day long and was happy for the
first time in her life.

The following Saturday Lois climbed up to the girls' window; he had come to see her, not Fanni. "Would you like to

go dancing again next week?" he asked her, and she said, quickly but shyly, that she would. But on Friday she waited in vain in her dirndl dress, freshly bathed and with her hair tamed into an artful coiffure. When Fanni was picked up by her friend, Marie didn't go with them, since Lois might still come. She sat on the front steps and waited with increasing despair and resentment. At ten o'clock she took the pins out of her hair and went to bed. Angela stroked her shaking back until she fell asleep on her wet pillow.

The next Sunday she saw him standing in front of the tavern with another girl, laughing. She passed quite close to them, but he either didn't see her or didn't want to see her; he whispered into the ear of his new flame something that caused her to blush and giggle in confusion. He never came back. From then on Marie saw him only at a distance, and always with the sense of a physical jolt and the feeling her heart would stop.

That spring two other young men were interested in her, but their efforts meant little to her. One of them, a seventeen-year-old farm boy from the neighborhood, amused her with his bashful adoration, the heart-shaped *Lebkuchen* he bought her at the church fair, and the little bouquets of jasmine he pushed through her window when he came to see her. She had known him since they were children, and what connected them was being the same age and from the same village.

The other one annoyed her, the son of a *Häusler*, someone so marginal that he had no land or livestock to speak of and had to support his family by outside work. The family lived in a small cottage in the woods near the Czech border. His brother had once worked as a farm hand for her father, but they had had a run-in and he had quit before Candlemas, the usual time for employees to give notice and change jobs. "Hotheads, these Kovacses, foreign riffraff—what do you expect?" people had said at the time. There were three brothers: an elegant dandy, who was old enough to have been in World War I and had a new elegant woman in tow each time he came from town for a visit; Ludwig, the hothead farm hand with the wild look in his eyes; and Friedrich, quiet, shy, all thumbs.

Even when everyone else was convulsed with laughter, Friedrich would only smile awkwardly in the background. He was different from the other fellows; he looked different, too, with his black hair and olive skin and his large eyes, which did not laugh even when his wide mouth, with its somewhat too full lips, exposed his teeth. He was a buffoon, who affected you in a strange and embarrassing way, as if, no matter where he showed up, he didn't belong, as if he were an old man instead of twenty-six. When he saw her picking raspberries in the berry patch adjoining his parents' homestead, he walked over to her and talked about the weather and the harvest in the villages, even though she turned her back on him after a brief hello and Fanni threw clumps of dirt at his fly. After that he showed up wherever he thought he might find Marie—on the church square after eight o'clock Mass, in the fields that lay on his side of the village, and finally he even became bold enough to come to the village and climb up to her window. Marie didn't know whether to be flattered or annoyed by his stolid courting. It lacked the element of play and camaraderie of the local boys' behavior; it was serious, meaningful, almost solemn.

One day he insisted on coming to the house in broad daylight to introduce himself as an official suitor for Marie. "What does he want, this *Häusler?*" her mother said contemptuously. "I'm sure he's not going to do me any honor." Her brothers imitated each of his clumsy, fumbling gestures: how in his embarrassment he wound first his wristwatch and then his pocket watch, how he put one foot on top of the other and kneaded his hands. Her father gave him a scornful glance, meant not only for the figure he cut but also for his social rank, and then ignored him. Marie wished she could make herself disappear. But when he left and the storm broke—"Are you crazy? What a clod, and a *Häusler* to boot; it would be different if he were a farm boy"—Marie found herself defending him; she even claimed that she liked him quite a bit. When she had seen him standing in the room she had recognized, in spite of the shame and humiliation his mere presence caused her, that they had something in common: both of them were loners, outsiders.

From then on she allowed him to walk her home, listening silently when he asserted that she was different from other girls and that he valued this, and when, on the lawn, he clumsily put his arm around her waist and kissed her, she let it happen. What was she thinking of, she asked herself as she lay in bed later that night, a *Häusler*, someone who was as much beneath her as she was beneath the townspeople, someone who worked as a woodcutter for the convent and whose siblings were servants, someone who was ten years older than she and didn't know what to say when he walked beside her—what was she doing with him? Get rid of him, she thought with irritation. But when his huge eyes searched her face as if pleading for the key to happiness, she shrugged her shoulders and allowed him to worship her. After all, she didn't have to make a decision yet.

The parish got a new pastor; the swastika hung from the roof of the community house; there were flag ceremonies with much yelling of *Sieg Heil*; people learned to use the Hitler salute; and one morning the village idiots, Aunt Pfleger and her son, had disappeared. The Gestapo had picked them up during the night, people said, and wasted no more thought on this except to conclude that that's the way things go and those two had been a hardship on everyone anyway.

A few weeks later, in the middle of the harvest season, came the draft calls. On the way back from church, where he was always lying in wait for her now, as if it was understood that he would walk her home, Friedl pulled a postcard from his suit, on which everything had been preprinted except his name and address. "What is that?" she asked and was irritated by his slow, ceremonious manner. "An induction notice." "Does it look like war?" "That's hard to say," he said, sounding mysterious because he was talking tough politics, men's business, and the induction notice gave him an aura of manliness. He had been recognized; someone had considered him important enough to address a postcard to him.

"Will you wait for me?" he asked her on the eve of his departure, when he kissed her behind the barn. Later she couldn't remember what she had said—probably yes, or maybe nothing. But when he was in basic training in Freistadt, she went to visit him. It was her first trip, the first time in her life that she stepped into a train and went away, and by herself at that. Because she couldn't bear to be without him? Because she loved him? At least that's what she claimed in the presence of her nagging mother and her mocking brothers and sisters. "I bet you'll come home with a little souvenir in your belly," Angela needled her and got slapped. "If you come home with a kid, I'll throw you out of every door in the house and you'll never darken any of them again," her mother said. Marie went off nonetheless. Friedl had rented a room for her for the night, but he himself never entered that room. They sat at the edge of the woods and said nothing; they sat on a grassy field and said nothing; Freistadt wasn't much different from the market square at home, and they had no money for shopping. He was in uniform, she in her dirndl dress, both freshly bathed and groomed, both embarrassed and silent. In the evening he had to return to his barracks; she left the next morning, bored and disgruntled: she could have saved herself the money. His first

love letters arrived: cards with views of Freistadt, picture postcards with baskets of sentimental roses, a heart surrounded by
forget-me-nots. "Sweetheart," that one said, "I miss you. I
wish I could be near you. Forever yours, Friedl."

There were fewer and fewer young men; Fanni's fiancé
was drafted, too. Their father was exempt: he was needed on
the farm. The girls' division of the Hitler Youth was recruiting.
On Sundays there were round dances in the athletic field
behind the school and evenings of folk dancing in the recre-
ation room of the church, where girls danced with one another
and were bored. Marie had stopped wanting to belong. She
distrusted the high-spirited camaraderie; she didn't like to march
in formation, wave a flag, and sing loudly in the church square.
She simply wasn't interested, and preferred on Sundays to go
to bed after lunch and then sit on the dewy grass behind the
house to watch the sun set and the moon rise. As she sat there,
with the meadow fragrance around her, the lone evening star
flickering in space, and the last flush of the sun turning pale
above the stubble field, she read the declarations of love on
those mawkish postcards, which gave her a vague feeling of
destiny and the warm, grateful knowledge that one person, the
first in her life, loved her.

War broke out. In the little village near the Czech border there
was no change except the arrival of soldiers' postcards from
Poland, France, and Greece. Finally Friedl had something to
report besides the fact that he loved her: We've been marching
all day; we are camped outside of a town with a Polish name;
tomorrow we march on. We will march on: so, too, sang the
Hitler Youth. Fervor, excitement, fanaticism: Marie did not
share in these. Her life continued its round of milking and
grass mowing and, in the evening, the hum of the hand-driven
machine that separated the milk from the cream. Her mother
became bedfast, but Marie spent little time in the room where

she lay against a stack of pillows. She spent most of her free time in the meadow behind the house or in the barn. Her newly awakened capacity for love, brief and unfocused as it was, settled wholly on her favorite animals: a ram with a snow-white coat, which was permitted to butt its curved horns into her stomach because it looked so sweet when it was getting ready to attack; a sheep for which she gathered the juiciest leaves from the unmowed grass strips and which she bathed every Sunday; cats; small farm animals. Even in winter she liked to spend her days in the barn, but then she had to tie hot bricks and cat skins around her hips, because her lower back was so painful she could hardly move. The doctor had said it was possible that the childhood paralysis would recur when she was around forty. During the long winter evenings she sat spinning, with her back pressed against the tiled stove, which was slowly getting cold. She wove dozens of linen towels, hard as boards; tablecloths in which she embroidered monograms; bedclothes, stack upon stack, edge upon edge: ecru-colored, rough-textured mountains of household linens for her dowry.

Even Fanni and Rosi had settled down, after their craving for excitement, dancing, and men. There were no young men left in the village. Occasionally one came home on leave from the front, in a freshly pressed uniform, brisk and dapper. They admired him and touched his uniform; he was sure to find a warm bed for a few nights, and then he was gone again. There were weddings, and, for those in a hurry, proxy weddings; there were christenings and deaths, and the endless chain of death notices from the front began.

"Pray for me," Friedl wrote from the Russian front. The imminent threat of death liberated his pen; he swore a thousand desperate oaths of love and fidelity. How could she drop him now, when he wrote that thinking of her was all that kept him alive, that he would gladly die if she broke with him? His letters grew wings; he began to compose bumbling poems for her.

For Christmas he came home on leave. His mother had cooked and set the table for him, for her favorite son, her youngest, whom God was bound to spare because she sat on the front steps every night praying for him, entreating the stars, the same stars that must be in the sky above Russia: Lord, send my Friedl back home to me. And now he was here, hollow-cheeked and paler than before, and he did not stay with his mother on Christmas Eve. He polished his shoes, bathed, pressed sharp pleats into the trousers of his uniform, and went into the village, where no one expected him, no one wanted him. "What does he want here again?" Marie's mother grumbled. "If he doesn't leave soon, I'll kick him out," the farmer said through clenched teeth. Friedl was ecstatic; he was sitting in a warm room in a farmhouse, hesitantly reaching for a star-shaped cinnamon cookie, and there was Marie, who had been on his mind day and night, on the marches and in the trenches: there she sat, large as life, and when she finally edged him out the door, afraid her father would grab him by the collar of his uniform and give him a swift kick, he got to kiss her quickly in the dark hallway.

No, I don't want him, she thought, when they walked home together in the ringing cold on Christmas Day. Both of them were shivering, he in his uniform without an overcoat, she in an unlined jacket, with shoes that had holes and were frozen stiff. During his absence she had fallen in love with his letters. She had forgotten that he was awkward, inept, and taciturn and got on her nerves. It wasn't him she had fallen in love with, but his love for her. And now she was so repelled that she couldn't even stand the idea of being kissed by him. He wanted to come back in the evening, but she said, "No, don't come, don't ever come back again; it isn't going to work out with the two of us." He left without a word.

On the following Sunday, when he was on his way back

to the front, his mother walked up to Marie and seized her by the arm. "What have you done to my boy? He sits at the table and cries, all night long; there's no point in staying alive any more, he said. That's how he went back to the front; what if he throws away his life because of you?" She turned abruptly and left Marie standing there, feeling like a murderer.

This was the winter of '42, and the death bell did not stop. Every day there were new notices of men killed or missing in action. The letters from the front dwindled, stopped coming. A neighbor's son, the one with the heart-shaped *Lebkuchen* and the bouquets of jasmine, had been killed. On Fanni's birthday in January she received an army postcard containing a thousand birthday kisses; a week later his mother came to the house: he had been killed on the Eastern front. Two months went by without a word from Friedl. Marie couldn't stand it any longer. For the first time in her life the farmer's daughter went to knock on a *Häusler's* door. "Have you heard from Friedl?" she asked. His mother took a printed notice from the buffet and things went black in front of Marie: she was responsible for his death. "Seriously wounded in the area of Orel," she heard his mother read; "took over the cannon after two of the men in the tank had fallen and fought, defying death, until he was seriously wounded." He was awarded the iron cross, first class. The old woman wiped her eyes with her sleeve: "He's alive and won't have to be at the front for some time." Defying death, Marie thought; he got the iron cross because of me, because he wanted to die.

Soon after, an army postcard arrived from the mountains, the Riesengebirge:

> Here I sit above green valleys,
> Sad and lonely in my room;
> You are all that's in my heart, dear,
> Without you there's only gloom!

She wrote him a long letter. He was overjoyed, and in his next letter he asked her if she would marry him when he came back from the war. She answered yes, she would marry him. God only knew if he would come back; God only knew how long the war would go on.

"The war is lost," people were saying after Stalingrad, but they whispered it behind closed doors and cupped hands, while knitting mittens for the *Winterhilfswerk*. "Shut up or you'll end up in a concentration camp": this fear had reached into the villages, too. And you cupped your hands in front of your mouth when you mentioned the Gestapo and the fact that they had been picking up people in the middle of the night again. Someone had denounced someone; no one could feel safe; everyone had enemies who might denounce him; everyone knew something he wasn't supposed to know. The Gestapo came in the night and the mailman in the morning, and both brought death with them, an invisible death.

"Gypsy whore!" a farmer's daughter who was in the Hitler Youth yelled at Friedl's sister right in the church square. "Everybody knows you are gypsies. Kovacs—what kind of German name is that? And your uncle has never stuck to any job, lazy drunken bum. And look at her with her black hair and lying eyes. They all belong in a concentration camp!" Is it true, people in the square were asking, curious and titillated. His mother was beside herself: three sons in the army, wasn't that enough? She had submitted proof of their Aryan purity in the village hall. Franziska Kovacs, née Leitner, daughter of Zölestin Leitner and Aloisia, née Loeffler, both Roman Catholic. "We are not interested in your side of the family," the official said and showed her some illegible scraps of brown paper. "What about Josef Kovacs, son of Jakov Kovacs and Marya née what? And Jakov Kovacs, son of Gabriel Kovacs and whom? Born where? Christened where?" Kathi, the oldest, managed to come up with the papers—no one knew how, no one talked about it. The sons were allowed to stay at the front because Kathi could prove that Gabriel had come from Hungary and so had Marya, from a far-flung pocket of the old monarchy, where they didn't pay much attention to papers, where grandmothers and great-grandmothers get lost somewhere in the steppes.

This satisfied the officials, but not the people. "Gypsy trash," the Hitler Youth girls hissed behind Lydia's back, Lydia with the black hair and dark down on her upper lip and legs. Racy, the boys called that; it was racy, but not racially pure. At stake were the few men who still came home on leave, and the gossip was that Lydia lay down with them among the potatoes and in the hay, even if it was only for one night, even if they were engaged to other girls. Fanni reported that Lydia had told her she ought to be naked when she was with a man, that was the best way. "There you have it again," Rosi said vociferously, "all gypsy girls are whores." "She has the evil eye," Fanni suggested, "and she puts it on a guy on his last leave from the front; she lies in the hay with him and hexes him." Fanni shot a poisonous glance at Marie, who was bending over a bowl of potatoes. "No wonder not one of *them* has been killed. Not that anybody would miss that bunch, but my Hans was the only son, and now there's no one to take over at home." Just one more thing, Marie thought, always one more thing; isn't it punishment enough for me that he has to be a *Häusler?*

During the summer of '42, Heini was drafted, and a little later Franz, the youngest. The house grew silent, with an oppressive kind of silence; there were brief, cautious sighs of relief whenever a letter from the front arrived. Their mother could not leave her bed any more. She had undergone one more operation, but was sent home without hope for improvement and waited for her slow death, supported by pillows, her face ravaged and yellowish. A silence composed of fear, uncertainty, and waiting, hovering over the whole village, assumed a palpable intensity in this room. There was the smell, its residue on one's skin; it was death, yet not only the death of a barely fifty-year-old woman whose living body was rotting away in the dark room. Without speaking, her daughters changed her bedding, put clean bandages on her deformed legs with their open sores, handled the bedpan. They ate their meals quickly and surreptitiously; her plate, always the first one, placed by Fanni on the nightstand next to the bed, was also the last to be emptied, untouched, into the pig trough. But when Marie's fiancé—"the bridegroom," as the maliciously smirking sisters called him—when Friedl came home from the field hospital with the iron cross, first class, on his sergeant's uniform, her mother still turned her face to the wall and murmured, "What does he want, this *Häusler?*" His sympathy gave out in the presence of her hostile, averted face, and later she complained bitterly that he still did not respect her.

Friedl himself looked like walking death, with his cheekbones jutting out, bluish shadows under his eyes, and his hands so narrow and bony that Marie dreaded his touch. But everyone looked at the new uniform and the iron cross, and after church he went to the village photographer and had himself photographed against a background of dark cumulus clouds—the returning hero, even though in this, the fifth year of the war, people had had enough of heroes and the weeping mothers of heroes.

It was no secret that the war would be over soon; only the men on leave from the front hadn't got the message yet. They still believed in the final victory, while the old men in the church square slapped their thighs and laughed: "Where are you hiding it, your final victory? In your pants pocket?"

"I've saved enough money to buy a farm with six head of

cattle," Friedl told Marie eagerly on the way home. By all rights he should have inherited the little cottage, but his brother had married in the middle of the war and Friedl had given up the inheritance in his brother's favor, because he was afraid of the brother's violent temper and because he thought, Who knows if I'll ever come back. He would buy a small farm for himself and Marie; there were certainly plenty of farms without heirs to be had. "Or perhaps we should settle in the Ukraine after the final victory," he said. Marie didn't care, just as long as she got away from home. He had brought her an engagement ring, silver with a fake blue stone, She had to wear it on her little finger, her fingers always being swollen from work. He had brought her earrings, too, and tried to pierce her ear lobes with a sewing needle. She gritted her teeth and hated him and his earrings. She consented to their first official lovers' pose, embarrassed and with one eye on the photographer, whose shadow falls broadly and indiscreetly on the lawn between himself and the sheepishly grinning pair on the bench behind the fenced-in vegetable garden.

In the fall of '44 her mother died. Everyone breathed easier. The windows were opened wide to let out the smell of death. The five daughters had black dresses made and enjoyed their freedom. Their father's freedom had never been curtailed because of his wife, but now he was officially eligible to go courting.

He was forty-five and still the best-looking man in the village. There were few young men left; twenty-year-old invalids came home with one leg missing, or both. They were as tired as the old men on the benches, more tired even, and they had no hope left and no memory except five years of horror. You could hear the bombers in the sky, but they were flying toward Vienna or Salzburg. The blackout regulations were carelessly observed. Only one bomb fell in the area during the entire war, a dud that landed in the meadows, a long way

from the villages. While the bombed-out people in the cities
fled through burning ruins and stood in long food lines, the
farmers did not suffer. Livestock was butchered illegally, a
quick, noiseless operation; the meat disappeared into the hollow space between the floor of the granary and the ceiling of
the tool shed. In the morning there was no trace of any nocturnal butchering. The number of refugees from the Sude-
tenland kept increasing; they came through the village with
handcarts and covered wagons, ragged, hungry, in tatters. When
Marie's father was not in the house, the refugee women were
allowed in; their children got milk to drink and they were given
bread and cheese to take along. But when he was home, the
gate was bolted shut. "We don't have a thing," he yelled; "get
out. We don't need any beggars; go someplace else." "You'll
see, the time is going to come when you'll have to start thinking
about things," Marie said to him before ducking out the living-
room door.

That time came more quickly than she could have guessed.
In February they received word that Franzl, the younger brother,
had been killed in France, and before the obituary and the
porcelain tablet for the grave were ready, a second announce-
ment arrived, catapulting their father from the best years of
his life into reality: Heini, the son and heir, the future farmer,
was dead. The autumn grave in the cemetery was still fresh;
there had been no time for a lawn to grow. It seemed as if
three dead were lying in the new grave when the porcelain
tablet was put in place, with the pictures of the two brothers
underneath that of their mother: in her fifty-third year, in his
nineteenth year, in his twentieth year.

By now the fourteen- and sixteen-year-olds were being
drafted and even the farmers were supplied with hand grenades.
The word was that the Russians were close, and by now the
refugees were coming from Vienna. While the civilian militia
were shooting at the approaching Red Army from trenches

along the main road to Bavaria, Marie ran for half an hour along an open road toward the parish cemetery one night in order to rescue the new porcelain tablet. This was her one and only war experience: to run back and forth between the two fronts, intoxicated by the thrill of flamethrowers overhead and machine guns behind her, to play a trick on death and, arriving at home, grin and wave the trophy, so disproportionate to the risk she had taken.

And then, one lovely spring day, the war was over. The deserters crawled out from under the hay, and those who came back put up with bell ringing and embraces. The old men on the benches had known from the start that the war was lost, and the parlors were now occupied by the Russians. Nothing changed except that the livestock didn't have to be butchered illegally any more and that the Russians were busy drinking and raping.

Friedl came home in torn civilian clothes. He had buried his sergeant's uniform and the iron cross, first class, along with his belief in the final victory, before he got to Wiener Neustadt. He was pale, tired, and thirty-two, and he didn't know where to go from here. The pay he had saved was swallowed up by the currency devaluation, and he had no place to stay, now that his parents had moved to their little retirement cabin. All he knew was that he wanted to marry the girl he had wooed for seven years.

□

"What was it like when you were young?" I asked my mother. Perhaps she would understand me, guess all my questions, if she would make herself remember desire and loneliness and the secret torments of love. "When I was a young girl there was a war going on, and when it was over my adolescence was over, too. Besides, what with the beatings and the work, who can talk about being young? It was no picnic." "Weren't you

ever happy; weren't you ever in love?" "In love, with *him?*
No; I loved him and was faithful to him, but you can see how
he's paid me back." I wanted to fill the gaps, make her more
human, imagine a young body longing for love. "That was
out of the question then," she said severely; "our father would
have killed us, and, anyway, what a thing even to think about."
No, her body defied my imagination with its armor of virginity;
no, I think, my mother was never young.

It was a love match, my aunts said, the grand passion of
novels. She didn't go dancing; she didn't look at anyone else;
she slapped anybody who made fun of him; she sat in the
living room night after night, writing him long letters. And
when they were together? Like lovebirds, couldn't take their
eyes off each other and sneaked off alone and must have had
something going before they got married.

"Those were the days, between '39 and '45," said Aunt
Rosi, who had been an aid in the air corps. "We were young
and free and there were plenty of soldiers. Only at the end it
almost got us; that's when they packed us like sardines into
the last plane, and the Red Army was all over the place already,
and when we landed in Ebernsee, they had just let loose the
inmates from the concentration camps and the maximum-
security prisons." My younger sisters—so my mother reported—were free and easy; they had no sense of decorum,
no morals; they stayed out all night, and when they went
dancing their skirts barely covered their bottoms.

But none of them was really affected by the war, neither
my mother, who did not wish to remember her joyless girlhood, nor Aunt Rosi, who could not understand how the
concentration-camp inmates could suddenly be running around
free. Was it really like that, an unhappy adolescence, crushed
by work and beatings and virginal unworldliness? Of course
not, my aunts said, and claimed to remember only the un-
believable pair of lovers whom I can't even imagine when I

look at the photos of him clumsily putting his arm around her waist while she pulls back slightly and looks down at him with a probing and suspicious look.

   And the war itself, the catastrophe, the great historical event that was carefully kept from us? The war meant death notices and good-byes and letters from the front. But what about the Nazis, whom nobody mentions to us? Everyone's eyes become defensive: We didn't know what was going on. Didn't you say, Shut up or you'll end up in a concentration camp when someone said that the war was lost; didn't you live in constant fear of being denounced? People who weren't there shouldn't talk about it, you say, giving us a stern, disapproving look. But I've seen the photographs of the Hitler Youth girls; I recognized my aunts in them—photographs, you understand, evidence. The three-cornered neckerchiefs, the figures in formation, the raised right hand, the evening meetings at which they sang patriotic German songs—there are pictures of that, too. And all those songs of which I know every word because my mother used to sing them in the kitchen like songs about spring or Christmas carols. *And we sail and we sail toward England, for today we claim Germany, but tomorrow the whole world.* But when I innocently played the old Austrian national anthem on the piano, not knowing *Deutschland, Deutschland über alles* had been sung to the same tune, my mother yanked my hands away from the keys: "My god, if someone hears that they'll think we are Nazis." Otherwise the only information I got from her was that her father beat her up just as regularly during the war and that she remained true to that oddball, my father, because she had no other opportunities.

   "What were things really like?" I asked my father, and I had the feeling I was tormenting him. "Didn't you see or hear anything, either?" "Oh yes, my first dead man, in Poland, someone who is lying on the street and has stopped moving; your first dead person, that's like the loss of your virginity; later you get used to it. And in Russia, the farmhouses that were chopped up into firewood and the boundless rivers."

"But what was your part in it?" His hope for the final victory, which prompted sarcastic remarks from his father-in-law, the iron cross and the newspaper clipping he kept, until he was wounded near Orel, in the same folder with his army papers and the forged ancestral documents. Those, and photos of tanks, burning airplanes, infantry formations; a war diary in an illegible cursive script. The war was his only career; he never worked his way up afterward, never stood out again. "What do you want to know?" he asks, sounding harassed. "What I'm supposed to tell your grandchild someday." "I don't have anyone's death on my conscience. Isn't that enough?" "What did you know? What did you see?" "The mass graves and the people who were hanged, the propaganda films and the rapes." And then, years later: "And still you're holding on to the clipping and your proud memory of the iron cross? And still you wanted to take your wife and settle down in the Ukraine after the final victory? How am I supposed to explain this to my daughter, who loves you?"

When I was small and wanted the attention of my remote father, I would ask him about all different kinds of weapons and then I would patiently not listen while he explained them carefully. At the age of six I could have been learning all there was to learn about armored scout cars, gun barrels, and tank treads if I had been listening, but that there were such people as Jews I did not learn until I was twelve and my girlfriend expressed regret that Liz Taylor had married a Jewish son of a bitch. So in '39 you didn't suspect anything, but in '45 you had said so all along and not been able to do anything about it, and you were punished just the same with hunger, currency devaluation, bombed-out cities, and occupation soldiers.

On New Year's Eve, over punch and herring, how they reminisced about the night bombings. "We had just got back from the shelter and put the children to bed when the next alarm came, and this time we just put our coats on over our nightgowns and ran back to the shelter, so tired we were ready to drop. We only went because of the kids; our neighbors stayed in bed—they had had enough for one night. And when we came out of the shelter we could see from far off that our house had been hit and, well, we lost everything." We looked at them, the survivors, with admiration, and at their children, hardly older than we, who had slept in their baby buggies while the cities were bombed to bits. How did you survive that without becoming a different species of human being; how can you sit there and recall these things so calmly when we who were not there are shaking with fear? "At supper I said to Fanni, 'Something has happened to Rudi.' We suspended my wedding ring above his picture, and the ring didn't move. During the night the picture fell down from the wall. Fanni said I didn't hang it right when I put it back; too bad about the glass, she said, but I had heard the rapping behind my bed and was already waiting for the postman to bring the news of his death." On All Saints' Day, when the village band played *Ich hatt' einen Kameraden*, the traditional anthem for the war dead, our skin crawled, while tears were running down the cheeks of the mothers and sweethearts. So many dead, and we wished we had known them, because we were supposed to look like them, and because we had to take responsibility for what they had seen and done.

What did your generation learn on the war fronts of the Reich? That you should jump into the hole made by a rocket because the rockets from the *Stalinorgel* hit in semicircles and won't land in the same place twice. My father tells me this, and that it is possible to sleep while you're walking, and that there is nothing you can't endure, and that everything else can be found in Konsalik's book *Stalingrad Doctor*. You've certainly done nothing to boost the international tourist trade. In the Balkans you soldiers were more afraid of the partisans than of the entire Russian army; Greece was dirty and everybody got seasick on the isthmus; and who knows if someone might not recognize you in France. You've all seen plenty, and when you get together over beers, you'll dramatize your last and only career for the rest of your lives: "Another Russian in the gunsight; bang bang, he's gone; what do young people know about life, always asking for reasons. And the way we lived then, like dogs, we never had it that bad again; what is a human life under those circumstances?" Why didn't I listen earlier on, when they were still talking off the cuff? Because I was too small to use their war stories as evidence against them. Later, when I began to ask questions, their mouths hardened and they looked away: "We didn't know anything, we didn't do anything, we couldn't stop them, we only followed orders, because we weren't dreamers like you, idealists, ideologues, we were just plain flesh-and-blood human beings."

☐

And suddenly it was over and one was once again a have-not in civilian clothes, returning to a bombed-out, starving country and a ridiculously average sort of life. Suddenly nothing was so beautiful as the dreams in the trenches, neither the murmuring forests of home nor the no longer quite so young girl one had to come back to and marry because the alternative would have been to start from scratch somewhere else, somehow or other. So life had to go on as if nothing had happened.

Friedl found a job in town as a streetcar conductor and a place to sleep on his sister's couch. His sister had got married and was pregnant and living with her husband in a dark two-room apartment. All Friedl had to eat was what he could get with his food ration cards, because his sister would empty his pockets and confiscate the small amounts of bread, butter, and bacon his mother gave him when he visited her, and he said nothing since, after all, she was pregnant and let him sleep on her couch.

He could have gone home on his days off, but that would have meant transportation costs and he wanted to put away money for his new life, now that he had lost his savings and the hope for a farm of his own.

Besides, what would be the point of going to the village on a weekday? They'd call him a lazy bum; weekdays weren't meant for love, only Sundays, between church and the evening chores. The thirty miles that separated him from Marie now seemed more of a barrier than the thousands of miles during the war. The town was as alien to him as the village; he felt displaced, cast off by life after six years at the front. He did not make friends with his colleagues and was in his sister's way. He started to look for a place to live and urged Marie to set the wedding date; after all, they had been as good as engaged for years. Thirty-two years old, he had never slept with a woman, had dreamed only about her, whom he had first seen in the berry patch when she was sixteen. She was his one great love, and she would change his life.

Marie still had her girlhood dream of becoming a convent teacher, but since her mother's death her father had been beating her even more often; he had started drinking, and when he was drunk there was no telling what he might do. The house was frequented by Russians, who bought schnapps from the farmer. "Why young lady not nice?" they asked, lifting her chin and touching her breasts. She was scared and spent many nights hiding in the empty stalls in the horse stable. Her sisters went dancing. At twenty-three she felt old, left over. She did not care to enter the competition for the few young men who had returned. Her father brought home his girl-friends, hardly older than she was, and they ruled the roost until the daughters managed to get rid of them. She couldn't take living at home much longer; in a few years she would be

an old maid, part of the household inventory. Everyone said
marriage was simply a new yoke, a new form of slavery, but
could things be any worse, and wasn't there always the possibility of love, even happiness?

In March the banns were read in church. A chill ran down
her spine when she heard her name from the pulpit: now
everyone knew and there was no backing out. At home she
took the calendar off the wall and counted how many more
days she would have to get up for the milking and walk out
into the dewy meadows with her scythe. But it did not produce
the expected sense of elation. Suddenly, after all the years in
which she thought she couldn't make it through the day, in
which she wished that the night would refuse to usher in
another morning, suddenly she was homesick even before she
had left the farm. In the evenings she stood again in the farm's
meadow, ran out into the fields that still lay winter-fallow.
She breathed in the clear air and the sunset and the twittering
of birds and thought: Never again. She was afraid and longed
for the security of the fields and the animals she had raised.
At night, when she lay in bed next to the sleeping Angela,
she was afraid of having to lie next to a man she hardly knew
who would have the right to lie on top of her whenever he
wanted. During these weeks her obsession with sexual purity
became even more fanatical. She reacted with something close
to revulsion when her fiancé touched her, and he respected
her fear, appreciated it as proof that she was still intact, that
the waiting had been worth it. Oh, to be free, she thought,
lying down in the spring meadow, her arms spread wide.

Freedom became a word like *virginity* for her, something
to which she clung desperately, all the while feeling like a
plant that was being pulled up from the soil. The others treated
her as if she had become a visitor and didn't really belong any
more, though she had helped to cut down the trees that were
now at the furniture workshop, being made into her dowry.

On Sunday afternoons she took the stacks of linens from the chest: bedding, towels, handkerchiefs, undershirts; a bottle of perfume given her seven years ago by the neighbor's son, which she had saved for the wedding; a cake of scented soap; a silk handkerchief. There was an argument about the feather bed. A *Häusler* didn't need such things, said Fanni, who had taken over the household; she took the feather bed away from her sister. "I took care of the geese and plucked them," Marie yelled. "I've slaved away in this house, more than any of you!" She got her feather bed, but one with inferior feathers, which stuck together in lumps. A table, a buffet, two narrow beds, two meager wardrobes, a washstand, and the feather bed: this was the dowry, her pay for ten years of work in the fields, the measly inheritance the richest farmer in the area squeezed out for his daughter. Her sister Rosi made her wedding gown, a long white batiste dress with tucks across the bodice, a high neck, and long sleeves. Her veil was made of tulle and came down to the floor.

May arrived. Friedl had found a place to live, in a farmhouse on the outskirts, far from the edge of town, whose owners rented out part of it. That way the change wouldn't be so hard on Marie. A lovely two-room apartment, he raved, only you had to get your water from a well and the toilet was outside, as was customary for farmhouses. She went to visit her future mother-in-law a few times and was surprised that a retired *Häusler*'s wife was so well off. Friedl's mother served her *Gugelhupf* and coffee and gave her a coffeecake and doughnuts to take home. What Marie didn't know was that she was showing off for the farmer's daughter and that she would live on bread spread with lard for weeks afterward. Marie was surprised and enjoyed being treated like someone special for the first time in her life, someone worth impressing, and she thought it must be true that they were happy she was marrying Friedl, pleased that someone from the ranks of the farmers would

cater to them. She felt like her grandfather on the church
square. I am somebody, she thought on her way back to the
village, I am a wealthy farmer's daughter. The thought occurred to her for the first time now when it was no longer
true, when her dowry stood ready in the workshop and her
name was posted next to her future husband's in the church.

During the final weeks, when her father let up on her and
she was becoming an outsider, she began to love her parental
home, her village, her roots, with single-minded intensity,
and to identify with them completely. Photographs from this
period show her standing tall, with her hair piled up in high
waves, elbows held out from her sides and hands barely touching, together only at the fingertips; head high, mouth slightly
open, lips pursed—an empty and vain face, the landed aris-
tocracy. On Sundays she even wore gloves and silk stockings,
but beneath the new clothes the rough linen underwear was
scratchy and the lice were as busy as ever within her sea of
hair. Friedl sometimes lovingly picked a louse from her neck,
but she hated him for it. She had learned to hold still in
church when the fleas in her clothes warmed up and the lice
scooted down behind her ears. She was ashamed when Friedl
jumped out of the bus on the church square and came running
toward her with his empty, flapping rucksack, right smack in
the midst of all the churchgoers, in the center of the stage on
which she was playing the role of "rich farmer's daughter
getting married and moving to town." Her mother-in-law approached her deferentially outside the church, but Marie, being
tall, talked down to her in a few grudging sentences, the true
granddaughter of her grandfather, the great Kajetan. Her sisters
giggled: "Once the beggar gets up on horseback, the devil can
no longer ride it." At home she slaved as before, doing the
work of two servants and without pay, but now she was doing
it out of a sort of family pride.

The wedding day arrived. The sheep she had raised on the

baby bottle and bathed in the trough every Saturday had been butchered. Its fleece had been hung to dry in the barn so it could serve as a rug in front of her bed in their new home. The furniture was in the barn, soft pine painted green; the tabletop had two cracks already.

It was going to be a small wedding, not a farm wedding, but a *Häusler* sort of wedding. It's supposed to have been a bright, sunny morning, and the bride was in white from head to toe, with myrtle in her hair, serious, pale, impatient. The wedding guests were standing around awkwardly in the living room; the wagon was ready, a hayrack with cross-boards to sit on; and the horse, part work horse and part Russian riding stallion, was scratching in the soft ground.

Everything was ready; only the bridegroom was missing, for he had to come from town, directly from his nightshift, and he had forgotten the bridal bouquet. When he arrived on his bicycle in the black suit of his older brother, he looked harried, absent-minded, and tired. The black suit made him look even gloomier and more corpse-like. Marie looked at her bridegroom and felt a wave of hatred and shame rising inside her. No bridal bouquet, and no enthusiasm in this dead man's face; she wanted to tear off her wedding dress and tell him to go to hell and catch some sleep there. She and Angela ran into the garden and picked her bouquet, whatever happened to be in bloom and a few green sprigs.

Marie stood beside him angrily, taller than he whether they were sitting or standing, taller and with broader shoulders. The bells rang. She was fighting back tears. This was supposed to be the most beautiful day of her life? They went inside the church. Never again would people line up on both sides of her as she walked to the altar in her long dress, myrtle in her hair. And what she felt, more than anything else, was that she had been cheated, had drawn the short end of the stick.

It was a Mass without the choir, without any music. Still, the guests were sobbing audibly, as guests always do at weddings and funerals. The rings Friedl took from his pants pocket didn't quite fit. He had bought them from a colleague who had come home from a Russian prison camp and found his wife in bed with somebody else. The dates and initials inside had nothing to do with them and their wedding. You could tell they were rings that had been worn. Her father and Friedl's brother were the witnesses: her father, who had beaten her for twenty years; his brother, who had cheated him out of his inheritance. Fanni wore a tight-fitting dark-blue dress and as usual was the most beautiful woman there. Then they went to the license bureau and the photographer. As the couple walked toward the exit, Marie saw her first and only love, Lois. He grinned and turned away and she felt herself blush.

Two solemn, scared faces look out from the wedding picture that hung in their bedroom for the first five years of their marriage. There is no infatuation, no happiness, not even a little pleasure, only fear, and a touch of arrogance in her face, a touch of sadness in his. I have searched all their wedding pictures in vain for a smile, a sense of elation. Even the guests look like funeral guests in the pictures. The Kovacs siblings have large, dark, hungry eyes. An accordion player tried to liven things up, and there was even some dancing, and someone whispered in Marie's ear, "Tonight I'd like to be a flea in your keyhole."

And then they walked up the winding stair to the parlor, which was reserved for family relics, Sunday clothes, and dowries, and there, on the window side, was the big double bed. Later she spoke of this night as one of the greatest humiliations of her life, as a loneliness endured in physical and mental anguish. In this bed began the slow death of her twenty-year-long marriage.

□

Grandfather: for my daughter that means a small white-haired man who always has time to stop and listen to her. His patience has no limits; "Let her be," he says. He beams with pride and spreads his arms wide, so she can run into them as if they were a harbor. He has delicate brown hands, which guide her gently from curb to curb. I wish I had had such a father, or at least such a grandfather. His faith in her is unshakable, faith in her uniqueness, her beauty, her rightness. Sometimes I think I should warn her.

This old man was once married to the young woman who overlooks the living room from the bookcase and who represents the concept *grandmother*. Why is her grandmother so much younger than her grandfather? Because the dead stay young, because our memories of them become frozen; we can look at them under their sheet of ice; there they lie unchanged, still and always a mystery to us.

My daughter is allowed to ask questions: "Grandfather, what was it like when Mama was little like me?" Yes, what was it like? I think, and hold my breath for the answer. Was he even present? Why don't I remember him? He reports that I was a good, quiet child, that I played silently for hours by the wall of the house, where no one could see me; you wouldn't have known I was around, that's how quiet I was. "Who is that?" my daughter had asked earlier, pointing to my mother's picture. "A woman," he had said, and his face had closed off all approaches. I had been overcome by sorrow then and by the need to be alone with my memories; I went behind the house, where no one could see me, to play silently with my speculations, my deep-frozen shadows.

To go back, past the endless nights when he stood by her bed and stared wearily into the darkness while she berated him and forbade him to leave the room; past my despair, night after night, in the adjoining bed and my silent prayers that he leave her just so I could sleep; past her full body under the thin negligee, bared for a few seconds with a provocative look (but when he reached for her she pushed his hand away). They kissed each other quickly, with closed, pursed lips, kisses like the ones you use to send children off to school.

Back past the tablets with their commandments, one of which says *Thou shalt not succumb to impurity*, to the wide bed near the window of the parlor. The tulle veil, two yards long, and the white batiste dress lie on the floor, at the foot of the bed, near the chamber pot. Did she insist on keeping the rough linen underwear on? Only a gypsy goes to bed naked with a man. The shame of a body that had never become aware of itself, the bottomless virginity of someone who despises herself. How can a body feel desire if it perceives itself as a nuisance? "You cannot fascinate me," he said later, and she sobbed and covered her face with her hands.

I wanted to ask what it was like in the big bed and later, until she found the courage to say no and stick to it for the rest of her marriage, using me as a wedge by putting me in his twin bed, next to hers. "Sex isn't all that important in marriage," she lectured. "What's important is that a woman know how to manage the household." And so they sat side by side, staring straight ahead, in the photographs taken at company picnics, at rest stops on our Sunday outings, and in the evening on the bench next to the house; the air was hard to breathe, it was so poisoned with unspoken reproaches and unbridgeable loneliness. This is probably how they lay next to each other all through their sleepless wedding night, each staring into a separate darkness, and their hands did not meet, not then and not later. For seven years he had waited for this night, and I will never have the courage to ask him how he felt when he sank back into his loneliness and realized that he had gained nothing, that there was nothing to be gained.

Well, who was the woman named Grandmother who smiles down on her former husband indifferently? "Did you like her?" the child asks and furrows her face compassionately, like a visitor in a hospital. He gets up and says, "I have to be going now." He believes the child has to be protected from all harmful influences. He conceals the hatred in his impenetrable face, which, when her name is mentioned, becomes the stony mask I remember from my childhood. "You love the new one more than my mother," I said to him angrily after his second wedding. "No," he replied, "you can love like that only once, but now I am finally happy." And you can hate like that only once. "She used to beat you," he says when I defend her. "And you were there and let her do it," I say. Then he says nothing and I scream and he says, "You are exactly like her," and gets up, and when he turns around and his back becomes unapproachable I feel the cold terror of abandonment. But I have learned that at this point screaming will do no good, nor will entreaties, because he is already out of reach as he walks down the street, slowly, as if for the last time, without a good-bye. Then I understand her again and her rage against his indifference, and this is the way I have been jostled back and forth between them for thirty years.

□

The day after the wedding they moved to town, with Marie and her goat sitting on top of the wagon in the middle of all the furniture. She was even more attached to the goat than she had been to the sheep that had come along as a throw rug; the goat's name was Julie and she would supplement their rations of milk. In the morning Marie had walked through the livestock barn once more, and she had cried. And as the village got smaller and smaller and the church steeple on the market square disappeared behind the hills, she cried again.

The new apartment was damp, so damp that fungus was growing in the corners and the pictures on the walls became spotted. During the winter, water ran down the stone walls. The bedroom was always dark. It had a large barred window at ground level, facing the farmyard. At night the farmer stood

in front of this window and eavesdropped; sometimes he slid
past, a dark shadow. A young married couple, but there wasn't
much to overhear. Above the joined beds hung the Holy Family: Joseph, busy with boards and a saw, in the background;
in the foreground Mary with a miniature grownup who fiddled
around with some boards with one hand and fed doves with
the other. A family idyll in front of a makeshift shelter, snow
on the mountaintops against the horizon. For sixteen years I
had to say my morning prayers in front of this picture and try
to emulate the little grownup in the knee-length white nightgown. I spent years studying him and hated him with a passion.
Later my main interest was in the red spots that had run the
edges ragged as the dampness affected the oil. The other room
was a combination living room, dining room, kitchen, and
bathroom. A sofa upholstered in green, a buffet, an old stove
that always smoked and in winter was the only source of heat.
The bedroom was never heated. Above the washstand were a
towel rack and a blind mirror. There was no running water
in the place, no bathtub, no drainage, and of course no toilet.

Marie could have endured this apartment, although she
couldn't get it through her head that the animal pens, the
barn, the whole farm belonged to someone else and that she
had only two damp rooms, which were rented at that. But
what she couldn't endure, and yet did endure for two and a
half years, were the people in the house: the farmer's wife, the
other tenants, the neighbors. From the first day on, it seemed
to her that everyone had conspired against her, and she withdrew shyly and truculently, drew water from the well at night
when they all were asleep, used the chamber pot to avoid
having to go to the outhouse when she heard someone in the
hall. She listened to every footstep outside her apartment as
if she were waiting to be picked up by the police, and breathed
a sigh of relief when the footsteps moved on; her stomach
contracted if the footsteps approached or, worse yet, came to

a halt. She told me that the farmer's wife dragged her through the hall by her thick red braids; fifteen years later the occasion for this had been forgotten, but the humiliation remained, merged with all earlier and later humiliations, and attacked her even at times when she was almost happy.

Marie walked along the strips bordering the fields, gathering leaves from the trees and clover and hogweed from the edges of the meadows for her goat, but when she got home with a full bag of the paltry fodder, the farmer took it away from her and emptied it in his grass shed. Once she was unwilling to give up Julie's meal; she stumbled and held on to the bag, and the farmer's wife dragged her through the whole farmyard.

Is that exactly what happened? It is what happened in her memory and tormented her until she died. What is reality compared to that? I imagined her being dragged through the yard by her hair hundreds of times and was ashamed of her helplessness. Over and over the story about the ink on the freshly washed laundry, about the farmer's wife tearing her bedsheets off the line and throwing them down into puddles, about the farmer cleaning out the stove when her white linens were drying there.

Why was she always surrounded by monsters? Laundry day meant scraping her fingers raw on the washboard, scalding them in the hot wash water, and then having them turn blue from the freezing rinse water. Contempt on all sides when she attended Mass on Sundays: look at her, the church mouse. Were the farmers at the edge of town the only ones who never went to church, not even out of curiosity? Or was curiosity already a form of contempt? I didn't ask her then. But she learned in slow lessons how to cultivate, extend, refine, and sublimate hatred. She walked through the subdivisions of the suburbs, where the first single-family houses were being built on small enclosed lots; hedges were beginning to grow along the brick walls. Beggars, she thought with contempt, they're all beggars; land reckoned in feet instead of acres, urban riffraff. But in the evening she dreamed of a small house at the edge of town, where no one could pour ink on her laundry because her property, though small, would be fenced in.

They led their separate lives. He was always tired, and often fell asleep sitting up. She demanded love, whatever she thought that meant; at any rate, it was something he deprived her of. Of course he loved her, wasn't that enough, what else was he supposed to do, what superhuman efforts did she demand from him? In bed he loved her as best he could, and she hated him for it. She felt abused and mistreated. Her back became stiffer, her face harder, more forbidding; when he approached her he provoked indignation. He shrugged his shoulders, sat down on the sofa, and dozed off.

"What's new?" she asked when he came home from work. "Nothing," he answered. She felt cut off from the world on this farm outside of town. To talk with the women in the neighborhood meant humiliation and concealed malice, which she would then brood about for days; she was afraid to run into them. "Why don't you go into town, especially since you get to ride free," he suggested. What was she supposed to do in town? She couldn't shop for anything, and did he want her to walk around looking at houses by any chance? "Beggars," she said, "they're all beggars; what do I want there?" He said nothing and felt hurt.

They were hungry. The food ration cards were not enough to satisfy their hunger. Marie had never had to be careful when it came to food; at home there was always something in the pantry, even if it was only bacon, cheese, and bread. To eat one's fill again, to eat something other than polenta! Food became an obsession; sometimes her hunger got so unbearable that she dreamed of secretly eating the contents of a pig trough, the garbage left from a farm meal: potato peelings, bread crusts, pieces of bone, soup, milk. Julie had tuberculosis, but they drank what little milk she produced anyway. Once a week Marie took a rucksack and went to redeem her food ration cards. On the way home she took the bread out of the rucksack—heavy, soggy bread—and broke off a piece, just a smidgeon, then another and another, until it wasn't worth putting the bread back. When she got home she had eaten the week's ration for both of them.

Unable to stand the homesickness and hunger any more, she went home. The train was filled to bursting with hoarders, townspeople who were trading food from the farmers for jewelry, clothing, china, whatever they could do without. Marie felt ashamed: nothing but malnourished, hollow-cheeked figures, who dozed apathetically and whose eyes spelled hunger when they had the strength to open them. She was one of the hoarders, one of the have-nots who travel to the farmers to beg, she, the farmer's daughter from a wealthy home. She was going home to beg and didn't even have anything to exchange.

At home they sat at the table, with all the food they wanted, a large bowl of cream soup and real bread, which didn't fall apart in your hands. She sat wrapped in a soft fog till she dropped off, swaying, while the others were talking to her. "What is it? What did you say?" She couldn't concentrate; her head was going around in circles; food, food; everything else was a phantom world reeling past. "The way you look," they said, "skin and bones." "Will you give me something to take along?" she asked her sister, burning with shame. "That'll be the day, when we feed you and your beggar of a husband," her father said. "Whatever you get from us is what you eat right here; you're not taking anything away." Fanni had had bad luck with the Sunday cake; she took it outside to feed to the chickens. "Give it to me," Marie begged. "That stuff isn't fit for human consumption," Fanni said, as the cake plopped into a puddle.

On rare occasions they went home together. Friedl looked
even more starved that she, his eyes large and glassy, his lips
too full in his shrunken face. "Don't you dare bring the *Häusler*
here," they told her at home. So the couple stayed with her
mother-in-law in the little house in the woods. But since the
wedding Marie's mother-in-law had stopped fussing over her.
Her son was unhappy; he looked as if he was starving; he hadn't
been this run-down and apathetic when he returned from the
front. Did the farmer's daughter, who was not used to thrift,
eat up his ration? What was the point in marrying a girl from
a wealthy family when her people refused to help her out now,
though they had more than enough of everything? "You're
letting my boy go to the dogs," the mother said. Marie said
nothing and hated the old woman. "Here," her mother-in-
law said, "go ahead and cook." Marie hesitated: she had expected to be treated like a guest. "Go ahead," Friedl's mother
said, with hatred and bitterness in her voice, "go ahead and
roast yourself over a hot stove; you're a housewife, after all."
In contrast to Marie's relatives, she gave them food to take
along, food she was doing without. "But this is for Friedl, you
have to give this to Friedl," she would enjoin Marie. "Here,"
Marie said when they were at home, throwing the butter onto
his plate, "this is for you, just for you." He shared with her,
but she hated him anyway, because she had no one who cared
whether she went hungry or not. She hated him for the stin-
giness of her own people and for his mother's hostility.

At harvest time she went home again. Since extra hands
were needed in the fields, they tolerated her presence. She
worked harder than ever in order to earn her meals, and so
she could take a few eggs, half a loaf of bread, and some bacon
home with her. After a week of the most backbreaking work
in the fields, no one could deny her some food in her rucksack.
Once, when she walked home by herself from the forest meadows, everyone else having left earlier, she encountered a young
woman sitting at the edge of the road, who pulled Marie by

the arm and, without asking, read her palm before Marie could draw it away. "You'll get pregnant soon," the stranger said; "you'll have a daughter and then a son. You'll live in a small house on top of a mountain; things will go better for you there than they do now. And then you are going to die; you will not live to grow old." Marie pulled her hand away. "Hey, what are you going to pay me?" called the woman. "I don't have anything," Marie said, lifting up her hands. "Oh yes you do; let me have that ring." The strange woman reached for her right hand. "Heavens, no, that's my wedding ring." "Well, the other one, then." But she didn't want to give up the engagement ring with the fake gem, either, for information she didn't believe in and hadn't asked for. "Then I put a curse on you," the woman screamed, and an icy chill ran down Marie's spine.

Only rarely did Friedl and Marie go anywhere together. They had no interest in walks and hikes. Nature was there for making a living, not for contemplation and enjoyment. They felt only contempt for the city-slicker point of view. During his two years on the job Friedl had made no friends whom they could invite over or meet with. No one had enough to eat; hospitality was out of the question.

At times when he was on call and had to stay in the dayroom, he played chess with a few of his colleagues; otherwise he sat silently and dozed. He was often summoned to the office to swallow some reprimand: passengers had complained that he called the stops too late or kept repeating the same stops, that he made change incorrectly, that he gave the signal for departure and allowed the car to start while someone was still standing on the steps. Afterward he would sit at home and brood, in a black mood. When Marie asked him what was wrong, he would murmur that nothing was wrong, not a thing. He wasn't about to let her reproach him for his errors at work, when she already held his background against him, as well as his inability to express feelings and the wretched conditions under which they lived. "I married you out of love," she wept, "and out of love I left a life of plenty and followed you to this hole, this persecution, this hunger." "You pauper," she screamed at him, "hunger doesn't hurt you, you're used to it." The gulf between them kept growing, and they had been married only a year. "If you think you can fascinate me as a woman, you are wrong," he said in an ice-cold voice. "I'll never forgive you for that," she said, weeping, and she kept her word.

During Mardi Gras they went to a few dances. Marie always came home dissatisfied and unhappy. She had looked at the other women with envy and thought, Why should they be having such a good time, why are the men crowding around them? They were dolled up and made up; they looked happy in their threadbare little postwar dresses, and Marie was again the seething wallflower whom no one looked at twice. Her husband sat next to her; he danced only with her, but his eyes followed the other women who flitted across the dance floor, laughing and feminine. Though he was faithful to his wife, he wondered what these dashing, fun-loving women would be like in bed. The liquor went to their heads quickly since their stomachs were empty. On the way home, around midnight, there was hostility and bitterness between them, but at home in bed the liquor made him aggressive. If she didn't want to participate, all right; he could get his own without her. She sensed that it had nothing to do with her, that he was far away. "Be careful," she whispered anxiously, but it was already too late. He rolled over on his half of the bed and fell asleep immediately, while she lay there open-eyed, counting back to her period. Please, no baby, not now, not with this poverty and hunger.

But it did happen. She had worn a menstrual pad because she had to go into town and then was going on to visit her sister-in-law. A few days later she tossed the pad into the dirty laundry, and her fear grew into certainty. She was pregnant. There was anger at him for his lack of control, and fear of bringing up a child in such wretched conditions, but perhaps also some covert pleasure, the secret excitement of something entirely new, a new sensation in her body, something that was growing inside her and would be entirely hers. It had to be a boy, she could tell for sure it was a boy, and his name would be Erich. He would be a calm, sensible child, who would understand her and give her the love she had known only in her dreams. She gained weight, but no one noticed; she kept it a secret for a long time. As time went on she and Friedl began to feel happy about their parenthood, and it brought them closer together; they felt affection for each other and for the third member, who had been conceived without love and yet generated something like love in them.

Her father was the first to find out. Could he imagine himself as a grandfather? she asked him in a portentous voice. He was forty-seven and about to be a father again himself. This time he actually planned to acknowledge the child as his and even toyed with the idea of marrying the woman; she was younger than Marie and a cousin of Friedl's, the sister of Kovacs the gypsy, who changed jobs, living quarters, and women more often than shirts and was faithful only to wine. The four daughters were sabotaging his plan with the same mixture of malice, scheming, and persistence with which Magda was trying to become their father's wife, and the daughters won out. His child was born two months before his first grandchild; it was a boy, someone to take the place of his two dead sons, but though the baby was given his father's first name, his last name was Kovacs.

As Marie's pregnancy advanced, she became more and more depressed. She would sit in her bedroom all day, crying. Then she would pull herself out of her brooding lethargy and travel home for some fresh air and nourishing food, but even there she sat behind the vegetable garden and cried. It was May, and the same flowers she had cut for her homemade bridal bouquet were in bloom; this recollection added to her unhappiness. Her sisters and even her father treated her more gently; in fact, her father made a joke now and then that referred to her condition, but—except for brief spells of wildly hopeful fantasizing—she saw only doom and misfortune ahead. With a child she would be even more dependent, at her husband's mercy. It seemed to her that she had to go through the wedding ceremony in all its inevitability for the second time, say yes for the second time, but now without any illusions about happiness or love. She clung to her vision of the child. Her child would help her escape from the misery of her marriage, of her whole life. Her child, her son, would not only be her comfort and support and give her the love she had hungered for for twenty-five years; he would also take her out of her present life into a life of wealth and recognition. He would achieve things she couldn't achieve even in her dreams; she would harness all her strength for this; she would sacrifice her own life for him and he would reward her royally. Through him she would make it after all.

☐

And if it had been a son, would she have made it? Was it disappointment that turned her against her daughter from the beginning? The question all daughters ask: *Would you have loved me more if I had been a son?* Would she have beaten Erich with such calculated thoroughness, intoxicated by the helpless child's cries of pain? And if she had found a way to express love, would that love have been less destructive than her hatred, hatred for whatever resembled her and would re-enact her destiny, her self-hatred? Later, when Fanni had sons—she bested Marie in this, too—and left them in her sister's care, Marie could imagine what it would have been like to have a boy. "I hate Aunt Marie more than anyone I know," Burkhardt, Fanni's son, said later. "Why?" we asked, dumbfounded. "She practically raised you." "Yes, and she was going to castrate me," he shouted. Too much undigested psychoanalysis? Burkhardt was a farm boy; he didn't know anything about castrating mothers. He meant it literally, and it came back to me, the time she stood there laughing, with the knife in her hand. "All right, now we'll cut if off; quick, get a big bucket to catch the blood," and the three-year-old stood in the corner, trembling and naked. I know I felt sorry for him then, though I could not match this with any comparable experience. I wanted to tell her to stop tormenting him, but I was afraid myself; I was eleven at the time.

Fall came, and the waiting became unbearable for her; her body became clumsier and clumsier, her back more and more painful. If the baby didn't come soon she'd need maternity clothes for the cool season. On the first brilliant day in October, when the contractions began, she put her nightgown into a cardboard suitcase and waited for her husband. The night was cool, there was a light frost on the meadows; she wore his greatcoat over her maternity dress. Carrying a lantern, since there were no streetlights yet at that far edge of town, they walked to the maternity hospital, a one-and-a-half-hour walk. Whenever the pains came, she sat down on the curb, fearful that the baby would be born right then and there on the deserted street. But it took another twenty-one hours. Friedl returned home so he could get a few hours' sleep before the early shift. At three in the afternoon, when the baby arrived, he was just returning from work. Marie's long, heavy braids were damp with sweat all the way down to the ends. "Don't be such a crybaby," the nurses said when they were stitching her torn flesh; "all redheads are crybabies." The midwife held

the squalling child up by its legs: a girl. "Oh dear, a girl,"
Marie said, and she let her head fall back, disappointed and
exhausted.

The women in the ward raised themselves up to get a look
at the newcomer. "I thought right away that you were from
the country," the woman in the next bed said, "the minute
they brought you in—those long, red braids." She spoke an
affected sort of High German, and Marie would have liked to
crawl under her blanket with her braids and her rural dialect.
Several hours later they brought her the baby to nurse. It
weighed about eight pounds and had large brown eyes, which
kept staring at her. "You little goat you," Marie said; she
found the situation almost embarrassing. Here was this
infant who stared at her and was her daughter. I am your
mother, Marie thought, and everything became even more
unreal.

They had to think of a name, since she had never considered the possibility of a daughter. Erika? No, there was an
Erika in a nearby village and she went to bed with the Russians.
Marie suggested Brigitte. No, Friedl had known a Brigitte and
she had jilted him; this was before he met Marie. Vera, Marie
said suddenly, remembering the black-haired refugee girl, delicate as a china doll, who had stood in their farmyard and
stared at her with eyes as large as those of the newborn. "Can
I help you?" the girl had asked when Marie lifted the ten-quart
cans of milk as she started to walk out through the gate. Marie
didn't know what to say, because no one had ever asked her
if she needed help, and the girl took one of the cans and
walked behind her to the village milkstand. She had to put
the can down every few steps, and she couldn't make the last
few yards at all, but Marie had been overjoyed precisely because it had been such a huge effort for the strange girl. "My
name is Vera," she had said and held out her hand when both
of them were catching their breath, leaning against the milk

bench. For a moment Marie was filled with a warm feeling of gratitude, affection, and the desire to protect someone. If she had known what friendship was, such a feeling would not have been so confusing, but since she had never had a friend, she was speechless and helpless in the face of the reverence she felt for the strange girl. "Her name will be Vera," Marie said in a voice that ended the matter, and that evening the new father filled out the papers. He had never heard the name, but if she wanted a Vera, it was all right with him.

Marie's breasts became inflamed and she developed a high fever. The pain from the hard, abscessed breasts, which seemed to be bursting with milk though not a drop could be squeezed out, was more unbearable than the delivery. Her sister Fanni had come to help out, cook, take care of the baby, wash diapers. She had also been chosen as the baby's godmother. But Fanni enjoyed her holiday away from home and soon found an admirer, with whom she went dancing every night. She spent the rest of her free time in town, and when she came back after midnight she was so tired that the baby's crying did not wake her. Marie lay in bed, weak and with a high fever, and felt only irritation and rage toward the crying baby, who interrupted her sleep morning, noon, and night. When she nursed her she could have cried out with pain, and as soon as she was through, the baby started crying again, crying, crying, crying. The neighbors knocked on the walls: How can anybody sleep? The farmer's wife barged in and threatened to kick them out without notice unless the crying stopped immediately. Marie and Friedl took turns walking the baby night after night, two hours apiece. When she quieted down they would put her in her buggy, but as soon as the buggy stopped moving the crying started again. They rolled the buggy back and forth from wall to wall, and sometimes, when exhaustion and rage overcame her, Marie pushed

it so hard against the wall that the impact made the baby
fall out.

☐

Childhood memories. The dim, damp-cold bedroom. The bars
that scissor the yard outside into long strips. The walls are very
high and gray. My parents' beds haven't been made yet. I am
lying in a crib painted green, waiting for day, which never
comes to the bedroom. Day is out in the kitchen.

The towel bar is painted white and is high up on the wall.
My mother lifts me up. I am sitting on the emperor's throne.
Mama and I are laughing.

I am sitting in the buffet. It is my house. I shut the door
and it is dark. I have taken out the dishes.

"Where is the key?" Mama asks. "Where did you hide the
key?" "Key gone," I say, wanting to go on playing. She holds
me by the arm; it hurts. "Where is the key? Bring me the key
immediately," she says threateningly. I am afraid but can't
remember. "Key gone," I say, crying, while she shakes me
back and forth. I would like to help, but I don't know where
the key is, and I know only these two words, *key gone.* When
she is cooking she finds the key buried in the flour canister.

The sun is shining in the yard. Mama is hanging up laundry, huge white sheets with holes. I play hide-and-seek with
the neighbor girl through the holes.

I have a rocking horse made of white, shiny material. It
stands in the corner next to the kitchen table. Lini Aggerl from
next door, who is several years older than I, has come over.
I show off my riding skills: I ride on the white horse and am
a princess. The horse throws me, but I don't cry, because
princesses don't cry.

Snow, nothing but snow, in broad, hilly waves all the way
to the village. It is evening and the snow is strangely blue,
blue as the Christ child; a touch of washed-out red lingers over

the last rise. I am wrapped up tightly and sitting in a sled; it moves, and Papa is pulling it, an endless journey into the blue evening. Never have I felt more secure.

Train rides in the evening. The hazy compartment lit by gaslight. The train jolts to a stop, often in the middle of nowhere, and starts again with another jolt. For me the lighted windows are white linen sheets fluttering along the tracks as we travel—landscapes for which, later, I looked in vain along this same stretch, magic landscapes. Mama must not be bothered during these trips; she is sick to her stomach. Toward the end of the trip, usually when the Danube has come into view and the lights on the other shore dangle into the water, she thrusts open the window and vomits on the passing tracks. She only gets sick on the trip back to town.

Daytime train trips from town to S. My panicky fear of the train. The hissing monster hitched to the cars; white steam curls around the wheels and rods below; I bawl every time we board. As we pass, dark underbrush and green meadows slip by; I stand at the window singing. But when it is dark and we have to leave the steamy warmth of the compartment, the train is a bad animal again and my panic is even greater in the dark. In the overcrowded bus I sit on Mama's lap; the ceiling light makes the bus cozy; the people are different from the people in town, more expansive and guttural in speech. There is a smell of farm animals. Mama is happy; I feel it sitting on her lap, and I am happy, too, when the lights go out and it gets dark and warm in Mama's arms.

The farmyard, which feels more like home than the apartment in town. The big room, warm as the belly of a cow, as it is getting dark outside and the drapes are not yet drawn. The fire in the stove, which flickers through the cracks of the door; the cats flitting by; the shadowy pictures of saints above the table. Outside, the dull lowing of the cattle, the rattling of chains, and the heavy clomping of wooden shoes on stone steps. Later, the housewife working silently at the stove, and the humming of the milk machine, which brings the sweet smell of fresh milk. The grownups are large, clumsy phantoms, and you must not get under their feet. They drag themselves over to the windowsill, where the cider glasses are, and sink down heavily at the table. The tablecloth is a dirty mountain landscape whose valleys hold crusted silverware, and somewhere far away, in the middle, is the big aluminum bowl with the cream soup and the bread cubes. The cats are moving around under the table; when one jumps up on the bench, it is pushed off by an elbow. At the end of the meal, the indistinct sign of the cross over eyes and mouth, and a monotonous, wonderfully soothing mumbling, which would have been perfect to put me to sleep—"Rest in peace, Amen." Monika and I will get our milk later. We have to lie down in opposite corners of the beat-up sofa and drink our sugary milk from bottles. In the night we fight a stubborn, silent battle over the blanket. We are the same age and share a crib. Later, when the fights become audible and we wake the grownups, Mama takes me into her bed. We sleep in the parlor, but it is always cold there, and again we pull the blanket away from each other in our sleep. And in the morning we are cross with each other.

On Saturdays we take our bath before the grownups get theirs. Both of us are put in a big wooden tub, and we are scrubbed with hot water. During the scrubbing, Angela, who is Monika's mother, says one can see right away that her child is a love child. Monika is sturdy and has blonde curls, hair like that of the baby Jesus. Quite early in my life I get the feeling that Mama is ashamed of me. I am a child that did not turn out well, and I am ashamed of myself.

In winter they come in the bitterly cold morning darkness and put overalls on us. We stand in the crib, our teeth chattering, and what we want more than anything else is to crawl back under the covers, even together. In summer we are awakened by the clanging of milk pails and the heavy treading of rubber boots. Then the rubber boots, plastered with wet grass, stand on the stove side of the room, while the grownups eat cream soup at the table. When one of the women gets us up, things never go fast enough for her. We stand around the room half asleep and are given bottles of lukewarm milk with big pieces of skin, which stop up the nipples. The ice-cold wash-cloths are slapped in our faces and somehow we wind up inside our clothes and are sitting, teeth chattering, on the side seat of the hayrack, which gets going with a high-spirited jolt and bumbles down the village street. Oxen are hitched to the hay-rack, and on the plank floor are scythes and rakes, and lunches wrapped in a cloth. Even later, when I have been a town girl for a long time, I am filled with anticipation of boundless adventure each time we ride down the village street in the early-morning sun and turn off toward the woods. When the grownups are working in a meadow close to the village, Monika and I are put in a cart. Sometimes, when we get up early, we are allowed to go along for the mowing, and then we can ride home in the pushcart through the dewy grass. When the hay is brought back we are lifted to the top of the towering load, and we teeter high above the heads of the oxen as we enter the farmyard gate. There are long mornings by shady streams with low bushes. Sometimes a farm hand brings us a young rabbit, a small grayish-brown ball with trembling flanks and quivering nostrils.

I never see much of Mama when we are on the farm. She is a vague presence with strong arms, a headscarf, and sun-burned skin, which you can pull off her arms in strips. She never has any time, and her stern, distant face issues threat-ening orders: "You must not go inside the barn; you must not run off; you must not play under the hayrack." She puts me down by the stream at the edge of the meadow, next to the bundle containing our lunch. "You are not to move away

from here!" The meadow is big and so quiet it is scary. Woods
all around. Slowly the shadows of the trees walk away from
me. The sun begins to bear down; the crickets chirp more and
more stridently; heat trembles above the field; my head is
spinning; I am getting sick; I can't breathe; I have been forgotten. The sun is painting colorful circles in the air; the
crickets are as shrill as sirens. When I come to, I am lying
under a large hazel bush in the middle of the freshly mown
meadow, a noontime bush, and Mama is giving me ice-cold
spring water to drink.

I was afraid of the animals. I did not like to go into the barn.
Only later, when I forced myself to rediscover the buried farm
heritage in me, my supposed roots, did I breathe in the thick
air of the barn and let the calves sniff my fingers. I felt a secret
satisfaction in seeing my daughter slip through the well-meaning fingers of her great-aunts and run screaming from the
lowing cattle. I was afraid of the rattling chains and the heavy
stamping of the hoofs. The ground was damp, and if you
slipped you would have brown stains on your clothes and get
a scolding. But I enjoyed sitting in the empty calf-stalls, which
were very narrow and padded with straw chopped fine, and if
no one discovered you, you could sit in that dark warmth,
separated from the large cattle by the central aisle, and breathe
in the warm, penetrating smell. That, too, was an instance of
feeling protected.

There were lots of hiding places, and you were always in
some grownup's way. There was some punishment for almost
everything you did on your own, from being put across someone's knee to being locked inside the black kitchen, which was
otherwise used for baking bread. Monika and I loved to sit in
the grain shed and bury ourselves deep in the kernels. If one
heap was too small, we helped ourselves to the grain from
another. We played with grain the way other kids play with

sand. That the different heaps were made up of different kinds of grain, and that you weren't supposed to mix oats with wheat, we found out only when we got a thrashing in the big room.

I was scared to death when they slaughtered the pigs. I barricaded myself behind baby buggies, armchairs, and foot-stools in the farthest corner of the room while the piercing shrieking and squealing was going on in the yard. I didn't emerge until the women came in with bloody tubs and troughs and the stove was hissing. Afterward a pig's bladder dangled from the ceiling for days.

Monika took to this environment better than I did. She stood in the crib and danced a samba, *Bimbo, Bimbo, you're a little black boy.* . . . The grownups were enchanted. The child of Marie's younger sister, the love child, the bastard who had brought the disgrace of illegitimacy upon them, laughed, sang, and was her grandfather's pet. And I, the child of marital obligation, sat dark-eyed and thin in a corner and pouted because nobody liked me. "A strange person," my grandfather said with disgust. He took the first plums of summer from his pocket, and we stood expectantly on the steps of the house, waiting to receive them. But only Monika's hands filled up, and I went inside the grass shed and cried. I nestled against Mama because I felt unloved and cast out, but she, too, pushed me away, with her elbow, as if I were an annoying cat. "Leave me alone; can't you see I'm sweaty and exhausted?" I sat on the other end of the bench and fought back tears. "Such a bad-tempered child," the others said, and Mama was ashamed of me. The farm was the place where I learned that I was unloved and in the way.

☐

How far back I have to remember in order to remember love, a tenderness and security that sprang not from things, but from people. Later my mother often told me about the convulsions

I had had at the age of nine months. She told me this so as to reproach me for my ingratitude, to point out to me that I had owed her my life not once but twice, so that there would be no end of gratitude. My parents had been on a company outing in the mountains. There are photographs of them on this outing, sitting side by side in an alpine meadow, a young couple. My mother was twenty-seven and wore a dirndl dress. Her figure was fuller than it had been for some time. They sit next to each other in the sun, free and alone together for the first time in nine months, but in their faces is the same mute, dull sadness as in their wedding picture. He looks at her with a questioning, almost beseeching look, knowing the futility of his half-turn toward her. She stares straight ahead with an absent look and a vague smile for the photographer. It is as if there had been a reconciliation that had healed and solved nothing. At that time they must have called each other by their first names. When I was little, I sometimes heard him call "Mizzi" when he came home. "Dearest Mizzi"—that's how the army postcards began. Later they called each other Mama and Papa, even when they were fighting.

On the day of this outing, they had left the baby with one of Papa's sisters, who was then newly married. But the baby had cried when they left in the morning and had not stopped by the time they returned in the evening. Next day the convulsions started; her small limbs cramped and her lips turned blue as she fought for air. Marie ran out into the open air with her child, a small bundle of wrenched, contorted hands and legs. The neighborhood women were standing around offering opinions and useless advice. And suddenly the convulsions ceased and the baby lay limp and lifeless in her arms. "Now she's dying," the neighbors said, nodding their heads; "now she is with an angel in heaven." "No," Marie screamed and took a bus to the doctor's office just as she was, wooden shoes, housedress, and denim apron. The baby was saved and indebted, owing too much gratitude to be paid off in a lifetime. "What did you do that was so special? You just went to the doctor," I said once. She turned away, silent and offended, and soon found an opportunity to beat me for my impudent answers.

□

Marie was filling out. She and her child spent a lot of time on the farm, and she couldn't stop appeasing the hunger of the postwar years. You could get more food now, even with the ration cards. But Friedl was still skinny and hollow-cheeked. There was open warfare between Marie and her mother-in-law. "You're letting my boy go to seed; he's always alone, just like he isn't married," the old woman complained. "I'm doing it because of the child—the damp apartment, the poor food; here she gets fresh air and good country food," Marie would say. Later she gave up defending herself. She stopped going to the cottage in the woods. How could the old woman comprehend that she sat in the town apartment crying, doing nothing but crying, unable to stop, that she could not muster the strength and courage to dress the child and take her out? She was afraid of the town, of the people; constant, undefined anxiety pressed down on her chest. How could she explain this anxiety to herself?

When Marie did take the child out, she packed her so tightly into blankets and wrappers that she could hardly breathe. She wouldn't let anyone look inside the carriage; she was frightened if someone said, "What a pretty child—such big brown eyes." Among the admirers there might be someone who coveted the child for herself. She was afraid of the evil eye, and her fear was as real and concrete as the fear that her child might catch a cold and die. The child was her only possession, which she guarded jealously and fearfully and believed to be in constant danger. When she brought the new baby home from the maternity clinic, no one but she was allowed to carry her: she was afraid anyone else would drop her. But she herself was afraid to hold her, and the reason for all the padding was that the baby would be safer.

Marie would watch over the crib gloomily, and when she could no longer stand the pressure, she would ram the baby carriage with its crying bundle against the wall, in helpless desperation. Then she would sit at the kitchen table and cry for hours.

Every winter the child was sick. In November she would come down with bronchitis, and she wouldn't get rid of her cough and troubled breathing until March. When I was X-rayed at the age of five, the doctor found scar tissue covering old lesions in my lungs. She put my head under a heavy blanket and forced me to inhale the steam over a tub of hot water: "Breathe deep or you'll get a licking." She put her own head under the blanket and inhaled with me, but that made my fear of the cramped, steamy darkness even worse. Day after day she went into the woods, carrying her child piggyback, to gather young pine shoots, which she cooked one evening: good for the lungs, all natural. Everything for her child.

But the child was ungrateful; she cried a lot, was pale and thin and reticent. A strange person, her grandfather pronounced. Marie looked at her daughter as she sat silently and glumly next to Monika, that sunny little bundle of mirth, and she had to agree with him. It hurt her that her sacrifices should go unrewarded, that they should earn her so much ingratitude. That's what happened when you had a child by a dull and homely man. "Yes, she takes after her father, she certainly is his spitting image," she would say, sighing, and then walk away when she couldn't bear the sight of me any more; or she would start to nag me about giving her so little pleasure in return for all her trouble.

After four years in the damp apartment inside the farmhouse, they saw an ad in the paper: "For sale: small house at the edge of town, the land to be leased." The asking price was manageable; the house could be paid off in a year or two. It was at the other end of town, a long way from the scene of their early defeats. A chance for a new beginning. A log house of almost three hundred square feet; one room with kitchenette and toilet on the ground floor, and upstairs two bedrooms, which you reached by climbing a ladderlike staircase. Marie was used to large, high rooms; in this house you could touch the ceiling with your outstretched hand. She felt as if she were crawling around in a doghouse, but there was running water, and no one could spy on her or mistreat her here. The land they would rent was spacious. "We could keep chickens," she said, "and maybe rabbits, or even a goat." The present owners, refugees from Hungary, were going to emigrate to the United States. The initial visit to the landowner was endless. I stood, holding my mother's hand, next to a chest of drawers in a narrow hallway. We were not invited into any of the rooms. "Be quiet," I was told, "stand still. Make a good impression. If you're good, we'll go look at the little rabbits afterward." I was good and waited impatiently for the little rabbits, but in the end we left without having seen them. Feeling betrayed, I couldn't have cared less about the new house.

Marie borrowed the money from her father and from Rosi, who was now a full-fledged dressmaker and had her own shop in the district capital. We often went to visit her, as we visited the farm, to have an excuse to get out of the farmhouse apartment, that hateful, damp hole. The shop was also her residence. She slept behind a curtain that shielded her bed from the customers, and there was a small room with a living area and eating table. "Free and easy," my mother called her place, with a mixture of moral indignation and envy. Rosi received male visitors. She had a record player on which she played us music to dream by: *Where the Wild Stream Runs, in the Forest*

Green and *White Swans in the Old Castle Pond.* A dream
factory, full of life, and without the bleakness I knew at home.
I felt good there, and so did my mother; she was more animated
and younger in her sister's free-and-easy quarters, sipping a
glass of cognac, which went to her head so quickly that she
forgot about my presence when my aunt recounted anecdotes
from her love life. Rosi made dresses for us, flowered pastels
with ruffles, ribbons, and smocking, which had to be kept
clean.

In the fall we moved into the new house. I was three years
old and was allowed to play outdoors by myself for the first
time. With no one watching, I could wander through the
woods below our property, lay claim to hollow trees and make
houses out of them, get my shoes soaked wading in the stream,
out of reach of my mother's strict instructions. I designed a
dream paradise that no one was allowed to enter. I played
alone by the woodpile behind the house, or in the woods below;
I built sand castles out of the fine Danube sand that was left
over from mixing concrete. My father, too, was wordlessly
happy; he built a summerhouse, a laundry room, and a chicken
coop next to the house, put in concrete flooring, installed
water and sewer pipes.

Things were looking up: a home of our own, more food
to eat, less quarreling. My parents rented a piece of some
publicly owned property in the river bottoms for almost nothing. You could have as much land as you could cultivate.
This spot, too, became a fairy-tale place for me. Water gurgled
behind the alders. When the snow melted, it pulled against
the roots and dragged the branches downstream in gray eddies.
In front of this there was a garden strip with beds for vegetables
and feed corn, which had to be wrested back from the river
each year, and which the river reclaimed from time to time,
leaving behind waves of fine sand you could dig your toes in
deep. Dune landscapes you sank into; sand castles driven into

the river by the wind. A cornfield, with stalks tall as men, and spears of light that the sun shot through the fleshy tassels; a jungle in which you could hide and be safe. On the other side of the alders, beside the path with the deep ruts, my father had built a wooden shed. It was dark inside, between the tools and the old clothes; a broken piece of mirror hung on the wall; in there I was the enchanted water sprite who let salamanders and round colored stones glide through her fingers.

In summer we had fresh vegetables from "our garden," and before long we had fresh eggs from "our chickens." "Our flowers" blazed at the edge of the path, and I held on to the garden gate, swinging back and forth: it was our garden. My mother was happy; she could cultivate the land with her own hands, and under her hands everything grew. When she worked in her blue jumper, bare-shouldered, with tanned, freckled arms, her hair held back by a scarf, she was as oblivious as I was in my kingdom. She did not notice the glances, from men across the fence, that rested on her ample figure, or the jealous looks of their wives. "You can't fascinate me," the one man who had seen her undressed had said to her, so how could others see her as anything more than a human machine at work? "Shame on you, you slut," a woman yelled at her from a window when she was tying her shoes alongside the path and bending forward in her blue jumper. Friedl was coerced into confronting the woman and telling her off on Marie's behalf. "Does she have to parade everything she's got right in front of our window?" the woman complained. "My husband's eyes are about to pop out; he's always at the window when she walks by." Friedl was embarrassed and apologized. For Marie, another lifelong enemy had made her appearance.

Things were looking up, though. Every morning we went to get fresh milk from a farmer. My father brought home bags of broken cookies from a factory, goods that had not made it through the conveyor belt and were given away or sold at low cost on certain days: cheese rinds, doughy wafer pieces. People no longer starved to death on food ration cards, and eventually no longer needed ration cards. Sometimes there was even enough money left over to fulfill some small dream. Marie could finally afford to have her hair cut and dyed. No one was going to call her "carrot-top" any more, not so long as she lived, and no one was going to know by her long braids that she came from the country. In church she wore fashionable clothes, hats, and a haughty face. At home she went around in wooden shoes, with her hair tied in a scarf and a denim apron covering her now more than ample figure: she could not stop appeasing her postwar hunger, and she was getting fat. An imposing woman, people called her. Friedl did not gain weight. "Your husband looks like he's not getting enough to eat," someone would say now and then. A strange couple walking to church on Sundays, arm in arm, one of them holding the hand of the child in her white stockings, black patent-leather shoes, and itchy woolen dress that must not get dirty because it had cost half a month's pay. This is what she lived for: that people should respect us, that we should count for something in the community, that people should see nothing, that people should have no cause to talk about us. A haughtily smiling façade, expensive dress fabrics bought in the most expensive stores and worn for five years without once being laundered, since Sunday clothes are something you watch out for and take off as soon as you get back inside the door. Straitjackets in reputable, middle-class taste, with which we bought people's respect, while at home we ate broken wafers, since no one could see inside your stomach. The greatest honor would have been if, on Corpus Christi Day, Friedl had been one of the four men who carried heaven; but he was puny, he counted for nothing, he was only a streetcar conductor.

Sometimes someone still used the term "beggarwoman,"

meaning her, in spite of the spotless dresses and hats on Sunday. "Why don't you buy some windfall fruit for the poor kid? They're selling it cheap at the market right now," a neighbor said, and earned Marie's everlasting hatred. She said nothing, she never fought back, but each time a few more muscles hardened in her closed face. After each such incident she struggled even harder to make a place for herself and her child among the engineers, doctors, architects, and professors of the community by means of her appearance, her queenliness, her unapproachability, her good taste—as far as that was possible with a husband who impressed no one, who was nothing and earned nothing. The joy of having her own home, of not going hungry any more, of being able to work for herself, did not last long. The old sense of discontent returned, and so did her ambition to rise in the world.

Now that we were almost somebody, we no longer had to visit the country as the poor, humble relatives. We wore our Sunday clothes and had to dust off the seats on the train with toilet paper before we sat down, but now she could step into the big room with self-confidence: The city folks are here. Nylons and painted red lips, and a triumphant smile that was wiped away as soon as she went to shovel manure in her rubber boots and mended skirt, her head covered. But those first moments of arrival—she made the most of them.

Neither her husband nor her child was useful for her high-flying dreams. The child pale, with large, dark eyes, so large and dark that you didn't notice the rest of the face, with high, jutting cheekbones which made fresh, round cheeks an impossibility, and always sullen. "Eat, so you finally look like something; eat, or you cannot leave the table; eat, or I'll beat you within an inch of your life." The table became a daily battleground. Boiled meat and red cabbage in the soup. I gagged on it, vomited, and was marched back to the table. Boiled bacon, turnips, and potatoes on the farm. I dreaded mealtimes, the stern face of my mother, the contempt in the eyes of the others. "That brat's not eating, our food isn't good enough for her, the *Häusler*'s daughter; look at what a good eater our Monika is. Child, you are ungrateful; it's for your sake that we've pulled ourselves up out of the worst; for you, all the sacrifices we're making." Please don't make any more sacrifices for me, I wanted to cry out and be released from gratitude. With my guilty face lowered, I waited for the moment when no one was looking my way and quickly stuffed the pieces of fatty meat into my apron. Later, when my mother was washing dishes in the kitchen, I shoved the meat under the wardrobe. In the afternoon I ate wild strawberries and sour clover. And when the moldy meat was discovered during housecleaning, I got a beating. Just when my corporal punishment began I can't remember, but at that time it was, along with the hassle of eating and Sunday clothes, an unalterable fact of life, like winter and summer and rain: you couldn't escape it; there was always something you had done that was punishable.

A beating: it never meant a spontaneous burst of anger, which might be followed by awkwardness and reconciliation. It began with a look that transformed me into vermin. And then a silence in which nothing had been decided yet and which nevertheless was past escape. The offense was swallowed up by the silence; it was never discussed. There were no alibis, explanations, excuses. There stood the misdeed, whether it was a banana stain on a dress or food refused—unatonable—and suddenly the misdeed was only a symbol for such an enormous wickedness that no amount of punishment sufficed. "Get me the carpet beater," she commanded; "get me the cudgel." This was a wooden stick the thickness of an arm, which split in two during the course of my education. The broken cudgel was itself significant evidence of a culpability so great that it could never be punished fully. Had she been completely just, she would have had to beat me to death. I owed the fact that she continued to let me live to her sacrificial mother love, which, like the grace of God, was not earned and could never be repaid.

Even when I had learned that it was a senseless gesture, I threw myself down in front of her each time, my arms clasping her knees, begging, *Please, please dear Mama, my dearest Mama, I'll never do it again, I promise, I swear, you can take everything away from me, only please, please don't hit me.*

She never bent down to me; her face remained remote, as if she were carrying out the work of a higher power. I never dared to disobey her command; I always went whimpering behind the curtain to the side of the stairs, where the cudgel and carpet beater hung from hand-crocheted loops; they had their special hooks. What happened after the moment when I hesitantly handed her the instrument of chastisement I don't remember; I only know all hell broke loose. This is what hell must be like: pain and pain and pain in a rhythm that the body recognized almost instantly and against which it could not protect itself, neither by turning aside nor by running off, because the pain simply struck another part each time.

Blind, I never saw her or the cudgel during the beating, only the smacks of wood on flesh, of metal-reinforced rubber on flesh, could be heard. Could it really be heard? Do I believe now that I heard it? How could I have heard it when I screamed, screamed as loudly as I could, from the first blow to the last? For sooner or later there was a last blow. Why this or that particular blow should be the last, I could not guess. It was God's will, it was her will: she didn't beat me in anger, after all; she beat me for my own good and to drive out my abysmal wickedness. The last blow was the well-considered temporary end of an atonement that would never end.

And then she let herself fall to the floor, breathing heavily and stretching out full-length, exhausted as from the completion of hard labor, and I stood there terrified, with my heart racing and the pain gone suddenly numb. Was she about to die of exhaustion, had she fainted, all because of my guilt, the hard work I had caused her? She had told me so often that I would be the death of her. "Take the cudgel away," she said weakly, almost gently, and her slack voice gave me hope that she would survive.

When I came home from my expeditions in the woods or from picking flowers, there was always the chance that my mother's grimly scornful face would meet me and that I would be sent to fetch the cudgel. In spring I brought home large bouquets of primroses and anemones in order to soothe any possible anger in advance: look Mama, what I picked for you, and she was touched. "But the dress—did you have to get grass stains on your dress? And the skinned knees!" The larger the wound, the greater the panic, the more vehement the anger and the blows. I danced around the living room, always in a circle, until I got dizzy and cut my lip on the edge of the table. The screams of pain stuck in my throat when she grabbed me and hit me in the face randomly, until her hands and my dress were bloody from my torn lip. I was sent to bed with a cloth over my mouth. The wound should have been stitched, the doctor said the next time I went for a checkup.

I spent much time in bed. I had to go to bed when I wouldn't eat or when I was bad, but how could you avoid being bad? How could you know ahead of time what was bad and what would earn you a benevolent smile? Soon I had found out that whenever I felt happy and carefree I was bad and had to be punished. "I don't know what's the matter with the child; she's always so sad and morose," my mother said. Being sad and morose was a fault, too, but I wasn't beaten for it.

I became timid and fearful. Danger lurked everywhere; every-thing was dangerous. For every possible adventure there was a story of a horrendous, usually fatal outcome. Every successful adventure was rewarded with a beating. There was her constant fear that times would get worse and we would be hungry again. You had to be thrifty; every discarded crust of bread was a sin, the concealed pieces of meat under the wardrobe a crime. Then there was the fear of neighbors and of talk: the beatings took place behind closed windows and locked doors. Fear of thunderstorms could be averted only by endless rosary prayers, for where should lightning strike but here, reducing our wooden house to a heap of ashes within five mintues. At the first flash of lightning I was pulled out of bed; the feather beds, our most valuable possessions, were carried into the living room, and there we sat in the dark by flickering candlelight and prayed until the thunderstorm was over. Fear of the devil, who could meet up with you at night, or even in the daytime, in the shape of a good-looking young huntsman in a narrow pass, betrayed only by his club foot, was nothing by comparison.

Then there was the fear of men, especially occupation soldiers; most dangerous, a jeep full of Russians on a lonely country road. Whenever we had to take the bridge across the Danube, I started trembling at the bridgehead stop, because in the middle of the bridge there was the shanty, the border control between zones, where foreign soldiers checked IDs. The streetcar emptied out and waited until the passengers had been cleared and got on again. But I had to remain in the empty streetcar, under strict instructions not to leave my seat unless I wanted a beating, and I had to watch my mother disappear into the shanty, from which she might never emerge while I waited in the streetcar. The epitome of debasement was a woman who carried on with foreign soldiers. There were examples of this on my father's side of the family, but what else could you expect from gypsies and *Häuslers*. In fact, to have anything to do with a man was the worst thing you could do. Whatever that meant, I knew it had to be something terrible, so terrible you couldn't talk about it except maybe in whispers. It was something I couldn't be accused of, base though I was, but was suspected of doing in the future and so was somehow guilty of beforehand. "How will I make my daughter really and truly understand what a jewel her virginity is?" my mother said to an acquaintance, while I played with my doll kitchen. I was afraid of this jewel, whatever it might be, for if it was that important I probably wouldn't be able to guard it well enough to escape a beating in the end.

Since we'd moved to the new house I had stopped sleeping in a crib and now slept in Mama's bed, back to back with her; I never had enough room and I couldn't wrap myself up in the feather bed. In the morning the sheet was wet; Mama would have to hang the mattress out of the window and was very angry with me. Such a big girl should not need diapers; after all, I was three years old and should wake her instead of wetting the bed. But when I woke up and felt that I had to use the chamber pot, I was afraid to wake her because that made her angry, too. "Can't I ever sleep through the night?" she'd say as she yanked me out of bed. Desperate, I lay next to her and prayed that the urge would go away, and when I timidly whispered "Mama" and waited, listening to her regular breathing, and touched her shoulder with my finger and again whispered "Mama," it was too late.

"Girls are toilet-trained by age one and a half; boys may take a little longer," she, the experienced mother of the best-brought-up child, said to young, inexperienced mothers. She had many bits of advice for such women, who wanted to raise a child as obedient and well trained as me. "You have to strike children or they won't amount to anything; if you love your child, don't spare the rod. Children demand it; they're always testing how far they can go. Even newborns tyrannize over their mothers, and all the more so when they reach the defiant stage; you've got to nip that in the bud. We never had any tantrums at our house; at the first sign of rebelliousness you start in, you whack them until you break them of it." When someone gave me a piece of candy, I said please and thank you with averted eyes, my face unhappy from the strain of the obligation. People were polite: How nicely she says please and thank you; they praised Mama and overlooked my scared, joyless face. But not everyone was polite enough to feign blindness, and once in a while a woman who understood children would say, "Like a trained monkey," and incur my mother's lifelong enmity. "Don't look so glum," people on the bus would say, and I would start to cry. "What black eyes you have; you must have forgotten to wash them," people would say to tease me, and at home Mama would say, "Eat more so your cheeks will get plump and you won't have such starved-looking eyes." I was afraid of people because I sensed my mother's fear.

□

We are looking for old toys, my daughter and I. If you stand on a chair at the end of the chicken ladder, you can lift up a lid that will admit you to the attic. Dust trickles down on your hair, the decay of thirty years, black as soot. And there they are, my seven dolls, my seven daughters, but I no longer recognize them. "You played with those?" Of course she is disappointed, my spoiled daughter. She is reconciled only to the eighth, the one I never wanted because she came to me too late, a walking doll that has eyes that close and says "Mama" and has hair you can style. My daughter puts aside my other children, with their stuffed arms and battered heads. Where is her imagination? Doesn't she see how good-natured Liesi is, how sarcastic and vain Greti is, how delicate and sensitive Marlies is? "Poor Mama," she says, "didn't you ever have any real toys? How could you play with such stuff?" Child, I've seen you play with your real toys from an expensive toy store; you were in the same world I was in, but it was a different world, and that's why I believed you would be able to break the chain. That's why your dolls don't have their heads bashed in and their hair pulled out. That's why you say, "Good night, Snow White," and cover her lovingly and send the dwarfs away so no one will disturb her sleep. My dolls never slept; all of them were Cinderellas, who had to work and be obedient and still could do nothing right; they were rebellious and obstinate and had to be punished until their noses were broken and bundles of their hair were loose in my hands. "What are you doing?" my mother would call from the kitchen; "You are breaking the doll." "But that's because she was bad," I said self-righteously. This time the power and the law are mine, because in my world I am the ruler of fortune and misfortune, and there is no good fortune in my world. "What has she done?" my mother asks, trying to insinuate herself into my world. "She won't turn the wheel," I say and continue my punishing duties, slamming the doll's face against the edge of her buggy until it is full of cracks. "And why should she turn the wheel?" "Because I say so." But she was obstinate and wouldn't turn the wheel, and now she gets her head bashed in and will go around for the rest of her life with these scars, to be taken out of a dusty box thirty years later with the wounds still not healed, though no one will remember where they came from. Everyone will see her as ugly, disfigured for life; only for me will she still be beautiful, because she wears my wounds.

"Why are all the dolls so battered?" my precocious daughter asks. *Because my mother beat me, because I am battered:* no, you can't say that to a little girl. Why turn her face into a face of horror and disbelief? "Because the dolls are old and things have been thrown on top of them." "What kinds of things?" Sharp-edged kitchen stoves, sleepless nights, blows on the head and on the heart, baby carriages and marriage beds and my God, the doll's face has become unrecognizable, the forehead is dented, the cheeks hollow; the eyes are dead, the mouth is only a thin line. "It happens to almost all dolls with time; it's normal."

My daughter is sitting under the stairs in the precise spot where I used to sit, unfolding doll clothes, a puppet theater, an old piece of brocade. But she plays differently from me: now she is the fairy-tale princess covered with a brocade canopy, and Punch is courting her. "You are beautiful, and you are beautiful, and you are the most beautiful of all," he says. "Dinner?" he asks. "No, the princess and I are going to a gala reception tonight; it's a lovely idea, and many thanks, but we're not hungry now." As I eat my sandwich by myself, leaning against the buffet, I wonder why Punch never courted me, never took me out to dinner. And if at nine o'clock Punch should say, "I'm sorry, but the princess and I aren't sleepy yet; we're going out for a walk"? What shall I do then, Grandmother? Then you'll have to hit her, because children should be in bed by seven o'clock, after their supper and bedtime prayer and after brushing their teeth. And if she doesn't want to? What do you mean, she doesn't want to? Who's in charge at home? You are a failure, your child won't amount to anything; she doesn't know discipline, respect, obedience, and one fine day she will start hitting you unless you beat her to the punch. You'll remember my words someday. Yes, that's what she would say. Grandma, you wouldn't have loved this child, either, I say, and wipe my greasy fingers on my skirt and laugh because I have the power to break the chain and cancel everything: the bedtime prayer and obedience, fear, and perhaps even hatred.

☐

In our house there were no unpolished shoes, and no dust motes floated in the sun. In our house mealtimes were punc-

tual; in our house everything was well regulated. When you
came home you wiped your shoes on the mat in the entrance
hall and then took them off next to the kitchen door: "Don't
you dare bring any dirt into the house." The bedrooms were
for sleeping; you didn't go up to them at other times: "You
don't laze around in bed; all that does is give you ideas for
mischief." As soon as you woke up you had to get out of bed
and have your face smacked with a damp washcloth. Everything had to move fast in the morning or you might miss out
on the day. After the washcloth in the face, you sat down on
a chair to have your hair fixed, a perfectly straight part and a
ribbon that held the hair away from the forehead. Every day
Mama ironed the ribbon, which sat on my head like a giant
butterfly and was a further reason for gratitude—what other
mother would go to the trouble of ironing her daughter's ribbons every day? Then there was breakfast: warm milk with
honey from a baby bottle until I was seven. And don't forget
the morning prayer; you can't leave the house without the
morning prayer. Our distance from the picture of the Holy
Family was set by an invisible ruler, and there we stood side
by side in the same spot year after year, our hands folded
against our chests, the sign of the cross at the beginning and
the end—not a sloppy, messy one, either, for we always have
time enough for a fine sign of the cross, touching forehead,
chin, and chest. Then she dipped her forefinger in the kettle
of holy water next to the toilet door and drew a wet cross on
my forehead. Now nothing could happen to me all day, unless
I was disobedient and received a beating. Evenings in the late
fall, when it got dark early, I played in the corner under the
slanting stairs. But I wasn't engrossed in my play; I was listening
to my father read to my mother from Ganghofer novels, such
as *Die Martinsklause*, in which a wild redheaded woman causes
disaster and someone severs the tendons of young huntsmen
in castle dungeons. The world of these novels provided more
vivid images than my doll corner.

On Sundays my mother sat on a bench outside the house and kept gazing down the gently curved path that led up the hill. It was a footpath between a grassy field and the edge of the woods, and there rarely was anyone on it, since the four houses for the Hungarian refugees, of which ours was the first, were in a cul-de-sac. If anyone came up the hill, it was bound to be a visitor for us or one of our three neighbors, the fifth house being a weekend cottage.

On rainy Sundays or in winter she went to the veranda door every ten minutes and looked down the path. I grew up with the feeling that every change, good or bad, whether relief from beatings or news of someone's death, had to come up this path. Only thunderstorms came from the opposite direction. But we rarely had visitors, and when a familiar face did come up the slope, the whole house shook with excitement, and the heavy, stony face of my mother took on life. Water for coffee was put on the stove and a piece of cake cut into four segments; the table was wiped and set and the denim apron hidden behind the curtain. My mother's family never came unless they were visiting someone in the hospital: it was too inconvenient for them to take the bus from town, walk up the hill, and let themselves be squeezed into such close quarters, only to take food away from poor people. But the Kovacs girls had married into the city; they lived in dark apartments and their children were pale and delicate. Marie's feeling toward them was one of kindly condescension that easily turned to scorn. They were lacking in humility, for, after all, they were the daughters of a *Häusler*, even if they played at being ladies now and had enough to eat, as was evident from the weight they had gained. But their low birth showed anyway, Marie said, what with Lydia shamelessly unbuttoning her dress on a crowded train to nurse her twins, without turning aside or covering herself with a cloth; sometimes when she came to visit she had forgotten to put on underpants. Also, they ate

whatever was put in front of them without much urging; they
didn't have the good manners to decline politely and pretend
they had just eaten, or at least to leave a bit of food on their
plates to indicate they had had enough.

Leo Kovacs's third wife came most often. She walked all
the way from town to save the bus fare, and with her she
brought her spoiled, delicate daughter, Lisa, for whom she
made dresses that seemed to come out of fairyland. This fragile
beauty with her manicured fingernails was a thorn in Marie's
side. What right had the daughter of a *Häusler*, who was a
ticket taker in a movie theater, to care for her hands, wear
beautiful clothes, and let herself be spoiled, when she, the
farmer's daughter, had rough, broad hands and had been cheated
of her young girlhood. This is how I want my daughter to
look one day, she thought, a well-groomed young lady. But
Lisa the young lady turned into Lisa the floozy, and she stopped
showing up until she had hooked an architect. After that she
was Lisa the great lady, and it was an honor to be related to
her.

Why did my mother get so excited about Lisa? Because
she wore crinolines and lace panties and low-cut dresses? No,
because she was one of those, a whore. What's a whore? A
woman who throws herself away, who does things before her
wedding that she shouldn't do until after, a woman who un-
dervalues her purity and is involved with men. *Dear God, the
jewel*, I thought and wanted never to grow up, never to have
lace panties and a bosom, because if I displeased her even
now, my punishment would be that much worse if I slipped
and fell, my legs helpless in the air, my spotless lace petticoat
soiled and the jewel lost. The terrible image of the dirty petticoat, the torn stockings, and the irretrievable jewel haunted
me in my dreams. I knew I was in special danger, for though
my mother was a respectable woman, all Kovacs women were
whores. That's why we had as little to do with them as possible,

and soon they began to stay away. When you ran into them now and then back in the village, on the church square, you acknowledged them reluctantly, with a cool hello. Otherwise they would sidle up to you and be familiar and burst into cries of admiration: "Look at the child, a real Kovacs, the spitting image of her father." But my daughter is going to be a respectable person, Marie swore to herself, not a gypsy like the Kovacs girls, even if she's physically a Kovacs ten times over. "She really wants her child to be someone special," the relatives said. I grew up with the impression that the Kovacs side of the family was something lower, something that might soil you, a flaw to be concealed. But how could I square that with the warmth and openness that came to me from my father's sisters, in contrast to the spiteful contempt that was aimed at me on the farm?

Marie avoided her mother-in-law. She would lead me up the dew-covered meadow lanes to the cottages in the woods early in the morning, but as soon as Grandmother's house could be seen through the young fir trees, she turned around. Later I used to go there alone in the morning, when the sun, still cool and slanting, sparked the dew, and did not go back until it got dark and Grandmother took me back through the woods. "You can walk across the meadow by yourself, all right," she said when the village came into view. I liked being with my grandmother; I much preferred it to the farm. She didn't talk much, but I felt accepted and safe. I was allowed to play with everything, and the food was much better than on the farm. She showed me how to make houses out of sticks and moss; the pine cones were cows and lay side by side in the barn. I built large moss houses along the edge of the woods. My cousins were older, but sometimes they let me watch them roast potatoes and sit in their rock caves, where they played cops-and-robbers. The flowers you could pick here smelled different from those in the valley around the villages; there were also plenty of berries, and you didn't have to put them in a bowl before you could eat them. The sun was not so hot in the clearings as in the meadows down in the valley, and I was allowed to go into the woods alone to look for mushrooms; in fact, I could do what I wanted, unsupervised, unreprimanded, and everything I did was appreciated. "Vera is so smart for her age," they said. "Well, she takes after her father." I was shown around proudly. "Her daddy's daughter," the *Häusler* women said with approval, and I was one of them and even a little bit better. In the evening I would return to the big room on the farm, which smelled of sweat and exhaustion, and Mama met me with the question whether the old bitch had run her down. "Of course they have better food in those little cottages," she would say sarcastically at the table, when I got sick trying to eat the fat boiled pork, and I felt lonely and cast out again.

Marie fell in love once more. She must have been thirty or thirty-one, married for seven years, and she had long given up the thought of love, especially the sensation of erotic tension, if she had ever known it. She fell in love with a farm hand who had hired on for the harvest season. I was repelled by him. The food stuck to his false teeth, and he was jokey in a suggestive, loose way. There was lots of laughter at the table, and Marie always laughed the loudest; they exchanged glances over the soup tureen and laughed. Every evening after work she took a bath—she had never bathed so much before— and then she sat in the big room in a thin muslin nightgown. You could see her large breasts through her nightgown and you could see that she was naked underneath. Sometimes she undid a button and you saw a bit of white skin, not tanned by the sun. That summer she had eyes only for this man; she pushed me away when I tried to cuddle against her: "Leave me alone; don't lean against me; I'm hot." I felt more cast out than ever. "Mama and the farm hand have something going,"

I said to my grandmother, sounding as if I knew it all, but not knowing what I was saying. I only knew it was something that took place between a man and a woman and that it was something evil, disgusting, and sinful.

I don't remember the outcome of this belated romance. All I remember is sitting under some sheaves of grain one evening after supper while the red-reflecting sun went down behind the fields and the sky, clear as glass, darkened, and there was something dangerous between my parents: awkwardness, fear, hurt. My mother was very quiet; she didn't scream as usual; she was not offended and reproachful but embarrassed and truculent, and in my father I sensed the wordless hurt with which he often withdrew behind his paper or into the woodshed.

Next summer Lois, the farm hand, was no longer around; they said he was working in a factory. Once my aunt pointed furtively to a skinny, worn-looking woman and a bunch of children. "Look," she said, "his wife and kids." "No wonder," Marie said and curled her lips disdainfully. Years later she would still shyly ask about him and blush when his name was mentioned.

☐

In the suburb at the edge of town, where the villas were suddenly springing up like mushrooms, the competition for status continued. The child was sent to kindergarten; she had to be better dressed than the others, better at crafts, more ingratiating and lovable, and most of all she had to make friends with the right girls, so she would have no trouble getting admitted to the right circles later. But at registration the father's occupation had to be listed, and Marie thought she noticed that the initial friendliness of the kindergarten teacher changed into coolness. "Oh dear, an only child," she said, and the child, who was hiding behind her mother's skirt and refused to utter a sound, was living proof that all her prejudices were correct.

I hated the school and, except for drawing, liked none of the play, least of all the group games. There, too, were blonde little darlings with curly hair, who captured the teacher's heart and were allowed to hold her hand when we went on walks. If someone told me first thing in the morning that we wouldn't be allowed to draw on that day, I said nothing but simply picked up my satchel and left. I didn't go home; instead I built moss houses in the woods. But someone always saw me and told my mother, and I got a beating.

It was at this time that she started to beat me regularly, on my buttocks, hips, and thighs, since those places were covered by clothes and the welts could not be seen. Next morning, when she dressed me and pulled opaque white cotton stockings over the blue-green bruises, she reminded me that I had deserved it and that I must not show it to anyone or I'd get more. "No, no," I screamed in despair. When the teacher said, "Vera, why don't you take off those heavy stockings, you must be awfully hot," I trembled and squeezed my pleated skirt between my knees. "No one is going to steal them from you," she said, laughing, but the panic in my eyes made her withdraw her hand and shrug her shoulders. A strange child.

"My daughter is so taciturn and glum," my mother complained to the teacher I would have in school the next year. "That might possibly be connected with the atmosphere at home," the teacher said cautiously.

I did enjoy drawing in kindergarten, and my drawings were tacked up in the hall, but that didn't make up for the fact that when we went walking no one wanted to be my partner, and that I wasn't invited to the birthday parties of the doctors' and architects' children. My best friend was the daughter of a blue-collar worker, who wore torn stockings and had mucus running from her nose in all seasons of the year. "Why don't you go visit the Reisinger kids?" my mother said, and I shyly rang the bell at the tall garden gate. But it was no fun playing in the Reisingers' park—you couldn't step on the manicured lawn, much less go inside the house—and after an hour I was sent home. I sat by the woodpile behind our house and felt cast out and unloved. "Our children have treadle scooters and Vera doesn't, and we wouldn't want our kids to fight"—this was Mrs. Reisinger's explanation for throwing me out. For Easter I was given a treadle scooter, but it didn't help; the beautiful gardens that belonged to the villas remained closed to me. At the table my mother would complain bitterly and vociferously that her child was left out of things because she, Marie, had had the bad luck to marry a workingman. But I actually preferred playing in the ditch, where the root houses belonged to me and I was not disturbed in my jungle explorations. Sometimes I let Irene, my friend with the unwashed stockings, enter my domain, but I liked being alone best: even Irene didn't see what I saw and asked stupid questions.

□

"That was the saddest thing for your mother, that you weren't accepted in the better social circles," our neighbor said, hanging her bosom across the fence. "Oh yes, I can't tell you how many times she was over here crying her heart out; she wanted nothing but the best for you, she grieved herself into the grave because her Vera couldn't manage to get a foothold among the better class of people and get ahead." "I don't remember," I said curtly; "it didn't matter to me." She brushed my washed-out jeans with a look that said, You still haven't got anywhere, you are hopeless; and left. The better class of people. She couldn't manage the ascent by herself, because it would take two generations. But her daughter had gypsy blood and no manners, and so the ascent from the petite bourgeoisie became instead a descent into bohemianism.

"My God, if your mother could see you," they said about my flying hair and dirty feet in hemp sandals, when I spent my nights in train stations, when I took off my shoes and swept the glasses off the table with my ragged skirt. Those expensive outfits, half a month's salary for the fabric alone; standing in front of the expensive dressmaker's mirror, I was the joyless image of my stern mother. I made miniskirts out of them, then later cut them into strips and threw them out. The subdued colors, the conservative designs—they seemed indestructible as they followed me, barring all entrances to real life, and I could not shake them off until I had destroyed any and all traces of my past. Then I sat in front of the big houses and high garden gates, shivering in my brightly colored feathers, and the world of respectable middle-class taste took its revenge and said, It was *you* who didn't want *us*; we were ready to let you in, but you laughed and walked away, swinging your hips.

She taught me to hate stability; right now they are putting their heads together, saying, Look at her, bumming around the world with no fixed home, just a loser, a gadabout; if her poor, decent mother knew. The smiling public mask and the death from lack of love in the dark bedroom: I have turned them around; I carry my heart on my sleeve. I say, *Stab me, if that's what you want, and watch me bleed, watch me scream, see how beautiful I am in the agony of death.* I have removed the cotton stockings from the blue bruises and am displaying my bloody welts, waiting breathlessly all my life for the next whipping. It's never long in coming, because wounds are like blossoms, red bait for birds of prey; they sink their claws into the wounds greedily and tear them open until they are sated and peaceful. I step across these birds of prey, thinking, that one must have overeaten, but I no longer think, *My God, if only he doesn't die of the pain he has caused me.* No, Dr. Shrink, I am not a masochist, I really don't enjoy being tortured, but I know I have to be punished because I am a bad person and unworthy of love. When you beat me, I know there is order in the world: no one can be trusted and I can stop suffering the pains of love; I can kick you in the teeth because your evident pleasure in torturing me incriminates you. Therefore I change mothers and lovers like shirts, and in the end they all have the same face in my disappointment, from which I rise laughing with pain because I never expected anything else.

To make up for the social fiasco of her five-year-old daughter, she bought even more expensive Sunday clothes, even greater delicacies for the snack her daughter took along to kindergarten and later to school. Ham rolls, butter croissants—things I never saw at home and didn't get to eat during break, either, because everyone wanted a bite. Everyone else had whole-grain bread and butter wrapped in waxed paper. "You get smoked ham and I haven't so much as tasted a slice of sausage for years," my mother said reproachfully to point out my lack of gratitude. I hated the pure wool Sunday dresses; they caused my skin to break out, and in church, where you had to sit motionless, they itched terribly. But if I objected to the wool dress on Sunday morning I was ungrateful, because it had cost half a month's pay. The white nylon for Corpus Christi Day was even more precious and any stain on it would ensure a beating. "Look how self-confident Ulrike Reisinger is, as if she owned the world, and you stand there hunched over, with your head down between your shoulders, looking as if you had just received a slap in the face," my mother reprimanded me. Somehow she had managed it so that I walked with the doctor's daughter in the first row in the Corpus Christi procession, and now, seen in retrospect on the photographs, I was destroying all her efforts. Every Sunday I sat in church, in the same row, in the same seat between my parents, next to the center aisle, trying not to scratch though the wool was as itchy as a hundred fleas, not to laugh though the woman in the row behind me couldn't sing in tune, and, most of all, not to give in to the enormous temptation of picking the straw flowers and plastic fruit on the large straw hat of the woman in front of me. In processions I never walked solemnly enough; I didn't know what to do with my hands and stumbled in my patent-leather shoes. I was like my father: I impressed no one; I did not amount to anything, would never amount to anything. My mother's stern gaze lay on my every step, every movement of my head, and said, You will never amount to anything, you are worth nothing.

I climbed on a chair and looked at myself in the mirror and decided I was beautiful, even though the world maintained I looked like nothing. "Get away from the mirror," my mother called, horrified, as if I were in extreme danger; "that's where the devil looks back at you." Pride goeth before a fall. Disgrace follows you everywhere. The only help was prayer, twice a day in front of the Holy Family, and in bed at night a round of the rosary. My posture was poor as a result of sleeping in her bed and often huddled against her, so I had to do special exercises on a regular basis. I now slept in bed with her, and my father slept on a bunk in the other room. We went to bed at seven every night—even in summer, when the sun was still shining—and we said one rosary, or sometimes all four of them, depending on how we felt. Our rosaries lay under our pillows; mine was white ivory; hers had shiny brown beads that looked like coffee beans. Long after she had taken her laxative, had put her hairnet over her permanent, and was making irregular snoring sounds, I lay awake and furnished my luxury villas with dream furniture and dream men. I loved those long sleepless evenings, with no one trying to spy on my dreams.

Marie had been away from home for eight years and still felt like an exile in the city. She was terribly homesick; this she confided to the few people before whom she let down her guard enough to talk about herself in a veiled way. The debt from the house was paid off, her father having let her pay back every penny; they were no longer hungry but still poor, and people said with admiration, "How do you do it, Mrs. Kovacs, with your family looking so good on a workingman's salary?" She managed to make juicy roasts out of the cheapest cuts of meat; she herself ate day-old bread, reduced at the bakery, while buying an eighth of a pound of ham and a roll for my school break. In the grocery store she pretended to have a cat in order to get cheap scraps.

For a short time she took in work by sewing together precut bathing suits, but the extra income was so negligible that she gave it up again. "What would you say to a part-time job, now that Vera doesn't get home until afternoon?" my father suggested diffidently. "Clean house for big shots," she countered angrily, "I'd rather die." She was a professional housewife and proud of her abilities. Every visitor confirmed that she was the best cook; the linens in the cupboard were snowy white, starched, their edges matching. Not a speck of dust on the furniture, the kitchen spotless, the floor so clean you could eat off it, her child clean and always nicely dressed, she herself imposing in good, expensive cloth and never a hair out of place. At home she still wore the blue jumper and the washed-out denim apron, and her hair was tucked under a headscarf.

She kept chickens and rabbits. When the rabbits got big and the roosters started fighting, they were killed. Killing animals was men's work—putting the hen's head on the whetstone and severing it from the body with an ax, with the headless body continuing to reel and the other chickens clucking excitedly. What followed was women's work: bleeding the chicken in hot water, plucking it, and cleaning out the insides. Men's work was caulking windows, making outdoor repairs, pruning trees. But most of all men's work was bringing home money. A man's worth rose and fell with his pay, with the prestige and standard of living he could offer his family. The home and the raising of the children were women's work, and

he had no say there. She fulfilled her obligations, no one
could deny that: every day a hot meal with soup, a main dish,
and dessert; everyone nicely dressed; her daughter so well brought
up that she didn't open her mouth unless she was asked a
question. My mother was above competition, meeting any and
all expectations one might have of a housewife. My father was
the one who kept her from rising into a better kind of life.
She despised him. He sat at the table and said nothing, fell
asleep after meals instead of amassing money.

Once the debt was paid off, she began to save, for she had
big plans and no intention of remaining in what was meant
to be a temporary shelter for refugees the rest of her life. These
savings were exacted from his meager pay and skimped from
her own food; she wanted money for land, a plot of one's own
that could not be taken away from one year to the next. When
she talked to the owner of their present land, she listened
nervously for any word that might indicate how much longer
they would be able to stay. "The little houses will be gone
soon," she heard the owner say to the men from the electric
company one day, while she was hanging up laundry a few
yards away. For weeks she couldn't sleep and talked of nothing
except what it would be like when we would have to tear down
the house and fill and level the cellar as if we had never lived
there. These were the holes of fear she stuffed with shillings,
and with every thousand added to the passbook she felt a little
less threatened.

Once we owned property at the edge of town, we would
build a house with brick walls and large, light rooms and an
American kitchen with hot running water and a bathroom
with tiles around the tub and a hot-water heater. Every Saturday night in summer we took a bath in a narrow aluminum
tub in the laundry room, where my father had installed a
drain. The water was heated on the stove, and since water and
electricity were expensive, Mama and I bathed first—she at

the broad, I at the narrow end of the tub, she wearing her denim apron, which floated on top of the water. Then my father took a bath in the same water, but you weren't supposed to see him naked. In the winter the aluminum tub stood in the living room and you had to be careful not to spill any water. All this would change once she had a pile of thousands, enough for a real house.

In the meantime there were small improvements: a closet, a washing machine, a refrigerator, and a moped for my father, so he could stop endangering our livelihood by walking home past the landing pier when he came from the nightshift with a pouch full of company money.

□

The child started school. New efforts to keep up with the affluent: school bag, fountain pen, pen box, all from the best stationery store, and smart new school dresses. But the child threw up her breakfast every morning on the way to school. As her mother watched her walk down the hill, smartly dressed, her satchel on her back, Vera stopped and, doubling over, vomited on the path. She never turned back. Later, when her mother went grocery shopping, the smell assaulted her. What could be the problem? At school the teacher said, "You look as pale as a ghost again." "Spook, spook," the other kids called and laughed. She was too shy to ask to go to the bathroom. "Something really stinks around here," her seatmate said, and Vera agreed eagerly, "Yes, an awful stink."

The teacher summoned her mother. "Vera is so scared that she soils her underpants, and there are traces of vomit on her clothes every morning. When I stop at her desk and point out a mistake, she starts to tremble. Do you threaten the child?" "She's always been nervous. I don't know what's wrong with her, either," Mrs. Kovacs replied.

"You cause me nothing but disgrace," she said at home.

"Why was I cursed with such a child?" When I did my home-work she sat next to me: Don't stray below the line, make nice round "o"s, *Schaufel* and *Schaukel*, "f" and "k," over and over in an endless procession, *Schaufel* and *Schaukel*, how can you mix up "f" and "k," no one else has any trouble. Tears on the paper, which blurred the writing. My mother grabbed me by the hair and, rubbing my nose in the blurred writing, thrust my face down on the notebook, on the table, until blood mixed with the tears, and sent me to bed.

Schaufel and *Schaukel*, I said in my dream and screamed under her grasp. "Can't I get a little sleep, you pest?" she scolded and sat up angrily in bed next to me. I lay awake for a whole long night, for many whole long nights, holding my breath. I would rather not go to sleep than cry out in my dream, wet the bed out of fear, be yanked out of bed and beaten because of my nocturnal transgressions. At dawn I would finally fall into a brief, restless sleep. "Since when have you suffered from insomnia?" asks the doctor who has been prescribing Valium for me for years; nothing else has worked, not counting sheep, not mantras, neither prayer nor sinful thoughts, since I mixed up *Schaufel* and *Schaukel*, since I became afraid that by sleeping I would bring on my punish-ment. But I only say, "Oh, for a long time, since I was a child."

I became a model student and knew everything the others didn't know, but that didn't reduce the fear with which I sat through the morning, with which at home I drew perfect letters. I brought home nothing but shining A's, capital A's, A's with exclamation marks, and I was rewarded with some caresses and, on occasion, the fulfillment of some modest wish, a quarter-pound of mayonnaise salad and, for a report card of all A's, a box of watercolor paints. Then I was Mama's good little girl and was allowed to sit on her lap and play with her hair after dinner. I was praised in front of others—"Our Vera is studying hard; she had all A's on her report card"—and I basked in the glory of approving grunts and nodding heads.

But deep down I felt those A's were the achievement of my mother and her exemplary way of raising me. When I got my first B I hid behind the garbage cans in the schoolyard. But my teacher discovered me and asked why I didn't go home. "Because of the B; I can't go home with a B or I'll get a beating," I managed in a strangled voice and then burst into uncontrollable tears in her arms. "Don't you think you might be a little too strict?" my teacher said cautiously to my mother, when she delivered me at my door. "A B isn't so bad." As I stood trembling between her and my mother, I was praying that she wouldn't say anything about the beating that awaited me. She said nothing, said good-bye in a friendly way, and Mama watched at the window until she had gone around the bend before ordering me to bring the carpet beater and bare my bottom. True, a teacher was an authority figure, someone whose judgment you didn't contradict, if for no other reason than to keep her well disposed toward your child, but I was in disgrace for weeks because of the criticism my mother had had to swallow in silence.

For this was the first commandment: whatever happened at home, it must not go beyond our walls; the façade had to remain seamless. We were a respectable family living in perfect harmony. When she announced that I was to be punished and I tried to appeal to unsuspecting strangers who just happened to be walking up our hill, I could count on an even more furious thrashing. Who is going to believe a bawling six-year-old who gets in your way during a pleasant walk in the country on a calm Sunday afternoon, yelling, "Help, please help me, Mama is going to hit me"? Who wants to get involved just because some naughty little kid is trying to get out of her well-deserved punishment? "There, there," the nice gentleman with the cane said soothingly, "it can't be as bad as all that; we've all been turned over someone's knee now and then and have turned out all right; it hasn't done us any harm." She did not come out, but waited inside for me, breathing heavily. "If you do that again I'll beat you to death."

I wonder how far my screams carried on beautiful summer days, when all the windows were open and only ours were carefully shut? Our neighbors heard my piano playing, but didn't they hear my screams, which couldn't have been anything like the ordinary crying of children? "My mother beat me," I later said to the neighbors and relatives, when they started in on their hymns of praise for the superior housewife and fine mother, but they looked at me imploringly and changed the subject. You hide your dirty linen before strangers; I had violated a taboo; we are a nation of abused children.

And the public-school doctor who summoned my mother to his office, what did he mean to accomplish, how long did he think he could protect me? One by one we were called into the school office, and this time neither panic nor pleading was of any use. "If you don't feel well, show me where it hurts; I'm the doctor and can make it better." "No, there's nothing wrong with me; I feel fine, only please don't make me get undressed." My teacher came to help me undress; she was an authority figure and you didn't talk back or offer resistance.

I caught the look that passed between them, questioning, horrified, abashed, knowing; her shrug, his hand pulling me closer, his cool fingers on my bloody welts, distinguishing between the bluish black and the greenish yellow of the bruises. "Does that hurt?" Denials, and tears of shame, as if I had been cast among the lepers for my unspeakably evil deeds. "Does your father beat you?" he asked; in a moment I would have to throw up. "No," I answered truthfully. "I just fell down." The washbasin near the window: before he can rescue his clean, shining instruments, I have thrown up on them. He looks annoyed as he watches the teacher help me dress.

On this day, as on any other, I had to go home; where else could I have gone, with the carefully sealed envelope in my satchel? I didn't have to give it to her: she found it herself, because she checked my satchel every day. I didn't dare look at her face when she read the letter; I crouched in my place under the stairs and trembled, not saying a word. That evening fear made both of us silent. My parents were whispering in the living room; they were banding together against me. "We'll go tomorrow," my father said, and there were fear and shame in his voice, too. "I'll take off." I suppose they must have gone; I never heard about it. She avoided looking at me; I felt the silence preceding a great tribunal. I hated the doctor; he wouldn't be there when she beat me the next time for my new transgressions and for her humiliation in having been publicly exposed, she, the world's best mother, who sacrificed herself for me unlike any other.

My mother chose my seatmate and best friend, Uli Reisinger, the doctor's daughter, self-confident and well mannered, un-afraid of bad grades, teachers, or classmates. To me there was something uncanny about Uli; I felt an aggressive shyness toward her, but my mother decided she was the only possible and suitable companion for me among all the first-graders. That is, until I slapped Uli's face for some impertinence that angered me—the only slap I gave, rather than received, in my life. Uli's mother came to our house that very day and com-plained bitterly. After that Mrs. Reisinger and my mother were implacable enemies. Not a day went by when her name wasn't mentioned with anger, derision, and envy. The doctor's wife, the "if-you-please" lady, had been in the store again and was waited on first, even though it wasn't her turn, and Mama's day was ruined. Before long she found out that Uli's mother, although she had married a doctor, had only an eighth-grade education and thus wasn't any better than Mrs. Kovacs, the

workingman's wife, to whom you could say with impunity that
even beggars had washing machines nowadays. Uli went to
the sports club, and Mama knew that Dr. Reisinger had been
de-Nazified and was still a Nazi. Nevertheless, we had to keep
up with the Reisingers; I was signed up for gymnastics and
ballet, in the hope of finding there even more distinguished
company than in the two-grade public school.

The woman who had leaned out from her bed in the maternity
hospital and said, "I thought right away that you were from
the country," came to visit and, after seven years of maternal
effort, the two daughters were measured against each other.
Marlene's mother's face shone with pride, and in my mother's
face I saw the disappointment and shame I knew so well.
Marlene played the recorder, so I received a recorder and was
enrolled with Marlene's music teacher. Soon after, Marlene
started piano lessons. My parents had long discussions. There
was a zither in the family, which we could borrow for free. A
piano cost a fortune, and where would we put it in our house
of only three hundred square feet with slanting walls? They
bought a piano anyway, because Marlene's mother laughed
derisively and said, "A zither, of course, that makes sense—
country music."

The spinet piano cost a whole year's savings, and I had to
prove myself worthy of the sacrifice. From the beginning I
practiced an hour every day, always the same monotonous
phrase, *There was a mouse ran over the house, trip trap.* My
mother endured it with bated breath, a torture she accepted
because it was worth seven thousand shillings and steered her
daughter into the right circles and the right career. When it
turned out that I had no musical talent, that I hated playing
the piano, and that the piano teacher was anxious to get rid
of me, the effort and the pressure were doubled. I was chained
to the piano for two hours and wasn't allowed to get up until

the alarm rang; until then I had to produce sounds, even though the notes were dancing in front of my eyes and neither rhythm nor melody was correct. After four years and three piano teachers, who confirmed my lack of talent with derision and slaps, I was playing Mozart sonatas. Then I started playing hooky, ate the box of candy I was supposed to give the piano teacher for her birthday, and prepared myself for the worst. The worst occurred: a letter from the teacher, who was being deprived of her fees, which I was turning into treats for me. But this time there was no beating; instead, a resigned sadness: "Everything is wasted on this child." Sometimes I still played Bartók in a slow, sad way for my father, because Bartók made him sit reverently next to the piano, and then the piano stood against the wall, overcrowding the living room—a reminder that the daughter had no talent and any effort in her behalf was pointless. But even my mother didn't want to go once more through the disgrace of attending a student recital and having her daughter be the only one on the podium who received no applause, because she hammered out two pieces without any feeling and got hopelessly stuck in the third.

☐

How did I come to have a musical kid? I wonder as I watch my daughter play the cello, ready to say at any time, "Stop if you're not enjoying it." "She's no genius," they tell me, to put a damper on my admiration. Who's talking about genius? I suppress the desire to tell her how grateful I am that she herself chose to do something I did only as a result of daily terror. It took me fifteen years to be able to listen to music again without resistance and a feeling of defeat. She plays the way I used to draw—oblivious of herself, of time, with her face turned inward in concentration.

She wants to be a famous artist or a ballerina, and when she listens to music in her room she turns the key. I know she

is dancing—I know by the smell of her sweaty leotard—and
this time I even know why she is dancing. She should not
have to hide, should not have to lie and say she is doing
homework. When she was little she sat in her playpen and
watched me dance; she was my most appreciative audience.
Later I used to hold her and dance when she was sick, when
she was unhappy, when she was too tired to play, and I thought,
If she forgets everything else, she will remember this.

Why should she now be so annoyed and embarrassed when
I ask, Have you been dancing? She is guarding her dreams so
she won't tire of them, so they won't turn into dutiful exercises
that can be measured in praise and criticism, my clever daughter. She is annoyed because she doesn't come up against any
locked doors which she could break down. And I feel excluded,
rejected, thrust into the realm of adulthood, where you don't
dance alone and just for fun, where everything is sensible and
orderly, where mothers are housewives and wear respectably
subdued colors, where the father is not a Saturday visitor but
puts his feet on the table every evening and is served his dinner,
where you don't have lovers sneaking out in the early-morning
hours.

"You had a real childhood," my daughter says, and she
means the house I lived in for seventeen years and refer to as
home without hesitation, a mother who was always waiting
for me with a ready meal and fresh laundry, a proper family
life. "Yes," I say angrily, "be glad that I saved you from that."
But she dreams of it, of an unbroken family in an unbroken
world, and she blames me. How is she to understand that the
unbroken world is a torture chamber from which I broke loose
with the courage of the damned, ready to break loose again
and again to save her and me? With what nostalgia she longs
for my childhood, how she accuses me: You haven't given me
security; you haven't given me support; you've just always
dragged me along on your escapades. "Yes," I say, "but I've

never hit you and I've always adored you." But those are givens for her. How could I not adore her, a gift of the gods, a prodigy, beautiful and smart and talented and capable of conquering the world with a single smile? Only if I were like her grandmother would life be perfect, she thinks.

□

At school I continued to be at the top of my class, and it was soon taken for granted that I knew more than the other kids and brought home nothing but A's. There was some letup of pressure; I was allowed to go out and play in the ditches again after homework. But now I rarely played in the ditches; the neighbor girl and I ran out in the street and threw rocks at surprised passers-by out for their Sunday stroll; I filched strawberries out of other people's gardens and hounded a frail, shy boy named Erich in order to torment him with threats and attempts at extortion. He was afraid of me, and terrorizing Erich, who was the smallest kid in class and never raised his hand, became my favorite sport until one day his father caught me on the way home from school and slapped me twice, right there in the street, leaving red fingermarks on both cheeks. A few hours later, my mother found out. Furious, she marched over to see Erich's parents, but she came home wearing a sad, resigned look that said, I have a wicked daughter. Erich was forced on me as a new friend; I was invited to a children's party at his house and allowed to play with his remote-control cars; he was invited to our house and I was bored to death. The friendship didn't last long: his mother decided I was too rowdy for him. Later I asked myself whether the incredulous look she gave my bare upper thigh, as I was bandaging a skinned knee, had something to do with her distant manner and the end of the invitations. What went through the mind of this gentle, refined woman, who lived in a large house protected by blue spruces, when she put her hand on the marks

left by the carpet beater? She quickly pulled my skirt down
over my knees and said, "That's enough for today." She guided
me out the door, gently and kindly but irrevocably; she wanted
to protect her unsuspecting child from violence.

Since my first communion I had sat in front in church,
next to my classmates, in seats reserved for children, and whispered witty, sarcastic remarks into my prayerbook, until everyone in the pew was giggling. We knelt, our faces in our hands,
holding our noses, and burst out laughing during the silence
of the consecration. After church I had to take off all my
clothes and be hit with the carpet beater until I lay on the
floor soundless and motionless, and my father said, "Now you
see where you get with your brutality; you'll kill the child."
But when I screamed, "Papa, Papa, help me," he had stayed
on the sofa, not daring to interfere with the punishment. From
then on I sat in the next-to-last pew again, between my parents,
sang along with the hymns, and came back from communion
with folded hands and lowered eyes. But I could never do it
right, run the gauntlet past all those benches. Once I stumbled
over the communion bench and then fell over the steps of our
pew; another time a button was undone, or I looked unfriendly;
I grinned stupidly; I gave people impudent looks or acted embarrassed. Every Sunday, when I held my mother's hand walking home, I could feel her disapproval, which erupted into
disdain and derision over our Sunday cake. When I was nine
she bought me a book on etiquette, but it said nothing about
correct behavior in church. For years I was pursued by the
same nightmare. I am standing at the communion bench in
my undershirt, and it will not cover my bruised thighs, though
I desperately pull it down, feeling my mother's look of anger,
disdain, and revulsion on me.

"Don't you teach Vera a little something about keeping house?"
my aunts asked when, on the farm, I didn't know how to hold

the broom to sweep the floor and was clumsy when it came to washing dishes. "Vera is supposed to study for school; I can handle the household by myself," my mother answered sharply. "But then she won't want to be in the kitchen when she's married, either," was the concern raised by my aunts. She cut them off by saying, "Vera doesn't have to marry; she is going to be a convent teacher."

By the time I was eight there was no doubt about it: I would become a teacher and enter a convent and so fulfill her girl-hood dream. For that you didn't need a household, you didn't need to be pretty and appealing; for that you only needed piety, obedience, and tireless study. These qualities were continually being reinforced by her stern face and the hand that wielded the carpet beater. She called it iron discipline and was proud of it. With this new point of view she took me out of ballet class: a convent student doesn't need to master pirouettes. I enjoyed ballet class; I had a friend there—a refugee girl from the Hungarian uprising, who didn't speak German but crawled underneath the benches and pinched the other girls' ankles—but I didn't dare object. When Mama went to town in the afternoon, I put on her clothes and danced in front of the mirror. I was still doing dancing in front of the mirror when I no longer had to listen for the sound of her key in the door and had long since given away her clothes.

Third grade went by uneventfully. My grandfather had stomach surgery. He was in the hospital for half a year, hovering between life and death, as my mother impressed on every stranger, and so gave me the gift of unexpected, delicious freedom. It seemed as if there was no end of sunshine during these six months, from the moment Mama quickly washed the dishes and changed clothes until evening, when she came home and seemed distracted. She hated her father, but she did what was expected of her. She was the only one of his daughters who lived close enough to visit him every day, and she did it with the same stubborn conscientiousness with which she kept house and thrashed discipline into me. She brought him her canned cherries and cakes and allowed herself to be tyrannized by his self-pitying moods. At home she wasted no words on him or his condition, but the household had to run as it always had.

I sat alone by the veranda window and daydreamed over my notebooks. I pulled the drapes and looked at my naked body in the mirror and discovered the first unsettling signs of femaleness. Following afternoon classes I once went down to the river with the boys to smoke, and for a brief time had a boyfriend who was willing to enlighten me sexually. We were standing in front of a former air-raid shelter and he was talking about making children, but I thought it had to do with the war and was picturing a children's crusade, and when I finally caught on and eagerly twisted my beret in my hands, my mother came from the bus and immediately smelled something impure. Afterward she often asked me about Günter and looked at me closely, but Günter's parents moved away and took with them the first threat to my strictly guarded purity.

□

When we attempt to define ourselves, when others try to sum us up in words, we fall back on our mothers. "You got your strong will and your rootedness from your mother," my aunt says, and I'm not sure what she means by rootedness, nor am I convinced that I inherited my stubbornness: it might be one of the many things she beat into me with the carpet beater. Along with, for example, my fear of every loud noise and sudden movement, and my fascination with anything that has the power to torment me. "My mother was a rebel," I say, "she didn't believe in traditional sex roles," and while I'm saying it I know it isn't true, even though she didn't train me for the kitchen and the household. But mother-daughter relationships are "in" now, and mothers are receiving the distinguished-service medal again. My mother was a tall, imposing lady, with good middle-class tastes, an impeccable housewife with above-average intelligence, discreet, correct in her behavior, a little bit arrogant.

Yes, that's how your mother was, chorus the neighbors and members of our parish. Why, then, do I begin to stammer whenever I approach her in words, when I try to use her as a mirror so I can see myself more clearly? Other mothers are tall, imposing, arrogant, and intelligent behind the kitchen stove, but their daughters can laugh and tell childhood anecdotes and put their mothers back into the toy chest with a friendly pat. But my mother is an emptiness that fills up with fear when I look at it; I have never been able to decipher her. She rises behind the words that are meant to exorcise her; she grows like an incubus, and I am paralyzed while she devours me. I can't even scream, because no one can hear me, and if they did they wouldn't understand. And I can't stuff her back into the toy chest because she is more alive than a mother you can visit in a nursing home or a dark apartment in town.

In a foreign city I happen to see myself reflected in a shopwindow, and there she is, her hair under a square scarf, her arms pressed against her body, with the strangely hesitant, melancholy movements of her head and her frightened eyes. My mother is my double, who just happened to exist before me. I need only to glance back over my shoulder to convince myself that she is re-enacting every one of my gestures, but her gestures are more meaningful, more majestic, more mysterious, like the shadow of a Javanese dancer behind a rice-paper screen.

My father tries to demythologize her: she was insane, simply crazy; who knows how long she had had the brain tumor that was discovered after her death. My feminist friend tries an ideological explanation: any woman in her situation would have to flip out and vent her frustrations somewhere; imagine no money, no love, just the household, the four walls, scrimping and saving, and no end in sight. The man I'm seeing tries to knock her off her pedestal: OK, so she was smart, read historical novels and books on philosophy, knew how to size people up coldly and shrewdly, sensed persecution everywhere and attracted it like a lightning rod; admittedly she had an unhappy childhood, a joyless marriage, never enough money, and great life expectations—but does all that give her the right to abuse her child? I defend her with theories about the beatings she received from her father, which she had to pass on, with her conviction that corporal punishment was part of education. My sense of my own worth depends on my defense of her honor. I cannot betray her, because if it should turn out that she never loved me, then I am a monster, something that should not be permitted to exist.

Therefore I don't say what I know and have known for a long time: that she is one of those who make our skin crawl and stop our imagination cold when we read about them in history books and documents, one of those who are expert in all branches of torture. She had the talent, though she was limited in scope; she had the tools, stored in an orderly fashion and always at hand; she had her mute sacrificial lamb, helpless and willing; and she had her secret, voluptuous pleasure, which released itself into a state of unconscious exhaustion after the execution of her task. She rarely allowed herself to be overcome by anger. She gave her victim notice—"Just wait until tonight"—but in the meantime I had to go to bed, where my fear would escalate into suicidal fantasies. Where did she learn that? What handbooks had she read? When the punishment began she expected self-control; crying and pleading just made it that much worse; self-humiliation set her off. Beating was a ritual surrounded by other rituals. Even her inspection of the red welts and bloodshot bruises, after the work was done, was part of it. Was she, in other words, one of those people whose careers are made in torture chambers and concentration camps? How shall I answer that question about her who was also my mother? The word *Mama* also meant the broad lap on which I was allowed to sit, the soft face you could kiss when you were good and brought home all A's. *Mama* meant pet names I never heard again in later life: "bunny rabbit" and "sugarplum"; it was the smell of Christmas cookies when I got home from school, out of the darkness into the warm, bright living room in December. *Mama* meant safety and peril; she could protect me from just about everything except herself.

☐

I was a sickly child with barely healed tuberculosis, susceptible to childhood diseases, with a nervous, oversensitive stomach and poor posture. My mother's devotion knew no bounds. Day after day she carried me on her back around the town's highest mountain, since the doctor had ordered mountain air and she couldn't afford a stay in a resort. When whooping cough brought on fits of choking, she sat at my bed day and night: "My sweet baby, my sugarplum, don't die." During the day I lay on the sofa, suffused with a pleasant lassitude, and she fulfilled my every wish, running to the store to buy me what I craved. She stood beside me and held my hand when I was given a shot or had to have a tooth pulled; I saw in her face her fear and the pain she suffered for me, and my own fear increased. For she was the only one who could fend off bad things; my luck and misfortune were in her hands. And she alone loved me; that had to be true, for she repeated it every day. She loved me more than anything and beyond words; she loved me even when she beat me and complained that she had been punished by having been given a prime example of homeliness and inferiority for a daughter. She had to love me; otherwise she could not have endured having a child like me. I was grateful

for a love I rarely experienced, but, then, it was my fault that
I deserved it so rarely, and I expressed my gratitude in homemade gifts, which I gave her for Mother's Day, drawings and
poems. *Oh, my sweet mother dear, life without you would be
drear; you, the one who gave me birth, are my happiness on
earth.*

When the school inspector came, I was called to the podium and asked to recite a poem. I knew the answers expected
of me: I tried to be a model child. What are you going to be
when you grow up? A convent teacher. What didn't fit in with
the concept of the model child: sexual curiosity; small sums
of stolen money, with which I bought chocolate and other
sweets that Irene and I ate in the woods; reprimands and de-
tentions I incurred for my wisecracks. These things I lied about
with a rich imagination, turning my face away. "Don't lie,"
she would say, "look at my face." But she didn't get the truth
out of me; I learned to hide my secrets like treasure and leave
a network of false clues. No one could wrest them from me;
I should have become a spy.

Christmas was the only time when there was no economizing;
Christmas was the only time when there was no quarreling.
It was the time when the Christ child came, at least until, at
the age of ten, I saw the tree in the laundry room two weeks
before Christmas. Suddenly I knew it had all been a hoax.
Even the doll with eyes that opened and closed, a doll I had
wanted for years, couldn't restore the old magic for me. On
Christmas Eve we ate sweet rice pudding for lunch, and afterward I had to go to bed, but I did it gladly because there
were rustling and crackling sounds from the living room as I
lay in bed reading a book. When it began to get dark, Mama
came for me, and what I saw when I came down the stairs
was the most beautiful sight of the whole year: the tree, lit by
the candles, which were reflected in the shiny round orna-

ments and sparkled on the tinsel, the fireworks of the sparklers, and the room, still in half-light, with the presents, which promised fulfillment of the wildest dreams.

My actual wishes were always modest, because during the Advent season I put letters to the Christ child on the windowsill, and greedy letters were not picked up. The Christ child fulfilled my modest wishes and added something extra, something unexpected but rarely disappointing. Of course, it never fulfilled the wishes that I didn't dare express.

Before we unwrapped our presents, we had to pray. We stood at the usual distance from the Holy Family, except that now the Holy Family had been taken from the wall and placed underneath the tree, on a folding stage made of cardboard painted to look like a stable. After the prayer the ribbons were carefully untied, the wrapping paper folded for reuse next Christmas, and the expected gifts displayed. Knee warmers for Mama: just what she had wanted for ages. Actually she had fantasized about a tiny mink collar with a bow that could be tied, or a pair of leather gloves. And a shirt for Papa: yes, he really needed that; the collars on his old ones had been turned twice already.

For nineteen years we ate the traditional Christmas Eve supper, frankfurters with mustard, a delicacy and an extravagance during the early years, and later part of the Christmas tradition. They were followed by open-face sandwiches and pastries, Christmas beer and soft drinks. Happy, drifting evenings of play, rewrapping and unwrapping presents; the only evening without a specified bedtime, and before going to bed a last look at the candles on the tree, the glitter and sparkle in the dark room, and Mama's full alto voice singing *Silent Night, Holy Night*.

She did not care to go to the Christmas Mass in our little church; it was too humdrum for her without a choir or a brass ensemble, without the kind of ceremony that shook the nave and moved the parishioners to tears. That's how it had been in the country church at home, and it had been even more breathtaking Easter night: white-gloved men removing the black cloth from the windows and the crucifix, and a *Te Deum* so tumultuous that it brought you to your knees, overcome. That was what religion meant for her: grand opera, a feeling of awe, splendor, and allowing oneself to be swept away by all one's senses. Other than that, you did your Christian duty, attended Mass on Sundays and holidays, ate no meat on Fridays, and went to confession and communion once a month.

She had not been a young woman for quite some time, even though she was only in her mid-thirties. Overweight and with full breasts, or—as she preferred to characterize herself—imposing, with short hair dyed chestnut-brown and a permanent, with the wrong costume jewelry and timeless clothes made of expensive cloth, she hadn't been young for ten years. "Don't look so grim," a streetcar conductor would say to her and incur a murderous look from her for his impudence. Who did this guy think he was, just because he happened to be a colleague of her husband's? "I'm fine now; I don't lack for anything; I see to it that we have everything we need," she said to her sisters when we visited the farm, which we did more and more rarely. "Look," she said to Fanni, who was watching her bathe, "I'm so well fed that every drop of water rolls right off."

She was the most distinguished among all her sisters, the most impressive figure, the great lady from town, who had made it further up the ladder than the rest. When she stood on the church square, her erect bearing and haughty face said, Look at me, all of you; I am here and I have made it; I am a lady. The knot in her neck scarf was perfect; not a hair was out of place; her lips were red, too red not to attract attention; and her skin was smooth and wrinkle-free, still taut and supple because of her fullness and the extra-rich skin creams she used, her only cosmetic luxury.

Her preparations for this appearance in front of the church

could take as long as two hours. She would check ten times to see if her stocking seams were straight and look at her hair in the mirror from every angle. And then the child. Of course the child had to keep up with her, had to walk demurely beside her, living proof that she had made it and how far. I looked like a miniature replica of my mother, wearing a hat or at least a large propeller bow, snow-white stockings, white nylon gloves, and a suit that came from the most expensive yard-goods store and the hands of Rosi's former dressmaking teacher, now seventy, which made me look like a pint-sized fifty-year-old. All I needed to do was curtsy and shake hands; my mother did the talking. In her imposing presence it always seemed like a privilege to me to be able to walk beside her and be her daughter. We walked back to the village satisfied and united. We had shown them once more; we had a reputation; we were somebody; we had made it. The privation and misery had been worth it. What farm woman had such smooth skin; what farm woman would splurge on such fine dress fabric?

When we went to church in our neighborhood of expensive houses, she wore the same clothes and hats and her stocking seams were as straight as pins, but her face showed anxiety and defiance. Who would slight her today; which one of the women who pushed her aside in the store, and whose children I couldn't play with, would walk behind her; who would be dressed in the latest fashion? Here we had to be twice as impressive in order to keep up, to be somebody; we, the only blue-collar family in the community. And here, of all places, I caused her the greatest shame with my unsureness, my constantly increasing fear of putting myself on public display. In the village we went to church without my father; in town he walked beside her, often arm in arm, wearing his best suit, a snow-white shirt, and always a hat. But his face was inscrutable, his eyes far away; he walked beside

her silently like a puppet, in sweet harmony. A close-knit
family.

Our buffet was covered by a scarf whose embroidery read: *Order and cleanliness, that's what a husband wants.* At our house there was more than enough of both. There were no clothes lying about; after school I immediately took off my school dress, put on the everyday dress that lay behind the curtain, and neatly folded the good clothes. My mother washed the dishes right after meals, in summer in front of the house so that no water would spill onto the wooden floor of the living room. Why, then, was my father not happy at home? He came home punctually, right after work; dinner was on the table, his shirts were ironed and starched, his shoes shined to a high gloss. He always walked into the house with the same inscrutable, closed face. When I was little they used to kiss, hastily and without a change of expression, before he left for work. Later that stopped. "What's new?" she would ask while she dished out the food. "Not a thing," he would answer curtly. He didn't read the paper any more, either: that was a thing of the past, and, besides, newspapers cost money. On the first of the month he handed her his paycheck and received a hundred shillings for his personal use. She took fifty shillings, and the rest was household money. Whatever was left over went into the savings account earmarked "Bunny"; that was me. The account was for my future; I was to have a better life someday. He sat at the table and didn't say a word.

When every bite stuck in my throat and the atmosphere was especially tense, she sometimes asked him to give me a slap. He rarely did, and when he did I could hardly feel it; he did it only to avoid words with her. But one slap from him hurt more than being beaten bloody by her. I hardly ever succeeded in getting his attention. I wracked my brains how I could awaken his interest and finally started asking him about guns and tanks because he had been in the war and I couldn't think of anything else. He didn't care about my grades; he listened to accounts of my successes at school with an expression that didn't change; my unruliness did not disturb him. He was a puppet whom I called Papa, who lived with us and slept on a bunk in the other room. But if someone had asked me whom I loved more, him or her, I would have said *him* without hesitation. He didn't beat me; he didn't put me down; he took no notice of me whatsoever, but I felt sorry for him.

While we ate he had to hear that Mrs. Reisinger ran three steps and walked two and said "if you please" in the store; that the vegetable seedlings weren't doing well; and, finally, as her voice grew louder and louder, that he didn't care about anything, that he didn't give a shit about his own wife, that he didn't love her one bit, never had, and wanted only one thing, but he could wait for hell to freeze over, and that someone should give him a thrashing—maybe that would wake him up and put some life into him. He listened to it all without a word; when the threats and curses started, he left. He didn't go far—usually behind the house to putter or work on his moped, or he sat on the bench, staring into space. Meanwhile she screamed and cried, first sitting on her chair, later in a heap on the floor, with the dishes still on the table and tears on the tablecloth, shouting, "You pig, you mean bastard, you living piece of crap!" I stood in the living room trembling, also bursting into tears, and didn't know where to hide. This would be followed by days of ominous silence, until he would start, "Look Mama, you mustn't get so excited; it's the way I am; I can't help it." And then it started all over again, the insults, the accusations, the curses.

Most of the scenes took place in the evening, when he came into our bedroom to say good night and get a quick kiss, which she permitted him as she lay in bed. He stood beside her bed, not saying a word. "Don't you dare leave," she screamed when he reached for the door. He stood there silently while she screamed and wept and demanded love. But she wouldn't let him sit on the edge of her bed, either; he had to stand. "Don't you go to sleep on me and don't look out the window; look at me, take a good look, this is what you've done to me!" I lay in my bed, less than two feet from her, and shook with sobs and fear until late into the night. Suddenly a good night's sleep and proper rest were no longer priorities. "Look Mama," he said, "I have to go to work at four in the morning and the kid has to go to school; why don't you stop and let me get some sleep?" Sometimes he sat up in the living room half the night because she had forbidden him to lie down. I would hear him move in his chair from time to time and couldn't sleep. More and more often he would put on his work uniform and leave; you could hear the moped start up in front of the house and I cried out in fear, "Mama, call him back, he's going to kill himself!" "He's not going to kill himself," she said and went to sleep. I lay awake through the night, all my senses overwrought, listening for him to come back, listening for a sound from the woods, a creaking tree limb from which he had hanged himself. He said he spent the nights in the dayroom of the car barn, and I have never doubted it.

On such nights I was being torn to pieces between the two of them. "Look what he is doing to me. Why don't you tell him what a bastard he is?" she requested of me. I cried more audibly and didn't answer. Why couldn't my parents see what each one wanted from the other, when it was crystal-clear to me? If only he could show a little affection and warmth, I prayed in the dark; if only she would leave him in peace. She told me he wanted disgusting, unnatural things from her; what could they be? I was right beside her every night; "my guardian angel," she called me. "Aren't you going to have more children?" the relatives asked. "The kid is lonely, and an only child turns out selfish." But she had always given away my baby things as soon as I outgrew them. Not another child, absolutely not, anything but that. Once there was a new, previously unknown, kind of tension in the air. "Is your conscience clear; is there nothing more you need to confess?" she pressed him. He sat on his chair with a guilty face and said, "I don't know if I'm completely in the clear." But this crisis passed and ended in relief, without any raging and crying. Nothing had happened.

If only they would get divorced, I prayed, kneeling in front of my little Madonna, who took care of all my wishes. Before every school exam I knelt down quickly in front of the porcelain statue with the white veil and blue sash—*Please, please give me an* A—and I got an A. When I had abdominal pain: *Please, please no appendicitis*, and the pain went away. *Please, please don't let Mama find out that I stole sugar peas from the neighbors*, and Mama didn't find out. *Make Mama not come back from town and hit me.* But she did come back, and I received the beating she had promised me, and my parents did not get divorced.

Later, after my mother's death—since you couldn't discuss sex with her—I asked my father when they had managed to be in bed together, with me sleeping right next to her. "Hardly ever," he said, and it was clear he didn't want to discuss it further. And later still, when I told him about my marriage and about the boundless contempt I felt for the man I lived with, he said, "When you start to despise the other person, you should leave; I should have left, too." But they stayed together because of the child and because of people and because she had no qualifications for a job and didn't want to be a cleaning woman. "We have a good marriage," she told the relatives, and he said nothing and looked at his fingernails. The only demonstrations of affection I remember between my parents took place before witnesses, ostentatiously and with forced grins, to prove their marital happiness.

Otherwise they went their separate ways. He earned the money, such as it was. She kept house, she shopped. She spent the money carefully and hesitantly, fingering each large bill before placing in on the counter with a heavy heart. She never made larger purchases by herself—not because she couldn't have done it, or because she lacked the necessary self-confidence. She took him along and then made her own decisions. "Why should I shoulder the whole responsibility? Why should I bear the brunt by myself?" she said. She was a first-class housewife, and it didn't occur to her to rebel against that, but large decisions and purchases like a refrigerator or a winter coat, as well as dealing with governmental agencies and attending parent-teacher conferences, those were a man's business. Yet she knew she could have handled it better, having more guts and flair, and she complained about that. We were in a store to buy material for a winter coat, and she chose the cloth, the thread, the pattern; she assessed the quality and knew how many yards it would take. He stood around and flirted with the saleswoman. They smiled at each other above her head, which was bent in concentration over the material.

He had plenty of opportunity to flirt with other women; he knew their routes to work, their hours, and whether they went out at night. A bus conductor in a small town knows lots of people. For New Year's some women gave him presents or money for some special service, like delaying a departure so they could get on, telling them it was OK that they had forgotten their pass because he knew they had one; for the way his eyes said, You look especially pretty today, and because he talked with them when they felt lonely; because he invariably recognized them and greeted them pleasantly. Otherwise nothing went on; he came home right after work, he had no friends and never brought home any co-workers and never went out, either alone or with my mother. Work and private life, kept strictly separate, and neither relaxing or fulfilling.

Earning money and supporting his family, and now and then a longing glance across the fence.

But all she saw were those longing glances. "You only have eyes for other women. What's going on between you and her? I know there's something; I can tell by looking at you." She tormented him with her jealousy. He was bound to have an outlet for love. He tormented her with his coldness—"Leave me alone; you cannot fascinate me." She spied on him. While he was on duty, she took a bus into town, found out which one he was on, and faced him triumphantly, suspicious of the women who got on, watching his gestures, his eyes. Because he had smiled at one woman, she spat in his face. She grew frightened when he wiped it with his handkerchief. That night he tried to choke her when she pinned him to her bedside with accusations and imprecations. It was 'the only time he ever laid hands on her.

She taught me to despise him. She wore the pants, and she said it was no fun having a hen-pecked husband. But then he fell asleep standing up; he had no opinions on anything; he was completely indifferent. She sent him to the agencies because a man was treated with more respect, but she coached him in how to act and what to say. He never did it right, never got anywhere. He had been a conductor for fifteen years; others, who had started at the same time, were supervisors. At her urging he took an aptitude test to qualify for advancement, but he flunked. Of course he flunked; hadn't she always told him, "You're a failure"? The same uniform for fifteen years, topped by the same listless face, and not one step ahead. His raises merely kept up with inflation and higher prices. He would have liked to earn more, but how? He might become a messenger; that way he would get more tips. She weighed the designations: "streetcar conductor," "messenger." "Streetcar conductor" was preferable after all.

His dream was to become a concierge, the kind who sits

in a glass booth and communicates with the outside world through an opening; not a single door, no handling of money, hardly even of people. But to get a job as a concierge you had to have connections. He had none. They didn't even have acquaintances, let alone friends. "We're not working-class," my mother said, "we are middle-class." The only question was whether we were upper- or lower-middle-class. She didn't want to socialize with working-class people, and not with the lower-middle class, either. "Mrs. Kovacs is stuck up," people said; "who does she think she is?" She tried to get on a friendly footing with the wives of the doctors and engineers. But they looked down on her with surprise: What business does she have, trying to sneak into our set? After her attempts to get chummy with them, after shamming and making the right noises, she felt hatred and bitterness at being rejected. Uli Reisinger couldn't talk to me any more. "We don't mix with riffraff," her de-Nazified father had said. Uli flunked her third year in the *Gymnasium*, and my mother was elated. The connection was valuable, nevertheless. She was a girl from the right milieu, even when she went to the less prestigious or ambitious *Hauptschule*, which precluded admission to a university. And I was a working-class child, even when I attended the *Gymnasium*.

Later, when I was going to the private school in town, I crossed to the other side of the street when I saw my father coming toward me in his uniform. Papa was hurt. "After all I have done for her! Who sends her to this school; who pays the tuition?" For days he wouldn't look at me. "You've hurt your father very much," my mother said solemnly, but I knew she understood me; there was no punishment, no beating; it was simply an embarrassing situation. She no longer went with him to the parent-teacher conferences; she couldn't bear for them to face the teachers together as a working-class couple, and she was afraid to go alone. He was used to being humble and wouldn't have been particularly unhappy with his position if she had left him in peace. But she heaped scorn on him: "You milksop, you failure." She demanded more panache: he should cut a more impressive figure, be more of a man. She compared him unfavorably to other men, tall and dapper, and well educated besides. She flirted and talked about it at home. About the man on the train who devoured her with his eyes and addressed her only as "lovely lady." Once she saw Lois in the street. His wife and children were with him; the children were better-looking than I, of course; the wife had no looks, and Lois was unchanged. For days she talked of nothing else.

She taught me to despise men: "Men need a strong hand." Once she slapped him. I held my breath, but nothing happened. "Men don't accomplish anything; they lie around and dream of the money they've lost, or of the money they could have made if only . . ." Yes, if only. "Their heads are filled with lewd thoughts and they don't have any sense." There was women's work and men's work, a woman's sphere and a man's sphere, but if the man was no good, the woman had to take over his sphere, too. Later I fell in love with artists, feminine men, dreamers whose dreams had fallen apart somewhere and who wanted to draw me into their dreams so that I could confirm them, make them real, but I saw through them, feeling contempt and disappointment, and let them go. "Men are failures; there's nothing you can do about it. It's crazy and stupid to depend on a man. You've got to be self-sufficient."

She taught me disappointment from the start. I was given a double message. On the one hand: housewife and mother, the world and interests of women, being feminine: "Masculine women are revolting." On the other: "You've got to stand on your own two feet. A man is no support; he's just a little boy." The answer to the dilemma was to become a convent teacher. But what about love? Love was the greatest hoax of all. Love, what is it really? How should I know? Love was what my

screaming, weeping, unloved mother everlastingly demanded
from my indifferent father. Love was the conscientiousness,
self-sacrifice, and brutality of my loveless mother. Love came
down to a poor, thin imitation: praise and a vague show of
affection for superior accomplishment. Love was something
that could be bought with self-abnegation, good grades, and
unrealistic expectations. The other love, real love, existed in
dreams, in popular songs and operettas, in stories you heard
about, and in the family films my parents had taken me to
since I was six because they had no one to look after me.
Except to the movies, they never went out together.

I learned about loneliness from her, and that marriage is
a state that gives you a modicum of protection, not a community of two. It's walking to church in a dignified manner,
with a straight back, arm in arm, wearing your Sunday clothes
and removing them and putting them away for the week immediately after returning home. A good marriage: they always
walked with their arms linked, she a little taller, not saying
one word to each other, since they had nothing to say except
the wild outbursts in which she cried out for love. Otherwise
she was alone, beginning at six-thirty in the morning, before
she woke her daughter, when she arose to clean the ashes out
of the stove in winter, to make a fire in the bitter cold, to
shovel snow. It was still dark, and she was in her housecoat
and wooden clogs, awaiting, after a lonely night, a lonely day
in which nothing would happen.

☐

What should I have done with this inheritance in the years
between childhood and adulthood? I postponed the decision,
lived in my dreams, in which the rules of my mother and her
world were irrelevant, and stayed away from people, especially
men. I had my mother, who explained reality to me, who kept
life away from me. I was never tempted to test her explanations

and distortions. But on a night when no one kept track of time, I threw her jewel into the ocean; the Southern stars came together above me, and it was neither terrible nor sinful nor humiliating. I wasn't even thinking of her—or perhaps I was, because she said into my ear, "I'll never get over the shame," but I was too happy to relish my triumph fully. I had finally won a victory over her. None of what she had told me was true; none of it would be able to touch me ever again; I was no longer vulnerable. From this night on I would not be her daughter.

But I was wrong. What she had said to me need not touch me, but what she had done to me repeated itself relentlessly, took its course with each new embrace. I was the victim who humbly chose the instrument of torture and exposed my tender, barely healed scars. Each time I thought, *This is the test; this man will spare me.* But none of them could resist the temptation, because I suffered so nobly and without any doubt that torture and love are inseparable. "I know you can't love me; I know I'm worth nothing to you," I said each time with bated breath. Who among the many would argue with me and cover the embarrassment of my nakedness? Who would lift me up? Would someone take the proffered weapon out of my hand and say, "You are the loveliest, I love only you"? Not one of them could resist the power I offered him; each used the tool I had picked for him, one with imagination and perseverance, another quickly and awkwardly, before becoming bored.

But at least I experienced love in body and soul and, silent and unhappy, understood why the words *heart* and *hurt* sounded so much alike. Sometimes I picked out fathers; that was worse, since nothing could awaken their interest. They smiled at me in a kind and absent-minded way, patted my head, and promised something for later. So I stuck to the tormentors, the ones who said, You are no good, look at you, how can anyone love you; who dallied with the successors to my merry blonde cousin

and said, Why don't you get lost, You're in my way. But no
one could take the place of my mother; no one could beat me
as she had done; no one could tie me to himself as she had
tied me to herself. I didn't stay with the bunglers—I got bored
with them quickly—and I saw through the overeager ones.
There were only a few whom I could use as vehicles for my
destruction, who could hold me with threats, with caresses
whose price kept going up, with bait that drove me to superhuman efforts. And then one morning I wake up as if from a
nightmare, and the pain is gone; love is gone; I am invulnerable
and can go looking for the next one who will take me to his
murderous heart. This time the insanity will last only as long
as I permit it, for this at least I have achieved: I am the one
who decides when it is over.

The one thing I wanted from the beginning was to keep
my child from this heritage of self-destruction. I did not want
her ever to be forced into anything, to be afraid of punishment,
to feel the humiliation of being the weaker one and the inability
to fight against it. "You are smothering your child with love,"
the psychologist said, "you are unable to let her go; you are
blocking her development." I wanted to say that it wasn't true,
but I said nothing and accepted all responsibility: I had failed
again. "She needs discipline, a father's strict hand," my aunts
commented self-righteously when my pigheaded daughter broke
into tantrums. "Am I supposed to beat her half to death, the
way I was beaten?" I yell over my daughter's yells. "Like mother,
like daughter," they say in disgust; "pull yourself together." I
have brought up a child because I have given birth to her,
and no one has told me how. I remembered my own childhood
and knew how I did not want to do it, but not doing it wrong
doesn't mean doing it right. She is twelve and keeps a diary.
I have sworn to myself never to do this, and yet I do it, with
a guilty conscience, quickly, so I won't get caught, my heart
beating with fear. God knows into what depths I may plunge.

My eyes flit across school days and school problems: a reprimand I never knew about for talking and disturbing, a D on an algebra test, which I never saw. I congratulate myself on being so generous in contrast to my punctilious mother. But then I find the entry for a weekend with her father, and my pride dissolves like the ink that dissolved under her tears: *I wish we could be a family. It's horrible always to be in the middle. Mama likes me all right, even though she nags a lot. She doesn't always have time for me, either. Sometimes she just sits and stares out the window. Or some guy is over here for supper again. He says things like "How're you doing, kiddo?" and looks at me in a dopey way. He hangs around Mama and I have to go to bed early. I'm no dummy. They think I don't know what's going on. And Papa likes me, too. He says to everybody, "May I present my daughter?" He says he is very proud of me. I don't like his wife. She's a stupid cow. But he usually doesn't bring her along when he takes me out. Yesterday he took me out twice, to the pastry shop and to the restaurant. Papa chose my menu for me and it was much better than at home. And the waiter called me "Miss"; I bet I blushed. Papa has lots more money than we; he has better stuff in the refrigerator, too. "Pick out whatever you want," he says. "Money is no object." At home we have to economize, and Mama is often grumpy because I'm not thrifty enough. Mama says she needs a new winter coat. But Papa says she's got her nerve, what is she getting the alimony for. They are always fighting about the alimony. Once the three of us went to a restaurant together, on my birthday. That was lovely. It would be lovely if Papa could live with us. But Mama says it's out of the question. I want to have a real family someday, a husband, two kids, and a dog. And a big house. I don't want to have to economize all the time. I'm sick and tired of it. Over and over I have to say my parents are divorced. Then people look as if they felt sorry for me. But really they are shocked. I can tell; I'm no dummy.*

At this point I should make myself close the diary, but I guiltily continue leafing through her short life. *Tonight is a beautiful, clear evening. If only my life were this beautiful! I'm angry at everything and everybody. I wish I could be by myself. But I'm really angry at myself. I could give up everything in this world, everything. Not to exist any more, that would be the best thing. I don't want to go on living in this repulsive room. Like a prison. The scratched-up folding table and the bed and the view on the dark alley. In the old apartment you could at least see the sky and the woods. I'm terribly unhappy. But Mama wanted to leave the old apartment. She always wants to leave. She said it was too expensive and too far from town. When we lived there I could play in the woods and pick flowers in the summer. I always have to tag along when Mama gets some new idea. Whenever she says, "I can't stand it here any more," it means pick up and move, change schools, forget the old life. Why can't I have a home like other kids?*

What made me imagine my daughter was happy? How can she suffer so in solitude? She lives with me and is unhappy and I don't see it; instead I find daily confirmation that I'm a good mother. How did I arrive at this presumption? Just because she rarely cries in my presence? But, then, did I ever cry in my mother's presence? My daughter goes into her room and cries into her diary, and when she was too young to write she lay on the floor with her blanket, sucking her thumb and staring disconsolately into space. She would refuse to speak, refuse to answer. "Unhappy and depressed," the pediatrician said and looked at me questioningly. "Did you move recently, or has there been some other significant change in her life?" "I am in the process of getting a divorce," I said. He did not spare me: "The children are always the victims, of course," he said. Those were the months when she stood by, her face frightened, as her father roared and tried to get his hands on me, and I threw dishes at him and ran out of the house and was not there the next morning. No, I have never beaten her, but I presented her with an unrestrained show of pain and rage and tears, of banging my head against the wall of fate, and I realized much too late that I was destroying her capacity for happiness.

And murderous rage, the temptation to give in to one's lurking despair at the very place where the demarcation between oneself and another person is weak and can be trampled down easily, where self-hatred can turn, unexpectedly, into destructiveness: I have known this, and also the profound shame afterward. I never beat you, child, but the day I shook you in front of the stone wall, mute in my fury, there was such a little space between you and the wall. I knew then that I was capable of pushing your head against that wall and, horrified, I let go. When you were little and cried and cried, I stopped my ears with my fingers and cried out loud myself in helpless desperation until I couldn't hear you any more. And I am surprised that you are unhappy? You don't know anything about all this; the struggle between us was silent and without violence, but no less guilty, not even free of hate. You only know you are unhappy; you press your fingernails into your flesh to convince yourself that pain is not the everyday form of existence; you pull back into yourself and few can reach you, and I look on, helpless and ashamed. I did not succeed in breaking the chain. Here, too, I have remained my mother's daughter.

☐

I had completed elementary school and my mother registered me in the town's convent school, in the *Hauptschule* division. I wanted to get into the *Gymnasium*, but the elementary-school principal said he couldn't see me as anything except a *Hauptschule* student, though a good one, of course. I wouldn't be able to pass the *Matura*, the *Gymnasium*'s graduation exam,

because working-class kids are handicapped: verbal deprivation, lack of cultural stimuli. Don't aim too high, Kovacses;
pride goeth before a fall.

When we went to register me, we wore our best Sunday
clothes, subdued blue and gray, high-necked and long-sleeved,
and we were humble and pious in the presence of the nun
who admitted us. A public school wasn't good enough; it had
to be a private school, even if the tuition had to come out of
our food bill. "So that Vera won't have to suffer for her faith,
as I did during those first years of married life," my mother
said; besides, I was to become a convent teacher. Four years
of *Hauptschule*, then novitiate; the convent was bound to pay
for the teacher training to follow. Mama tilted and bowed her
head slightly and smiled more sweetly than I had ever seen
her smile—like an angel, said the Mother Superior, who asked
me to sing *Let There Be Sunshine in Your Heart*. We practically
dissolved in meekness and reverence; even back on the street
I was weak-kneed and thought people could see the halos
around us.

But during the summer, when Uli passed the *Gymnasium*
entrance examination, along with five other socially well-placed
students whose academic records did not approach mine, I
managed, for the first time in my life, to have my wishes
prevail over those of my parents and teachers. "Let's let her
take the exam so she'll feel better," my father said. Lisa, my
beautiful, notorious cousin, was a secretary in a jewelry store;
my other cousins were, or were training to be, saleswomen.
A secretarial job was a good job for a girl, a step up from the
blue-collar into the white-collar world. A teacher, however,
was an authority figure; she commanded respect and stood
above the rest of the community, just below the parish priest.
She had control over the school-age children and therefore
over most families. But what good was the *Matura*, what did
it qualify you for? When you graduated at eighteen, after eight

years of higher education, everybody else had already settled into an occupation, and where would that leave you? You weren't even a teacher; your *Matura* meant only that you had graduated from the *Gymnasium* and were eligible to attend a university. Who could afford to send a child to a university— a daughter at that, who would after all get married? University: the concept was too abstract to engage the imagination and arouse fantasies. Who attended a university? Clergymen and doctors. But was being a doctor really so much more prestigious than being a teacher? Worth the expenditure? "Maybe she won't pass the entrance exam," my father said. They hoped that I wouldn't. I was surprised and triumphant when my name was posted on the bulletin board. I had shown them; I had succeeded—my first independent decision.

For my mother the stress of competing lessened when I went to school in town. She didn't see the other students, didn't know how they were dressed, who their parents were, what kind of marks they got. And I didn't report the humiliation, on the first day, of having to stand up in almost every class and give my father's name and occupation. Just for orientation, the teacher said, but I noticed the light in their eyes when the fathers named were famous surgeons, owners of large businesses, the secretary of the army, and a few scattered aristocrats who could afford to leave the "von" off their names because everyone knew who they were anyway. A private school, an elite school, and again I was the only working-class child and had to show them, or they wouldn't believe it. "There are some students in the room who don't fit in," Sister Therese said and looked at me so that I blushed. "We must practice Christian charity." The daughters of the aristocrats and industrialists nodded magnanimously.

I had to get up at six-thirty every morning now, and in winter it was still dark when I took the bus to town at ten minutes past seven. The other students from our area took the

seven-thirty bus, but I had to be more than punctual and could
not slide into my seat when the first bell rang at five to eight;
I had to prepare myself intellectually, tune myself emotionally,
half an hour before classes began. During recess I took out
my ham roll and the bankers' daughters pounced on it: "Let
me have a bite, just one." When I came home, lunch was
ready, always punctual; my father also had to adjust his sched-
ule to mine. I changed out of my school clothes and hung
them up; then we ate. I didn't have to be whacked in order
to come to the table; I killed time and got through the meal
by imagining myself stirring everything on the table into a
mush, mixing everything with everything. Then I had to digest
my food. I lay on the sofa and was permitted to put my feet
on Mama's lap. She sent my father to the bathroom and turned
the key from the outside. He was too stupid to join in our talk
anyway. So he sat out there, or perhaps he stood up, until it
occurred to her to let him back in. At the time I was not struck
by his accepting such treatment without a word. We talked
about school, and she often told me about her earlier life,
about the farm before I was born; soon I knew her whole
childhood by heart, and also about the various acts of persecution during the early years of her married life. The pain-
fulness of it all made me cry. The hatred that traveled from
her to me tied my stomach in knots.

I loved her for her suffering, and I felt her humiliations;
I wanted to make it up to her; I wanted to take revenge for
her, even on Papa, who denied her love and asked unspeakable
things of her.

Then she washed the dishes and I went up to my attic
room with the folding table by the window and placed my
notebooks in a row on Papa's bed. "Mama, don't sing, I can't
concentrate," I called down to the kitchen. The singing stopped.
Later I said, "When I know someone is in the house, I just
can't get myself together." So, after doing the dishes, my mother

would get dressed and ride into town. At five o'clock she came home. "Your mother goes to town at the same time every day; is she working part-time?" the neighbors asked. I didn't think about how she might be spending the afternoons, summer and winter, in all weather. She had no money for shopping. Did she walk up and down the streets, did she sit inside churches? Sometimes she went to the cathedral library and borrowed historical novels; she brought home books by Karl May for me. Sometimes she visited the Kovacs aunts, though she had broken off contact with them some time earlier; they did not return her visits.

No one came to visit us, except the grandmother of a girl my age whom I couldn't stand. The grandmother was the only one to whom my mother sometimes hesitantly spoke about herself, and for whom she developed an affection, which got on the old woman's nerves. We often went to visit her, and if my mother sensed that she was at home, she rang, knocked on the windows, and crept around the house for hours, until the woman came out and pleaded, "I'm begging you, not today; I don't feel well today." Then she moved in with her son at the other end of town and visited my mother only once a year. She would not receive return visits, saying her daughter-in-law objected. Now Mama was left without anyone again. Still, on Sunday afternoons she peered down the road every half hour, just in case somebody was coming.

The various neighbor women who moved in next door tried for a friendly relationship with Mrs. Kovacs, including an occasional chat across the fence, but my mother mistrusted more and more people; she envied more and more women their houses, their husbands, and their children, and she violated even common courtesy in her determination not to let anyone see into her life. She was cool and unapproachable, and the hesitant smile appeared on her lips more and more rarely and froze more quickly, froze before it reached the earnest, distrustful eyes, which never smiled. The first sign of danger—the first sympathetic question, the first remark that sounded patronizing or critical—brought on a cold look, an icy smile. People respected her. She was always properly dressed; she always paid cash in the stores; we went to church on Sundays as if we were the Holy Family; everyone could see that her child meant everything to her and that she gave her all to the child.

I knew she gave her all to me; she told me so every day. I had become used to the fact that I could never be grateful enough. Nevertheless I tried to express my insufficient gratitude, on her name day, her birthday, Mother's Day, Christmas, with hand-painted greeting cards and with presents I had bought on money my aunts had given me for candy bars. Then she was so touched she wiped the tears from her eyes. But when she found drawings on the last page of my math book again, when I got D's on my homework, when I brought home my half-eaten school snack and balked at wearing the hard-won, expensive Sunday clothes, she turned away from me in disgust again: "You wicked, ungrateful wretch, what's the use of sacrificing for you?" Before my first D I could sit on her lap, touch her face, kiss her, and feel secure with her arm around me. But with the first D at the end of the first *Gymnasium* year our meager bodily contact, the last remnants of tenderness, broke off irrevocably. I was eleven at the time. It would be twelve years before I touched a human face again.

During my second year at the new school many things happened, things she had not expected and I was not prepared for. When I was nine she had told me that Aunt Fanni was expecting a baby and therefore had a big stomach, that babies grew in the stomach and then were born. No doubt it was a struggle for her to impart this information to me, and I could tell by looking into her eyes that I should not ask any questions about how babies got inside the stomach and back out. Getting inside must have to do with something unchaste, and I knew any thought of that was sinful and had to be brought up in confession. To get out they must have to use the largest bodily opening, and that was the mouth. I came to the conclusion that babies were disgorged.

But when I was eleven other things began to trouble me. My breasts were becoming visible under my sweater and bounced embarrassingly when I walked. When I touched them I felt an extremely disturbing sensation, which I could not explain. On my way home I went out of my way to pass the porno movie houses with their still photos; true, I looked at them furtively, out of the corners of my eyes, but with an avidity that drove me to walk down that same block, past those same pictures, again and again. When my mother went to town in the afternoons, I could hardly wait to take off my blouse and look at myself in the mirror. I would wake up with my body throbbing, and in trying to reproduce the state of arousal I discovered masturbation, with my mother asleep next to me.

Of course I fell in love. With movie stars, whose deftly concealed pictures I carried around with me, and with a *Gymnasium* student from my neighborhood, two years older, about whom I dreamed day and night. The degree of my happiness or unhappiness on any given day was dependent on whether he made an appearance between the time I left the house early in the morning and my return home in the afternoon. The days that were transfigured by his appearance were circled in red ink on my pocket calendar. I never spoke to him, but I would have recognized the sound of his voice, which had just changed, anywhere.

My mother knew nothing of all these torments, only that my grades went down from A to B and finally to C. During the first semester I received a warning, and around Easter the dreaded letter came, telling my parents that their daughter would not pass the math course. Both of them went to the conference at school and had to listen to their child's being described as lazy, untalented, and poorly behaved. They shyly put a hundred-shilling bill on the table, which was rejected indignantly by the math teacher and pocketed by the nun in charge with a God-bless-you. They talked about taking me out of school. My conscientious mother started punishing me for every bad mark again.

She beat me in a way that was different from before. Now it wasn't only the pain and blue bruises I tried to escape by spending long afternoons riding the streetcars in town; it was most of all the humiliation of having to undress in front of her before receiving the blows, the humiliation of having to reel, screaming and helpless, from one piece of furniture to another, with my body bare below the waist. Once I tore the cudgel from her hand and saw in her horrified eyes the same fear with which I cringed under her arm. For seconds we faced each other, the animal fear of being beaten between us, until the enormity of the situation registered in our paralyzed consciousness and the natural order was restored. "You wouldn't dare," she gasped and yanked the stick out of my hand. That time she forgot to aim for the places that were normally covered by clothing. Over and over I was hit on my arms, back, belly, calves, with the full force of her strong peasant hands, until I cowered in the corner next to the piano, fighting for breath, my arms above my head. There were ironclad rules that went with these ritual beatings, which I would not have dared to break because I was convinced that the punishment would escalate into something unthinkable, unsurvivable. I was not allowed to hide behind furniture or under the table, nor to escape by running up the stairs or out the door, and I was not allowed to put any object between me and the tool that served as the means of my punishment. After all, each beating was a serious, even solemn act, a service carried out in the name of a higher law, which must not be ridiculed by games of tag or hide-and-seek. I had to receive my blows in the full consciousness of my wickedness and worthlessness; they were divine judgment, not the random explosion of a thunderstorm.

She went through my notebooks every day now and slapped my drawings—the result of my dreams and a talent noted with approval by the art teacher—in my face before tearing them up and throwing them in the stove. I found better hiding places for my art work; there were cracks everywhere; behind almost every chest there was enough space for the charcoal pencils and watercolors I had secretly bought with candy money from my aunts and an occasional larger sum from my grandmother. A daughter with artistic ambitions, that would be the last straw, when it took so much effort even now to save her from disgrace, to thrash the ways of virtue and diligence into her so she would become a respectable person and would have a better life than her parents. Drawing in school notebooks brought corporal punishment; artistic talent was undesirable.

When I had a D in my schoolbag I rode the streetcar from one end of town to the other all afternoon long, considered suicide, and finally went to my aunt's in the river-bottoms housing development and confessed that I didn't dare go home. After that I felt better, and I did go home. My mother could sense my bad conscience already from the way I walked down the gravel path. We had stopped talking, but her angry eyes, her disdainful mouth, no longer caused guilt feelings in me; her beatings created only hatred and fear. I stayed away from home longer and longer, bummed around town, hung out in the train station, and made anonymous phone calls to teachers, aided by my friend Eva. At home I lied about makeup classes to my mother and avoided looking her in the face. I knew she wouldn't dare check with the school. When one of the nuns threw Eva and me out of an empty classroom and we fled to the washroom, where we were also caught, I acquired the reputation of being a menace to the morals of my fellow students.

This reputation followed me from year to year, all the way to the *Matura*. But my mother knew nothing about me in spite of the daily schoolbag check, nothing about my drawings, my roaming around town, let alone my dreams. She only found the notes my seatmate and I had passed under our desk: "I'm bored, you too?" "Yeah, that Fifi is a dope." "Have you done your math problem yet?" "No, and I'm not going to. I'll copy it tomorrow morning." Once she found a glossy movie magazine, but she didn't know that the tears on the paper she tore to shreds were for a movie star I adored. During vacations she opened the letters I received from school friends, and I was not allowed to seal the letters I wrote until she had read them. Privacy did not exist. I became an expert in transmitting coded messages: I learned the Greek alphabet; I sprinkled my letters with innocuous-looking English sentences. Nothing could be gleaned from me; I averted my eyes and revealed nothing. Only facts could be thrashed out of me.

Until she found my diary she knew nothing about me. When I came home after school and saw the offended look on her face, which said, You have dealt me a mortal blow, I knew instantly. *I am unhappy*, I wrote in my diary. *I am homely and no one likes me. I must do something about it*, it said on every other page. *I'll start by cutting my hair in bangs, and maybe some new frames for my glasses would help. Mama doesn't like me*, I wrote, but the excuse followed immediately: *It's no wonder, because she doesn't deserve such a homely and morose daughter. My cousin Monika was visiting us, Mama said she had become so pretty, and I so homely by comparison, but I don't really agree with that.* And then I went so far as to write this sacrilegious admission: *It's not my fault that I was born; I would rather not be here.*

The diary lay on the piano, clearly visible. I picked it up furtively and took it to my room. We never talked about it, but her ominous silence, her grim, contemptuous expression, the coldness that precluded any approach were worse than a beating; they lay between us for weeks, and nothing could soothe her or resolve the tension between us. I had had the audacity to be unhappy when she did everything for me and sacrificed her entire life for me. I had had the audacity to find my existence painful, when the meaning of her life depended on my existence. I was ungrateful, spoiled, and wicked, abysmally wicked. At this point she could have stopped rummaging through my schoolbag, searching my room, leafing through my notebooks; now she knew enough. But there was nothing she could do with her knowledge.

When I didn't behave, she still reached for the carpet beater, but more and more she substituted daily slaps, kicks, and punches for systematic beatings. All the things she had so carefully protected me from sought me out, drew me with the special lure of the forbidden. I found time for secret visits to the movies; three of us sat behind a bush in the convent garden, avid and horrified at once as we stared at a porno magazine; and I cleverly acquired pictures of movie idols and pop singers and even the Hit Parade behind her watchful back. School friends invited me to their homes, and we listened to popular music instead of doing our homework. Listening to music on the radio was a normal activity for them, but I was breathless and couldn't get enough of it. "I'm not allowed to listen to the radio at home," I would say, ashamed to admit that we didn't have a radio.

My mother was at her wits' end. Suddenly she had lost control; suddenly she could not keep her child in line with either beatings or hurt looks. Suddenly the dreaded "You just wait" brought defiance rather than fear to my face. Now the defiance, which had been forbidden in my house during the "defiant stage," could no longer be whipped out of me. She consulted her sisters, who were unanimous in urging her to take me out of the *Gymnasium*. "Why should a girl be a scholar? All that does is give her big ideas." But defiance was good for something: I caught up during the last few weeks and squeaked through.

One afternoon after school I stood on the streetcar platform, doubled up with abdominal pain. I was sure my appendix was rupturing, and I almost fainted when I saw blood running into my stockings. "Now you are a woman," my mother said when I showed her my underpants. "From now on you are fertile, and if you have anything to do with a man you'll get pregnant. That would kill me." I felt a sense of power, of autonomy, and also some fear: I had a weapon that could kill her. Like her I now wore a sanitary belt and a cloth pad between my legs, which was only changed when it was completely saturated. The pads would stink after a while because you couldn't take a bath during your period, not even put your feet in water, or you'd come down with epilepsy. You couldn't wash your hair, either, and I was excused from gym on those days and could sit against the wall with the other initiates.

When I took off my undershirt, my mother was repelled and told me I looked like a nightclub dancer, a prostitute, with my petticoat and bare bosom. I was ashamed, and my posture worsened as I attempted to hide my breasts. Some time or other I was given a modest cotton bra, which went all the way to my collarbone. My father always had to leave the living room when I changed clothes; he wasn't even allowed to see me in my underwear. In fact, she turned the key after he left to make quite certain my chastity was secure. From now on all my clothes were cut so as to hide every curve that might have made me distinguishable from a woman of fifty. Loose overblouses with cuffs and Peter Pan collars, shapeless calf-length skirts—everything sewn by our seventy-year-old dressmaker from the finest cloth bought in the best stores—and flat-heeled shoes. My aunts rubbed the dress fabrics between their fingers and clicked their tongues approvingly: "She's got good taste, that Marie, and nothing is too expensive for that kid." In school they laughed at me; I had the most old-fashioned clothes. I was so ashamed that I told my mother we now had to wear school smocks; that way I could escape being teased about the sacks that hung on me.

There was a new hatred, which I did not understand and for which I did not feel responsible, a completely new kind of cruelty. Not the cruelty of brutal beatings but, rather, of small acts of harassment: hair pulling, scorn and revulsion in the presence of my naked body, the hostile way she yanked me around and punched me when she got me dressed, the wary, contemptuous look that told me, wordlessly but incessantly, how wicked I was. I sensed that it had something to do with the fact that I was no longer a child, that I was becoming a woman like her, with breasts, with pubic hair and monthly periods; for this reason I was suspect and automatically guilty, tainted by a primeval guilt, a curse that could be removed neither by beatings nor by contempt.

I had a vague sense that she felt threatened by my emerging female sexuality and that I might be able to evade her hatred by making myself as unattractive and inconspicuous as possible. I knuckled under, put on the ungainly skirts and maternity blouses without offering resistance, pulled my shoulders forward, and made my face look impenetrable and dull. But then she held up other girls as models, lively young things who were discovering life for the first time and, dizzy with their discoveries, exuded joy and youthfulness. "Why can't you be like that," she asked reproachfully. "The other girls are so cheerful and energetic, and you're so gloomy and depressed. A person who is not thankful for the gift of life, a young girl who is not cheerful, has to be abysmally wicked." I didn't know the cheerfulness she demanded—I had never experienced it—and she had shut off my zest for life with her prohibitions and punishing looks. In my dreams I was like those girls, only wilder, even more avid for life; in my dreams I outstripped every one of them with the joy and freedom of youth.

My sleepless nights offered me much opportunity for dreaming. Often I slept only one or two hours, lying awake from seven at night until four in the morning, counting sheep, praying more and more desperately for the relief of sleep, because tomorrow was a school day and I had to be rested; a bad mark was unthinkable, inexcusable. For years I suffered from insomnia and never said a word about it, nor did I dare to toss and turn in bed; in my despair I cried silently, trying not to wake her as she snored softly next to me.

In the morning my schoolbag had to be packed ready to go; only my snack was still to be added. After breakfast I sat at the table, erect on a straight chair, and she did my hair. First she combed out my braids; then she worked on my scalp with a fine-toothed comb; then the hair was pulled away from my face and braided again. Sometimes it was caught in a ponytail, with my high forehead left bare and white. The ponytail hung down my back in reddish-brown waves. "If only her hair doesn't turn red," my mother worried, and looked down the road after me as my copper ponytail bobbed in the morning sun. In two days the hair was oily; then it was put up. A bunch of hair that had fallen out was fastened with hairpins and the fine, live hair was draped over it, just enough of it to hide the matted ball underneath. With this hairdo you couldn't run, exercise, or swim; a gust of wind was a catastrophe. Not a single hair could stray from this coiffure.

Every Saturday she bathed me thoroughly in the aluminum tub—behind my ears, under my arms, around my neck. I was not allowed to touch myself; the idea of self-abuse was not to be put into my head. It entered it anyway, at night, under the blanket, when she was asleep. But in the daytime she kept me away from my body. She got my undershirt out of the chest and pulled it over my head. It would not have occurred to me to object to the cotton undershirt that came up to my collarbone, or to my bloomers with their elastic legs. Only whores wore underwear that was made of lace and nylon and was offensively revealing. She hooked my bra and inspected my underpants every day. You had to be quick getting dressed, though you could linger over the outer things: cover your breasts quickly, don't look at them; it's sinful to have breasts. A future nun needs no breasts.

I became overweight. She praised me; there were no more fights at the dinner table. She didn't have to beat the food into me any more. The more she praised me, the more I ate; the more I ate, the more she praised me. I ate until I felt sick in order to make her like me even more; courting love, I stuffed myself with food. Self-sacrificing, she refilled my plate over and over. Only much later did she dare to admit that I ate her and my father's food, that I would eat seven schnitzels all at one time and leave only potatoes for them. I thought I could make her happy by eating so well; I only wanted to prove my good will. Later, when it was too late, she said, "Sometimes I thought, The child is inconsiderate; she eats and eats without asking if anyone else might be hungry." At age thirteen I weighed 144 pounds, was clumsy in gym, and nearly drowned in swimming class. Faced with my mother's pleading eyes, our family physician wrote "circulatory problems" and "nervous-system dysfunction" on my note for school, but he said, "Just between us, lots of exercise and a little less to eat." I was excused from swimming. During my summer vacation I lay in the lawn chair and memorized Latin vocabulary and grammar. Mama brought me layer cakes and creamy puddings, and I ate helping after helping, obediently asking for more. How could I have refused her cakes, her devotion, her love, though it changed my body into a lump of fat? After two months of incessant eating and studying in the lawn chair, I was the heaviest kid in my class. My legs were shapeless, with stretch marks making white cracks in the skin. Mama felt my thighs and was pleased; her devotion was bearing visible fruit—the child was well nourished.

I was the class joke. "Greaseball, fatty," they called, laughing, when after five tries I couldn't make it across the buck in gymnastics. Inconspicuous, gangly kids had become fashion-conscious young women; they opened like buds, had secret rendezvous, suffered the pains of first love, let themselves be kissed, and shrugged their shoulders at bad grades. I remained matronly, with my hair in a bun that expanded with the ball of cast-off hair, wearing maternity blouses and loose skirts. The greaseball with a receding chin, overlarge mouth, ears that stuck out, and black-framed glasses that made the gloomy face look even gloomier. But I suddenly turned into the best student in my class, the eager beaver from whom the others could copy the assignments just before school started in the morning. My mother was delighted: the crisis of puberty was over. No more movie magazines among my notebooks; I came home right after school and did all my assignments perfectly; the D's disappeared from my notebooks and A's became the norm again, as in elementary school. She had won this round, too. "Vera eats all, Vera studies hard, Vera gives me a lot of pleasure now," she told her sisters.

I was fourteen when she hit me for the last time. I had openly questioned the purpose of my existence. "It isn't my fault I'm here on earth," I had said. "That's the thanks I get," she sobbed and made her last attempt at beating into me gratitude and zest for life.

Otherwise the conflicts had become fewer. The notebooks for my homework were no longer inspected; they were clean, immaculate; besides, my parents could not keep up with the material I was studying. They could not have helped me now, and tutoring would have been too expensive: Either you learn or we'll take you out of school. At age fourteen other kids start to learn a trade. I knew that I really belonged with those other kids, who at fourteen begin to contribute to the family earnings. I was privileged. Not many parents were willing to support their children until they were eighteen, so that they could study. What's more, I was a girl. I had to prove myself worthy of the privilege. Beyond that, I had to show *them*, all those who were convinced I wouldn't make it, all those who said working-class children couldn't pass the *Matura* because they came from a culturally deprived home environment.

The amounts expended on me were counted out; I nearly died of guilt and awareness of my insufficient gratitude. Eighty shillings a month for tuition was a lot out of a wage of less than two thousand; and then there were my clothes, made of the best material; weeks in the country with my class, during which I never closed my eyes because I was homesick and afraid of the black mountains; skiing lessons and a complete skiing outfit. The expenditures grew into gigantic sums; when a four-figure number was named, a wall of horror lowered itself in front of my imagination and cut off my ability to think. Three figures mean wealth; four mean approaching ruin. My grades in math had only improved when we got to imaginary numbers, to integers and differentials, which did not require a connection with the real world. Only then did I feel capable of handling numbers, released from responsibility.

Like everything else, the ski outfit was managed by scrimping on food: boots with inside slippers, the finest skis, safety bindings; sweater, hat, and scarf were hand-knitted (of the best wool, of course), but the parka and ski pants were bought in the most expensive sporting-goods store. Added to this was the bag of provisions—rolled ham, salami, whole-grain bread, things we never had at home. I lay on my cot and ate and ate, weighing 153 pounds. "The greaseball is eating again," my schoolmates scoffed, but how could I let the precious salami go to waste? The hard-boiled eggs started to stink; "Phooey,

throw them out!" But you don't throw out a gift of God, and
food is a gift of God. On the slope I stood in a helpless panic
on my expensive skis. "Help me," I cried in despair, "why
don't you help me? I always let you copy my homework." But
the others were downhill already. I slid down on my bottom;
I shut my eyes and shot right into the deep snow. I hated the
the expensive skis; the safety bindings did not work when I
fell. But I came home with a sunburned face and reported
that I had had a good time, and my parents were glad that the
sacrifice had been worth it: "To think the child has the chance
to experience so many things we couldn't even dream of."

□

So many substitutions that simulate love for us, that are meant
to cloud our eyes and satisfy our hunger with surrogate nourishment. A whole life filled with substitutions for love, and
the recognition always too late because love remains an unknown quantity, which is measured in degrees of closeness,
but remains a remote abstraction frozen into a smile on the
big screen, Hollywood's dream of unhappiness for two. Love
needs to be earned; nothing on this earth is free. How could
I have doubted this premise, when my self-worth was grounded
in it? "There is a treasure in your vineyard," a dying father
said, and his sons dug for seven years and wound up rich as
a result of their hard work.

As long as I sought her love—long after she was dead—I
was praised for my hard work, my perseverance, my accom-
plishments; I got ahead and could be proud of myself. But one
day my battered, mutilated self lifted up its head defiantly and
said, *I don't care about your approval, I want out.* Then things
went downhill fast. Mama's good child tried to grasp the reins
and save whatever could be saved, but the defiant child yelled,
*I want to live, I don't want to be good any more, I want out
of this prison.* Again and again I have found a safe haven, but

overnight it becomes a prison and my other self, the rude gypsy, the tough little devil who cannot be killed or controlled, ends up victorious. The little devil and my mother fight for supremacy; I myself am on the sidelines; I do whatever is necessary to catch a few crumbs of love. My hunger has not yet been satisfied. There is a terrible hunger for love in the world; all of humanity has gone unsatisfied. Who am I to complain?

First I ate for the sake of love, then I fasted for the sake of love. "Eat so you'll grow tall and strong," my mother said— so the love I can't give you will manifest itself in fat cells. "Don't eat so much; I need more than you; besides, you're getting fat," said the man who taught me to unlearn love. So I stopped eating. He was right. Hadn't even my mother said I was so thoughtless I was eating them poor? "I am too fat, I've got to lose weight," I said, and started taking laxatives after every meal. "But you've become a skeleton," my friends cried in alarm and put bread and butter on my plate. I got annoyed: "I don't eat bread; I don't eat butter." I ate only carrots and hard-boiled eggs and weighed one hundred pounds. My hair fell out; I never slept more than six hours a night; my periods stopped; I suffered from migraine and neuralgia; but I still insisted that I was too heavy and vomited after meals. I looked at my boyish figure in the mirror: breasts gone, hips gone, period gone. The aggravation had been removed; now she could love me again, let me sit on her lap; I was a child again and she no longer needed to feel threatened. She had won; I had given in. She could have my sexuality in return for a little slice of love that left me hungry.

For seven years I refused the force-feeding, the substitute love of my puberty, washed it out of my body with laxative teas, felt naueasted when I thought of my mother's voluptuous body and her terror by food, inducing me to become a eunuch, and went right on fasting. Sometimes I ate secretly, at four in the morning, gobbling up everything inside refrigerators, grocery bags, pantries; I couldn't eat fast enough as I greedily devoured anything and everything, sweet or sour, with no regard for the flavor, with no witnesses; I even went through the garbage; then I tried to allay my indigestion and guilty feelings with laxatives. I was hungry for love and refused all food indignantly, refused it as an encroachment, an affront, an infringement on my freedom to destroy myself. My lust for the forbidden food was as strong as my revulsion. I dreamed about luscious cakes and then threw up; I couldn't see enough of the glossy color plates in cookbooks, but I swore that anything made with butter or other fats caused me to vomit. I knew the caloric charts by heart. I lived on inexpensive vegetables and diet cottage cheese. I would have obeyed my mother's unspoken command; I would have extinguished myself if the obstreperous little devil hadn't broken out now and then and driven me to seek out food against my will.

During these years I never touched my emaciated body; I ignored it and its needs; engaged in a quest for love, I was incapable of awakening it. "My God, are you skinny," my lovers would say—my one-night stands—and be gone. A female hunger artist, an erotic corpse. I went on starving myself without an audience in my dogged self-hatred; reduction was the key word of my existence. But I was tough: against my will I survived. In my daily battles for my mother's approval, I destroyed my body and drove my mind to peak performances. Sixteen hours of work without interruption; hundreds of books, until the letters danced before my eyes, until I was blinded by the sunlight that I sometimes guiltily indulged in. Self-destruction was the title of my research project; suicide in literature, through literature; regression; loss of self; overstepping and avoiding the boundaries of the self. Here I found myself in good company; here I was not alone; the editors praised my capacity for empathy. My intellect was agile in jumping over my shrinking body; every day I let my body jump over its sharp edge, the perfect executor of my omnipotent mother's will. She praised me richly. She did not have to turn over in her grave for my sake; she could be at peace: My Vera is studying hard; she is even punishing herself now; my work is over. I finally understood what she meant when she said she didn't deserve such a child. I was not fit to live; I had no right to food, to happiness, to love; I had to make myself inconspicuous, invisible; I had to put an end to myself as much as I was able, because if she didn't want me, how could I dare to want myself?

Again and again I have extinguished myself and carried out commands; I am an obedient victim. Who do you want me to be, I ask my lovers, and disappear into the roles they like best. I am Ophelia, Desdemona, or Lulu, according to their wishes. I extinguish myself in my battle for love and, desperate, step out of my role, get stuck, can't go on, am chased off the stage, a bad actress. No matter how willing, how obedient I am, I always lose the battle, because behind the roles I am starving and want applause for myself, not for Lulu, Desdemona, or Ophelia. But when I emerge from the costume, nothing is left except a small, emaciated body and a small, revengeful soul, and there is no way of breaking hearts and winning love with those. Then I'm ashamed and creep backstage to punish myself for my worthlessness, and the audience is outraged at the scandal: We want to see an actress, not an exhibitionist. Continuous self-punishment, my whole life long, and there are plenty of helping hands.

☐

Not much changed in my mother's life. After her child left for school, she would straighten up, then go shopping early— between eight-thirty and nine—safe at that hour from meeting doctors' wives, the owners of villas, who appeared later since

they slept later and had more and larger rooms to straighten.
Then she cooked, making a lot out of a little: a good sauce
out of flour, water, and cream, a roast out of a cheap cut of
pork, and always soup before and pudding after. I hated soup;
I hated soup for thirty years. She ate a great deal; she tasted
while she ate; she ate up all the leftovers; she became obese,
weighing 178 pounds, sometimes as much as two hundred,
but she didn't care. Her obesity was a visible sign that she was
well off. "What I've got outside and inside of me no one can
take away from me," she said. Imposing, people called her,
because they wanted to avoid the word "fat." Her sisters told
her how well she looked. "I don't want for anything; I'm well
off," she said, self-satisfied.

Once a week she did the laundry. It was a luxury to take
the clean laundry out of the washing machine, and she couldn't
get used to it. No more boiling things on the stove, no scalded
fingers, no washboard. To pull the hot, wet wash out of the
machine with tongs and hang it up, how simple that was. She
hung the laundry in the yard, summers and winters. In the
winter it was frozen stiff by evening and her fingers were blue
when she put up the clothesline in the living room and changed
it into a forest of laundry for the night. I loved those rows of
laundry, which divided the small room twenty times and darkened the light.

She fed the chickens and cleaned out the chicken coop;
in the summer she also kept rabbits. All this reminded her of
home; she was in her element and would sing softly. She had
a beautiful contralto, but her singing infuriated me; it pursued
me through the house and left me no freedom for my dreams,
which, as much as possible, had become my refuge.

"You deserve to spend something on yourself," said the
few people whose insight penetrated the façade, who glimpsed
behind the Sunday clothes and hats the denim apron, the
threadbare blue jumper, and the scarf tied above her forehead.

Twice a year she went to the hair salon, but her ungovernable red hair grew rapidly, the red color showed through the tint, and her permanent became frizzy in the dampness of the laundry room. Losing patience, she pulled her hair straight back and gathered it in a short braid, which she fastened at the back of her head. On Sundays she changed this into an artful coiffure.

She did spend something on herself. A spring suit of leaf-green linen, with a beige hat, beige gloves, a beige purse, and beige shoes. In summer she splurged on a dark-blue part-silk dress with flowers woven into it. Her daughter was always outfitted at the same time; my summer dress was white with woven flowers, and there always had to be a bow somewhere, in front, or on the belt or the skirt. Her cosmetics comprised two tubes, one a rich hand cream, the other a rich night cream. Smooth hands, which did not show the work of the housewife, the slave, and a smooth face without wrinkles, which did not show long nights of weeping. This sufficed to satisfy her idea of beauty. In earlier years she had made up her lips. "For whom?" she said. "No one is going to look at me anyway."

On Sundays, after the dishes, we rode into town in our Sunday clothes, mother and daughter, both overweight, in matching dresses, arm in arm, our purses dangling, serious, careful not to brush against anything with our lovely, costly clothes—a quick glance at the seat, a casual dusting with the hand; our shoes and stockings unsplattered; four straight, parallel stocking seams which had been checked at home before we left, for you didn't adjust your stockings once you got out in the street. In spite of her corpulence my mother had slim, beautiful legs; mine were fat, and the relatives said that the mother was still prettier than the daughter. We could ride free on the bus and the streetcar, but we walked from the stop under the bridge all the way down the main street. We stopped at every store window, wishful, not saying much. I don't know what she was thinking, but I imagined being allowed to pick the most beautiful object in each display, and that any of these objects—garnet earrings, silk scarves, lingerie—could make the difference and transform my homeliness into the youthful vibrancy we saw in the passing groups of girls, who giggled excitedly and didn't look at the display windows, but whose lively eyes were on the lookout for the admiring glances of boys. We went down the main street, arms linked, I on the inside, close to the store windows: "Look, that spring coat would be good on you." I stopped before bookstores and Mama, bored, put up with it; we had no money to spend on books; you read them only once, and, besides, you could borrow them from the library.

"You don't need cosmetics at your age," she told me and forbade even a quick look at drugstore displays. In the end she did buy me a black eyebrow pencil in a heavy gold case; I appeared unfriendly and threatening, looking out from under black, bushy eyebrows. The lipstick she gave me for my four- teenth birthday was bright red and had to be wiped off as soon as it was put on. What could I do to be young and pretty like the others? Hair makes all the difference, I thought. "Why don't you change your hairdo?" my classmates said; how could they know my mother did my hair? I wanted short hair that could fall into my face casually. In the hair salon's mirror I couldn't recognize myself. Mama sat next to me and confirmed the success of the venture: I looked twenty years older. The wavy copper-colored ponytail was taken home as a souvenir. But the splendor collapsed at home on the first day: the high, teased hair had to be combed out; the comb was sticky with hair spray, styling lotion, and wave set, and my hair hung over my ears, lifeless and sticky. "Like a convict," said my mother, who always came up with exactly the right expression. My homeliness was an irrevocable fact, and my hair grew slowly. When it was shoulder-length, my mother pulled it together over the nape of my neck and fastened it with a barrette covered by a black velvet bow. That was the Mozart braid; her beautiful sister Fanni had worn one, and I was still wearing it after her death; it was two years before I dared to wear my hair loose. Once your hair comes down below your ears you can't wear it loose or you look unkempt, like a gypsy.

At the intersection we turned right, toward the cathedral, Sunday after Sunday, to attend evening Mass. It was our second Mass that day, but where else would we have gone, what else would have justified our weekly stroll around town? We went to confession; no one knew us here. I had become so devout that I had only one sin to confess: I hated and envied my fellow human beings. This led to long discussions about the inability to love, and the confessor referred me to Saint Francis of Assisi and an endless string of holy virgins. With superhuman effort, I managed love until communion. Here in the cathedral we had a regular place, too, but no one knew us; here you could be as openly devout as you wanted, kneel from the consecration until communion and beseech God to give you the miracle of happiness. The fervor of unacknowledged misery. Piety gives one's features an inner glow, said my mother, who was no longer quite so sure of my religious vocation. I was determined to become even more pious so that after school one of the boys on the bus would look at me the way other girls were being looked at.

After our feats of piety, we walked around the main altar and out the back entrance into the darkness through the old part of town, past the café where we would stop someday, when I was earning money and perhaps had a car and would take my old mother out. This was her favorite dream: her daughter, with a prestigious job and a car, taking her mother to a café out of love and gratitude. Today, when I walk past the café in the old part of town, I'm still assailed by nostalgia and guilt.

In time she had become lonely. She had been in the same
house in our suburb for more than ten years, but she had no
acquaintances to speak of. She kept her distance from the
common people who were her social equals; she was haughty
and had no contact with the families of the doctors and architects who shut her daughter out; sometimes she was friendly
in a patronizing way toward several unmarried women who
belonged to the Catholic Women's Club, but she took care
not to get too close, not to show her hand. A brief friendship
with a young woman in the neighborhood ended quickly because the woman was too self-confident, too impertinent, tact-
less, and had the nerve to criticize the way she was bringing
up her child.

If initially friendly relations with new people turned out to
be a mistake, if they did not keep a respectful distance or made
a slighting remark, she withdrew, tight-lipped and contemptuous, and hated them with an intensity, a dogged ferocity
quite disproportionate to the slight. In the store there was an
argument with a new resident of the area over a ten-shilling
bill lying on the counter, which each claimed as hers. My
mother was wrong—the ten shillings belonged to the other
woman—but having been embarrassed was cause for hatred,
and that hatred lasted until her death.

Grocery shopping became torture for her. There were more
and more wives of attorneys and engineers who ordered their
groceries by telephone and picked up their baskets by car, more
and more rude young women who did not treat her with the
proper respect, more and more mothers of children who supposedly were better, prettier, and smarter than I. Wordless
enmities multiplied; friendships cooled as a result of her distrust, her suspicious reserve, and came down to chitchat about
salad greens and recipes for casseroles. "Mrs. Kovacs was always so reticent," a neighbor said later. "I would have liked

to get closer to her, but I didn't dare." She greeted people in a pleasant, calm manner, hardly smiling; her movements contained a barely controlled vitality, strength that had no outlet and lay on her chest as a ball of bitterness and disappointment.

She had trouble breathing, especially on hot summer nights. It had started when she was thirty-two, on a hot August day, on the train going home to the farm. Profuse sweating, shortness of breath, choking spells, gasping for air. "Goiter heart," the doctor said; "someday you will have to have surgery." "It's the closeness," she said, "the tiny rooms, the low, slanting walls, the crowded conditions." On the farm the choking spells stopped; there, where the rooms were tall and square, and the fields stretched far and away, the air could be inhaled in deep breaths. Who could take her shortness of breath seriously? She looked like life itself, strong, red-cheeked and well fed. She still did the work of two people in the fields, and she was not a complainer. But at home she sat on the bed with her head stretched forward, her chest pulled in, and her mouth gaping; the air wouldn't get down into the lungs, but she didn't want an audience, least of all her daughter, with those eyes of everlasting, helpless horror. "It's over now."

She was never sick. Who would be there to cook, wash the laundry, get the child off to school, feed the chickens, take care of the house? Illness was a luxury for lazy people. Once she did have the flu and a high fever. "Are you feeling better, Mama?" I asked, sitting on her bed. Her face was burning; her hand trembled on the blanket. "Yes, I'm better; the temperature always goes up in the late afternoon." "Shall I call the doctor?" "No, I'll be all right." "Mama, do you know what I feel like eating right now? Christmas sausages." Her temperature was 104 degrees, but she got up, got dressed, and went out so I could have my Christmas sausages that evening. Who else would take care of the child?

She was a strong, energetic woman, and did not indulge

in self-pity. For ten years she suffered from constant migraine; unbearable headaches destroyed her reason. "I think it has to do with, you know . . . My husband and I have an unhappy marriage; he doesn't love me," she told the family physician, who knew my father as a quiet, modest man. The doctor grinned. She got up without waiting for the diagnosis and never went back. "He laughed at me when I talked about the excruciating pain; you don't dare confide in anybody," she said bitterly. She went to other doctors and was in treatment for two years. She received daily injections against the inhuman headaches, but she spoke to no one about their origin; no one was told of her unhappy situation—not any more. Nor did she discuss the headaches themselves with anyone. Headache—what's that? An imaginary illness, an emotional illness, something in your head. You didn't talk about that; it wasn't worth talking about, nothing real like sciatica or rheumatism. After two years she had had enough of the injections; they hadn't helped, and you could learn to live with anything, even headaches that drove you crazy. "I'm fine," she told the relatives. "Thank heaven we can buy whatever we want." My father had sciatica, and he got radiation therapy; when he came down with the flu, she fixed compresses for him; he had kidney stones and she visited him every day in the hospital. He was often sick; she took care of him and worried about him. She said that to have something happen to him would be the worst thing. He was the provider; our existence depended on his survival. She didn't matter; no one cared anyway.

There was turbulence in the lives of her sisters. Marie was the solid rock; in her life everything was flawless: the money lasted until the first of the month, and there was something left for the savings account; her child was a good student; her husband didn't drink or play around with other women; she had a good marriage, walking arm in arm to church and back on Sundays.

"What you don't know won't hurt you; don't let anybody see your hand; people think you deserve the bad things in your life and envy you the good." But the others washed their dirty linen in public, at least before the family.

Fanni had married a disabled war veteran, because the farm needed a man and there were few men left after the war. You could hear the fighting and screaming all through the village. "You whore, that isn't my kid; you jump in bed with everybody!" The child died while the parents were beating each other up; she managed the second one, but there were arguments about the paternity of the third, because the husband had been gone at the crucial time, away for treatment of the bone tuberculosis he had brought back from his imprisonment in Siberia. Then who was the child's father? "How can you ask?" Marie said, casting a significant glance toward the retirement quarters, where the farmer was sleeping off last night's bender. "He'll climb on top of anything that can stand still for at least five minutes." "You drunken pig," she said with contempt when he reeled into the farmyard at eight in the morning, his trousers covered with brown stains, and threw up on the manure pile. Even then he mustered the strength to beat her up, to hit his thirty-five-year-old daughter with his wooden clogs and his fists, and to loosen one of her teeth before he fell unconscious on his bed. "Pig," she said once more and spat the blood in his face. Fanni washed him and took off his shit-stained pants. "It's his baby," Marie said, getting her revenge after all. "Take a look; it has his face already." "Look at my smooth skin," she said to Fanni. "Not a wrinkle. No one would take us for the same age." Here, too, she had her triumph. Fanni was aging rapidly; all the responsibility for managing the farm rested on her; her father was usually in an alcoholic fog, her husband paralyzed and on crutches; there were two little kids; the hired help never stayed longer than a few months. "That's how God punishes pride,"

Marie said; "God is just." Now it was Marie who attracted
attention in the church square. People no longer looked at
Fanni, with her run-over heels, her old-fashioned, shabby
clothes and wrinkled, sun-dried skin. Even the gossip about
her died down, the more haggard and worn out she looked.

Rosi had become tired of her free life and her free-and-
easy quarters. She made a good match, marrying a teacher
who wrote poems, a dreamer with a sweet, boyish face. Rosi
became the wife of a schoolteacher and moved from one god-
forsaken whistle stop to another along the Czechoslovakian
border, living upstairs in one-room schools located in the middle of woods and fields, and sometimes sewed work aprons for
farm wives in return for a chunk of butter and two dozen eggs.
Mostly she sat in the darkened room of their teacher's apartment and wished for the old days, listening to the old records
from the free-and-easy time; the white swans in the old castle
pond were now definitely a thing of the past.

As in the old days, Marie went to visit her. One day, in
Rosi's absence, she couldn't turn off the record player—it got
stuck in the past. In the middle of the night she was thrown
out of bed by the drunken teacher who was returning from his
weekly night on the town. She would have left immediately,
but, modest as she was, she couldn't get out of bed in front
of her brother-in-law, who posted himself before it and sere-
naded her with every single stanza of "Ave Maria."

After three turbulent years of marriage, during which she
often fled to our house with swollen eyes and bruises, Rosi
left her husband and filed for divorce. She did the unheard-
of, was the first in the family to break the holy bonds of
matrimony, screamed in front of the whole family assembled
in the big room that she would not live another minute with
the masturbating, whoring pig. Someone took hold of us kids
and got us out of the room before she could continue her
shrill, uninhibited recital of further embarrassing details from

her married life. "Keep your mouth shut, you crazy nut," my mother said disdainfully and with pointed calmness. "Do you think you are the only married woman who has to put up with things?" But Rosi wouldn't stop raging, not even when the room was filled with horrified, outraged silence: a hysterical female, with no self-control, who refused to accept the lot of womanhood as she was supposed to—unresistant, good-humoredly, with a song on her lips.

Rosi, thrown off-course, looked at askance by the family, minus free-and-easy quarters, divorced, an outlaw, was seeking refuge with Marie. She was given asylum, but sympathy was denied her. I could tell from Mama's face as I stepped in the door and she said, "Rosi is here." The corners of her mouth were disdainful; her hands gestured impatiently. How could one lose control like that, act so undignified! Without an umbrella, soaked through by the rain, there Rosi was one evening on our doorstep, disturbing the hard-won peace of our house. "I lay down on the train tracks; I lay there for two hours and the train never came." No one seemed to think it particularly funny that the suicidal Rosi got bored with her wait on the tracks. She was given a dry nightgown, and my mother made up the couch—where she lay for three weeks, since she had caught a cold on the tracks. Just as she had visited her father punctually every day in the hospital for six months, so Marie now took care of her nutty sister, conscientious and unmoved. Food, clean laundry, a place to stay— her sister was entitled to those things, and Marie would not let herself be faulted. But compassion, understanding? Surely that was too much to ask. Understanding for what? For leaving her husband, rebelling against her destiny, bringing disgrace on the whole family? She should be ashamed of herself.

"You, too, are an uncontrolled hysteric like Rosi," Mama said to me, with contempt in her voice, when I threw down my schoolbag in a temper. "Someday you'll see, you'll think about my words; you'll end up divorced, too." To end up divorced was almost as bad as coming home with an illegitimate child.

Rosi rented a room in the old part of town; she had to keep her curtains closed all the time, because her windows faced the passageway with the toilet and running water. But she had a hotplate and a washstand in one corner, and the old seating arrangement and record player from the free-and-easy days in the other. In no time at all she had re-created her free-and-easy quarters; the wild stream was running through the forest green once more; even the white swans were in working order again in the old castle pond, and you could get a glass of cognac at any time. Marie enjoyed visiting Rosi again and felt young and carefree listening to the old-fashioned tearjerkers.

Two years later Rosi married a man who was twelve years younger than she, with whom she had shared her narrow bed for some time. Marie was glad not to have to wash Rosi's bedding any more, but she did not go to the wedding: it was only a civil ceremony and contrary to God's will. As far as she was concerned, Rosi's marriage was an illicit relationship, and God would punish her for it.

Marie was the best off of all the sisters; she gave the least cause for gossip, criticism, or pity. Angela had brought the greatest disgrace on the family, by giving birth to an illegitimate child; what was more (and God's justice failed here), the child was pretty, cheerful, and lovable, much prettier and more cheerful than Marie's own daughter, who lacked for nothing, absolutely nothing. But the priest had told the pregnant Angela during confession, "You will become this man's slave," and that's exactly what happened, so there was justice after all. When Monika was four they were married; she was not in white, since she was obviously no virgin, but wore a dress of lilac velvet with a black collar, and Monika was stowed away in her grandfather's retirement quarters until the wedding was over. Afterward mother and child moved to the husband's farm, where they had not been admitted before now and where the now dethroned mother-in-law was looking forward to giving the young floozy and her by-blow a rough time.

Angela had it hard. She was pregnant year after year—six births in eight years—and her husband beat her, pregnant or not, whether he had reason or not, while her mother-in-law stood behind the door, eavesdropping and grinning. The hired help didn't stay long because of the nightly fighting, cursing, and thrashing. On the basis of their old sisterly closeness, Marie went to help out every year when Angela delivered—did her work in the barn and the fields and took care of the older children. But eventually there was a quarrel. In her brother-in-law Marie found her match. She spat on the ground in front of him, and he slapped her and said to Angela, "Why don't you take off with that city trash?" To which Marie replied, "You won't set eyes on me again," and didn't even change clothes, just had a neighbor drive her to the train station as she was, in headscarf and apron. There was no reconciliation, not even Christmas greetings. I didn't meet Monika's younger siblings until fifteen years later; Mama never set foot in the farmhouse again, a woman of her word.

What had become of the beautiful, proud daughters of the farmer? Nothing at all. Grandfather had been right when he said, "You'll be beggars, all of you." Two farm wives who were drudges and were beaten regularly, one divorcée, and two who strove to get out of their rented quarters and buy something of their own, scrimping and saving for the sake of their children. Ironically, it was the youngest, who had never paid much attention, who had grown up motherless and flitted around the postwar dance halls in wild abandon, with skirts that were much too short and a fresh head of curls every night—she, of all people, became Marie's only serious competition. She was seven years younger, almost another generation. A generation that didn't object to couples' sleeping together before the wedding night, as long as nothing happened; a generation for which duty and the need to escape from home were joined by love, so that the first few years of marriage could be got through; a generation whose new life did not begin with ration cards and hunger, because the worst was over by the time they married and moved from the land of plenty into the rented flat. True, Heidi also married a *Häusler*'s son, and one who'd been born out of wedlock at that, a fact that was never forgotten; but he was too young to have been a war casualty; and he had his youthful strength and enough sense not to seek his livelihood in the bombed-out cities. He went to work for the Customs Office and was given free living quarters in a customs house along the Czechoslovakian border, where only rabbits and deer crossed his path. He led an easy, relaxed life in the Bohemian woods, and his money went further than it would have in the city. Heidi suffered no deprivation; she did not remember any humiliation, either here or back home, and their child, after two years of marriage, was planned, wanted, and loved. When they went to visit the relatives on their motorcycle, they would put the baby in the warm hollow between his back and her belly.

It was all right to compete with Heidi, who dressed like a lady, had to budget a monthly paycheck and keep house. Both Heidi and Marie had been struggling—at first unconsciously, later deliberately—to remove themselves from the quicksand that sucks you in; they began to hoist themselves up frantically, filled with stubborn ambition. They taught their children to speak standard High German from the beginning, and to watch out for their pretty clothes, wash their hands before eating, try not to get dirty, and keep their rooms in perfect order. One's place in the ranks of the petite bourgeoisie, and whatever further reaches one could climb into, was no longer figured in terms of milk cows, bulls, and acres of ground, but in terms of money in the bank and the mortgage from the savings-and-loan association, of plans for one's child's future and the chances for their realization. With this in mind, with ground and a house of their own in mind, they economized on food, gave up vacations and clothes, and engaged in a race: who was the thriftiest, who would get there first? Which of the two could afford more treats in spite of being thrifty, offer her child more? The competition created a bond of friendship that made them stay in close touch: otherwise their efforts wouldn't have meant nearly as much. Marie invited Heidi's children to spend a week with us, and when Sophia was in the hospital, she brought her freshly made schnitzels every day. And I went to the customs house every summer for a week and was waited on; there were meat and dessert every day, there were walks and the feeling of being someone special. Marie didn't have to pretend in front of Heidi, either; she knew about feeling closed in and the exertion of becoming upwardly mobile; this, too, joined them together.

Rosi tried to climb along with them after her second marriage. But she settled down in a ready-made nest, so it didn't count. And besides, after her escapades! How could they ever be forgotten or forgiven? She was plain lucky (God's justice had somehow failed again), spoiled and pampered by her mother, by fate, by her young husband, and—this was the least forgivable—by herself. Oh yes, she had a good time and had never had to do a lick of hard work; she wasn't keen on self-sacrifice. She had it easy; she sat down at the sewing machine and outfitted herself; she made her household and pocket money by sewing for a few hours and not reporting her earnings; she didn't know what thrift was, or respect for money, or the weary humility that sprang from sleepless nights in which you lay dreaming about having your own land. Now and then she would make a suit for one of her own sisters, who'd say Thank you and nothing more, though at least a yard of material was wasted in the process and the clothes looked sloppy, pieced together, carelessly seamed, with badly inserted zippers; this didn't keep her face from looking reproachful when she told them that for a mere "thank you" she'd spent night after night at her sewing machine.

Still, we went to visit her often in her new house, which was located in a spa, and it was always something festive, an adventure, even though she had stopped serving cognac and her free-and-easy quarters had turned into a bourgeois living room. The half-hour train trip cost quite a bit of money, and if you were going to spend money you had to enjoy yourself; you didn't spend money on ordinary things, and if it cost money it wasn't ordinary. Then the walk through the park with its well-dressed hotel guests, which required no entrance fee. Usually we went directly to the swimming pool, because Rosi didn't like to cook for guests. We had splurged on red and purple bathing suits for this adventure, and the bodice with the foam-rubber bra inserts was three times as big as my bosom; it gurgled when it filled up with water. The water in the shallow end of the pool was so warm that you shivered afterward in the August sun, so we stayed in the warm sulphur water for four or five hours, stood along the edge, immersing our torsos and letting our legs float straight out; we swam three strokes and were pleased and kept pushing back the dirt that drifted toward us, the waste products of hundreds of other patrons. "Eighty-percent urine," Rosi's husband said and wouldn't even dirty his toes by putting them in the water. The locals went swimming in the river, where you could see down to the gravel bottom. After five hours in the warm water, in the burning sun, we ate the sausage sandwiches and tomatoes we had brought, but then we had to get back into the pool, since you had to pay an additional fee if you wanted to lie on the grass. "I'll learn you how to swim," my father said, and he held his wife up horizontally; but his eyes strayed to slender young bodies, tanned shoulders, breasts barely covered by bikinis, and her head went back into the water so that she thought she would drown—drowned by her husband, who was diverted by the flesh of other women. This offense turned into one of the unforgivable crimes that came up every week and were retold and embroidered. It was the last time he came along to the spa. Our pool tickets were good for seven hours; afterward we sat in the train completely exhausted from the sulphur water and the sun, our backs hurting and our shoulders as red as lobsters and our heads ready to split. Under these conditions there was always bad feeling; I was ashamed of the greedy hunger with which she wolfed down what was left of the sandwiches on the train, and she accused me of being inconsiderate and ungrateful. By the time we got on the bus, a hostile silence lay between us; that's how most of our joint excursions ended.

For we always came home, up the hill, to the house with the slanting walls, the three hundred square feet of space, *our* house for thirteen years now, our modest little hut, the last stop of our adventures. When she opened the door she immediately fought for air, threw open the porch door, pulled off her clothes. "I'm stifling; this place is stifling!" I didn't understand what she was saying; I was afraid of large rooms. Standing in the middle of a large room was like standing on a stage, a public square; I longed for a corner, a niche. I had suggestions for beautifying our house: a wall vase, an umbrella stand, a new lampshade. But she wasn't interested; that would have been a waste of money. After all, we were saving for land and a house with straight walls and large rooms. But for me this house was our house.

☐

The house continued to enclose me. I broke through to the interior. That's where I found unsuspected spaces: the ocean

I had never seen shone magically in the moonlight; bridges
connected me with foreign countries; I even penetrated into
the jungle, into its noisy half-light. She thought that in a castle
she would turn into a fairy queen, but I knew even then,
looking into the far distance from my balustrade, that her
enchantment would always remain black magic. I waited behind the curtain with a knife in my hand, but I lacked the
necessary courage. Even in a house seven times as large, the
doors would have opened only from the outside and the mirrors
would have shown me the same misshapen, hermaphroditic
creature. I have tried them, the other kinds of houses; I have
left nothing untried—the tiled bath, the built-in kitchen, the
heavy drapes, the Art Nouveau furniture in the living room—
and she looked back at me from the mirrors with her mad
eyes, her features blurred by weeping. Then the shout of triumph
stuck in my throat; I rushed to the door, but the door had no
handle, as I should have known—not even a keyhole to peep
through—and I banged my sleepless head against the shim-
mering tiles.

Nor, later on, could I find the hidden doors to the inner
rooms. Why didn't anyone tell me that in houses where love
can be bought there are no hidden doors, no dreams from
whose banks one sailed on the moon-enchanted ocean toward
new islands and far, pure peaks? By locking me in you taught
me how to break out. When they sealed the tomb, it was
already empty, always. How often the house of my love has
become uninhabitable and I have peered through the pali-
sades, icicles refracting moonlight. Whenever I was ready I
first had to defeat her and, with suicidal recklessness, plunge
into limbo, where I was overcome by blackness refracted in a
hundred mirrors. "This is hell," she said with the incontro-
vertible knowledge of the dead, "when you can't measure the
distance between yourself and the rest of the world, when you
stretch out your hand in the dark and grasp only emptiness."

But I knew she was lying, that hell was filled with corpses, with vampires that fed upon my fears and failures. In the house of mirrors called loneliness there has to be a door. The trick was to find it: a touch of my hand and I would step into freedom. Once I understood this I could return to the first house, the one with the picture of the Holy Family and the tiny kitchen window with its striped curtain, and I could say, *This is my home for the time being,* because the doors could now be opened from the inside and I could dance in front of the mirrors without turning into a hideous beast. Now, when I leave, at shorter and shorter intervals, I do so almost without fear; each time there is less to lose and still much to gain. The shorter the days, the more open the country I still have to cross, and no one lures me to his house any more. My luggage is light; I wipe the morning dew from my mirror; I have almost everything I need. Almost everything. My body casts a shadow; my car casts a shadow; the shadow says, *You have betrayed me, you are bringing disgrace upon me, and disgrace will get you on the open road.* But, then, I did not expect to get rid of her, and when the sun is at its highest point, I let my wheels ride over her.

□

It was always "Once the child is through with school," "When she earns her own living," as the child kept becoming more expensive. Tuition raises, a class trip to Vienna for a week, and then the dancing lessons. You had to pay for the whole dance course when you registered, and beyond that were the costly dresses, sea-green silk, light-blue silk brocade—at least five new dresses or the dancing teacher would talk down to you—and if possible, a visit to the hairdresser for a fresh set before each lesson. What had happened to my vocation for teaching at a convent school? I didn't have a boyfriend yet, though I had been dreaming for four years about a small blond gentle student who was about to graduate; my mother didn't know about that. "Vera doesn't care about boys; Vera only cares about studying," she said appreciatively. When she went downtown in the afternoon I made drawings of myself dressed in tulle and silk, sitting in an opera box or on the deck of a luxury liner, surrounded by elegant men. But no one saw these drawings. I wanted to be a professional fashion designer, and during recess I used to sketch dresses for my classmates, but I didn't dare speak about this dream, either. The subject of convent-school teaching was moot, even though I got up at four-thirty every Friday morning and took the first bus to town so I could go to early Mass in the cathedral and confess my envy of my classmates and come away with a face made radiant by piety.

There was never any doubt about my enrolling in the dancing class like all the others—how else could I become socially acceptable? Since my fourth year my mother had been trying to introduce me into higher society, the only society that counted, to sweep me into it, slot me into it. Now there was another opportunity: the dancing lessons, the debutante ball. But I didn't make it to the debutante ball. I wore the most expensive dress among the forty girls; my hair was in a bun; I wore no makeup except for the black eyebrows and the too-red lips; I was overweight; and when I walked toward the wall mirror in the ballroom my heart stopped: *My God, there's Mama!* All the dreams that bloomed surreptitiously in my drawings ended in this room; the trees stopped growing into the sky of love. My father escorted me to the lessons; my father took me home. In between there was the onslaught of black pant legs and white gloves—"Gentlemen, choose your part-ners"—and the endless repetition of the experience of being a wallflower, the only one left sitting at the the mirrored wall, among forty empty chairs. "Gentlemen, promenade"; forty couples pass me arm in arm, an endless circle, and I hear scraps of conversation: What school do you go to . . . are you going to graduate next year . . . yes, I enjoy that, too. . . .

There were never too many boys, always too many girls. If there were two or four too many I was almost consoled: at least I could learn the dance steps—one, two, three, forward; one, two, three, forward. I was the "gentleman," of course, since I was tall and wore blue, the color for the male baby.

At the end of the lesson I was the only girl fighting for her own coat in a stampede of escorts, each one wanting to be the first to present his lady with her coat and scarf; my contact with their black suits was limited to being poked in the chest or the ribs. Here the gentlemen were among themselves, seventeen-year-old boys in a gym; "Hey, you pest, get lost." Two by two they drifted out into the October night. Only one was picked up by her father; one fought back her tears and at home wept uncontrollably on her pure silk dress. "Watch that expensive dress; those spots won't come out!" "I'm not going back, never again!" "And what about the fee for ten lessons, with no refund if you drop out?" "I don't care, I'm not going back!" "Well, at least we won't have to buy the ballgown. There's nothing to do. Pull yourself together!"

An annoying episode for my parents, just like the piano; "Well, maybe it has its bright side; at least her head isn't filled with boys." For me it ended any illusion of being like the others. "Yes, I know I'm homely," I would say in class, but I made up for it by being so funny that the girls were still giggling after class had started. Vera the intellectual, Vera the class clown; the world of genius awaits you.

Why had the convent-school-teacher idea been dropped, even though the well-developed sixteen-year-old daughter showed no interest in boys and had suffered such a painful defeat in the dancing course? When there were no secrets between mother and daughter? When the daughter learned so well and so eagerly, wrote the best papers in German, English, and Latin and would have been at the head of her class if it hadn't been for those four-figure numbers? When she went to early Mass every Friday, and the only entertainment for her and her mother was the late Mass every Sunday afternoon? Of course there were occasional visits to the movies, where she turned her head in embarrassment during the kissing scenes, even though the films were rated as acceptable for young people.

We finally had a radio and were in touch with the world outside, through radio plays on Wednesday nights, dramatized novels on Sundays, request concerts, and travelogues involving automobile travel. Listening to the radio instead of, or while, studying was strictly out and would not have occurred to me, and the Hit Parade was taboo, but listening to American country-and-Western music after evening Mass on Sundays couldn't do too much harm.

In the Catholic Women's Club she met a woman whose daughter had just left the convent; though she had been a teacher, she was now married, pregnant, and happy for the first time. Mama wanted to spare herself that sort of disgrace. So much, then, for the dream of entering the novitiate at sixteen? The novitiate of an order whose nuns told a worker on parents' conference day, "Why bother, working-class children can't make it," and who said to her daughter, "There's someone in this class who doesn't fit in"? The order of a church that was on the side of property, had always been on the side of power, even during the Third Reich? She had found Hochhuth's *Deputy* in the cathedral library and was neither edified nor particularly surprised. After thirty years of heaven-directed faith, who or what had made this forty-year-old woman doubt the justice proclaimed by the Gospels, caused her to bad-mouth the church, whet her sharp tongue on its servants, and even reach the point of not expecting much from God, the old patriarch, who had come more and more to resemble her father? "The last shall be the first," she said bitterly, and "His eye is on the sparrow, and that bullshit about the ninth hour—sob stuff, injustice that stinks to high heaven, pie in the sky for peasants."

Not that this stopped her from going to church or joining the Rosary Atonement Crusade. As always, we stood across from the Holy Family with our hands folded each morning, and I was sprinkled with holy water and sent on my way to school with a brief, fervent prayer "in God's name." Of course she was a good Catholic; it was just that the hocus-pocus of the church service, which she herself had been passionate about, got on her nerves—all that ceremonial activity. At home she made fun of the bigoted women who carried God's blessing in their shopping bags, just as the neighbors had made fun of her twenty years earlier. Sure, God is just; so why didn't she have a little plot of her own after twenty years of scrimping and saving; why was she still waiting for the happiness she had only heard about? And as for the blessing of children: if she had gone with the encyclicals, she would have ten starving kids by now.

Marie, what do you think about religion? "You don't need a priest to be devout; I can do without the church. All that to-do about the Pope and the clergy, *ubi et orbi* on the radio, and the money that's thrown away, and then you're supposed to kiss the Pope's toes. Catholic, OK, if it has to be, but why Roman? Money—the whole church has the stink of money taken from poor people's pockets: church taxes, home collections, sacrifices. Isn't a whole joyless life filled with sacrifice enough? They can go to blazes."

From Edith Stein, whom she had found in the cathedral 'library, she graduated to Husserl, and suddenly she was reading Engels and thought (and even told her daughter, in strict confidence) that Marx had the right idea. Education? No, she had no education. She listened to what I told her we had

learned in philosophy class, and then she went and read up
on that at the library in town. She listened to the things the
religion teacher had to say about the working class, and she
heard the parish priest become adamant when he preached
from the pulpit on election Sunday—or, rather, from behind
the communion rail, since he had become too lazy to climb
up into the pulpit: "Anyone who votes red is committing a sin
against God and should by all rights be excommunicated."
Politics from the pulpit, because religion is the politics of the
wealthy; to understand that, you don't need to study theology
or political science; all you need is an eighth-grade education
and a lifetime of struggling to get out from under and not
being able to do it. In the end she voted black, because she
was afraid of God's punishment, and because she herself wanted
to own some property and didn't want to identify herself totally
with the working class, the fourth, last class, the dirt at the
bottom of the heap. But that they were the dirt at the bottom
of the heap, and that there were no rungs left for them to
climb on, that she knew by then, and next time she would
vote red; it was just that she had caved in inside the voting
booth.

Heidi and her husband had bought a large, beautiful plot of
land in the country, at the edge of some woods, and the
blueprint for their house was ready for the builder. In the fall
they would start digging, and Heidi was working full time now
and not buying any clothes, absolutely none. "We actually
have enough money for some land, too," Marie said to her
husband, who had no opinion on the subject. There was a
possible plot at the edge of town on the other side of the
Danube; he said it would mean a long way to school for their
child and that a lot of energy and money would be used up
in the work of grading the steep slope of the land, and she
accused him of indolence. Every free day they went in this or

that direction to look at property on the outskirts of town, to where the bus lines stopped and the countryside became flat and desolate. "I wouldn't like living out here," she said when they walked past the fences of a housing development with its tightly packed houses; "everybody can see inside your house, and there's the dusty alley right in front of your kitchen windows." "Well, what do you want? We can't afford a place in town," her husband said. Then she started searching by herself, went to look at houses instead of store windows.

There was an old house, large and spacious, a sort of villa; the staircase was in bad shape, but the repairs would be manageable. The house belonged to an old woman who was lonely and wanted to move into a retirement home. A two-story house in the woods, quite isolated, with an unobstructed view of the Danube valley, a dream at sunset. Every Sunday after evening Mass we walked past the house, as if it already belonged to us. Only a million shillings. You would have to take out a loan and rent out one floor, but you would be spared the drudgery of building a new house. In the evenings, after homework, we walked around looking at the villas in our area; we could see, through the lace curtains, the television sets flicker in chandeliered rooms; we looked at wrought-iron garden gates, brick walls and an occasional open fireplace. Dreams. After our rounds it was back to our house, with the slanting walls and no hot water in the kitchen. Dreams that took shape in my drawings. In the meantime my father had fixed up a bath: a built-in bathtub, imitation tile, a hot-water heater, and a hand-held shower head. I played telephone with the shower head. We still all took baths in the same water—why waste electricity? I was sixteen, and my mother gave me shampoos, scrubbed me from head to toe, fixed my hair—no reason for me to touch myself, no need to look in the mirror. "My daughter doesn't need to learn household chores; she's busy using her brains; any fool can iron, and, besides, what would

I do if my daughter did my work?" "Talk about spoiled," the
relatives and neighbors said. But she was proud: "My daughter
doesn't have to dirty her hands; you don't have to learn how
to do slave labor, and there's more than enough time ahead
for dirty work." For the time being I sat in my room and
dreamed of a fairy-tale prince and the castle he would give
me, in which I had nothing to do except wait for him. Of
course I would marry when I was twenty, like everyone else,
and have a baby at twenty-one. Before this, the miracle of my
turning into a woman would have to come to pass, because
in my present state I was hopeless, and there was no young
man, no Prince Charming, anywhere on the horizon. Besides,
first of all I had to show *them* and pass the *Matura* with honors.

☐

The scenes of her life all lay within a radius of sixty miles;
she never moved beyond that. Nor would she have dreamed
of moving beyond. Travel, what for? When she traveled on
the local trains to the farm and to her sister's spa, she had
trouble breathing. Once she went on a pilgrimage to Mariazell,
for no particular reason; she bought holy medallions, roamed
through the souvenir shops, and looked forward to going back
home.

When my father had his vacation, we went to the Bohemian woods for a week and stayed in my grandmother's retirement cabin. Grandmother had been dead for years. We
slept in the attic, which was hung with wasps' nests and bats.
Half of the house had collapsed. Bricks, rotted wood, and
impenetrable, moldy darkness. Only the main room was still
usable, with its cool, tight stone walls; balls of dust lay on the
floor; my mother swept them up, swept the benches, swept
the spiderwebs out of the corners. "The smell in here is unbearable; open the windows and let out the smell." When she
knelt in front of the oven door and smoke filled the room, she

still cursed her mother-in-law, the damned witch who had told her to roast herself; and now the stove wouldn't draw, as if the old witch, the old gypsy, was still playing tricks on her. My father and I looked sad and remembered how warm and cozy the room had once been, how delicious the mushroom goulash had smelled, back when the rusty stove was still drawing.

That was our vacation. Even more work for her, since the walk to the next village was steep and the little local store stocked only rice, noodles, and candy; she had to lug the groceries up the steep hill in the noon heat, up to the group of cottages, which, in her unbroken farmer's pride, she still looked down on. In the morning, without a bath and with her hair undone, she had to go to the outhouse and brush her teeth at the well, and both the outhouse and the well lay in the morning shade of the house, which now belonged to her brother-in-law. A friendly grin was in order when, during the brushing, her sister-in-law stepped out of the house, herself ill at ease with the farmer's daughter, the town lady. "Would you like some milk and butter?" Always embarrassment on both sides: "Marie doesn't like us." "Why not? We aren't bothering her," her brother-in-law said. Friedl knew why not, but he said nothing. "To have to bow and scrape and say 'Thank you' to those beggars," she said vehemently behind closed doors, holding the decorated chunk of butter in her hand. "She is only trying to honor you," her husband objected and, full of hatred, remembered Marie's mother on her sickbed, when he stood in the big room during his leave from the front. But she didn't want to be friendly with that riffraff; it was humiliating to have to be friendly and say "Thank you," and anything that humiliated her aroused her hatred.

What do you do for a week in the woods on your summer vacation? Her child and her husband enjoyed themselves; they felt at home. But she? Looking for mushrooms, cleaning them, picking berries like the poor people after the war, and then

pretending she was having fun. Wearing out her feet on six-
hour hikes along the Czechoslovakian border on smugglers'
paths her husband still remembered from his childhood, looking down on the villages from bare bluffs, across the waves of
foothills, to the distant chain of the Alps, and finally sitting
down before descending again. And her people must not know
that she was up here in the woods lazing around and getting
her feet blistered instead of helping them with their good,
honest harvest work. Secretly she agreed with them, but you
had to make some sacrifices for your family. Secretly she felt
homesick when she looked down over the villages. A few times
she had helped the *Häuslers* with their work in the fields, but
that had led to tension and barbed words: "Farmers don't stroke
every stalk; they work fast, fast; they don't bundle a few puny
stalks together. And the fields, so small and full of stones—
you call this work? I'm not used to this." Her brother-in-law
said that one could learn anything, and she gave him a hostile
look and laid down the rake. The next day we left without
saying good-bye. Only my father sneaked over to the house
and tried to explain that that's the way she was and that he,
too, suffered under her farmer's pride and always had.

She withdrew more and more; she let herself go more and
more, since no one came up the hill to see us these days
anyway. Mrs. Kovacs, the taciturn one, the reserved one—
she liked it that way; people respected reserve. Why, then, did
she still look down the road in the afternoons? What was she
waiting for? She wore the same threadbare blue jumper for
days, went weeks without washing her hair. At home she tied
a scarf around it; when she went to town she covered it with
a hat. Her hair regained its original red color, but no one saw
that under the hat or scarf. She lost her tautness, her majestic
bearing, her imposing stature; she spread sideways. Nobody
looks at you anyway; you're just a nothing, a nobody, no matter
where.

Since the dancing lessons I, too, had lost all hope, all

belief in the redeeming power of tubes, boxes, brushes, and stylish clothes. I lived in a different world from that of my fellow students, withdrew more and more from what fell under the catch-all rubric of reality, though I could now navigate inside this reality because I was no longer seeking a place in it; sometimes I came up with wise, precocious remarks, and the girls would say, "Where did you get that?" The teachers pricked up their ears and said, "She's gifted, full of promise, too smart for her age." I took my place as the class sybil, calm and blasé, concealed my dreams, did not mention my loneliness and disgust with life, read Kafka, Trakl, and Camus, and found my other self, weary of living, a pale young woman in a barge at night. Longing for death, we walked on the edge of the abyss, this other self and I; we needed few words; we loved the dark, the sunsets; we were close; she was the only one who understood my thoughts and did not say, *You are morbid*; she said, *Yes, that's how it is*. At night we woke from our dreams at the same moment, sat across from each other, and talked in the language of dreams. She read my face; I could conceal nothing; I needed to conceal nothing. Depression and thoughts of death, the plummeting of instruments gone blind after midnight—we shared all that; there were no secrets. On our Sunday walks to the house we mentally inhabited but no longer planned to buy, we wove a snug cocoon of nostalgia, melancholy, arrogance, and unfulfilled, unfulfillable longing around us. I was facing the *Matura*; she was facing death. She prepared herself for death long before she suspected it, and I went along with her; I was obedient, had learned obedience for seventeen years, through blows to my body and my conscience, and eventually through the gentle current that separated us from the world, from life.

□

"I don't want to go on living," my child says and turns her head to the wall. She pushes me away when I touch her; she says, "Leave me alone, you don't understand." She has dark shadows under her eyes and her mouth is blurred from crying. "Your food makes me puke," she says, "your ideas make me puke, the way you act." I am standing in the doorway, my arms hanging down. "You were a happy child once; even a year ago you were a happy child; what has gone wrong?" "I'm not a child," she screams. "I was never happy." Now it's no longer a secret in her diary; she was never happy. She won't talk, she won't eat, she won't leave her room; she huddles in her bed, shredding paper between her hands, and whispers, "Go away."

"Go away," she screams, but she doesn't move; she holds her breath when I stretch my hand toward her. What have I done, child, that you had to go so far away from me? Never will our paths come together. She has run away from me and is lost in the thicket, in the thicket I have planted without knowing it. Now I cannot find her any more, and she answers my calls with scorn. "You never loved me," she cries and buries her tear-stained face in the pillow. How can I defend myself when the intention doesn't count, only the result? "You always loved only yourself." Yes, she is right; I always loved only myself, even in my love for her. She will not hold my hand any more; she pulls away and runs off and doesn't look back at me when the road turns. Our conversation has stopped; our house is as silent as a grave. My echo makes shrill sounds in my ear; she shakes the meaning out of my words and throws them down before me with contempt: "Is this what you wanted to give me, to take along in my life?" Then she says nothing more, just hugs herself and rocks back and forth because I have forgotten to rock her. I open the curtains; she turns to the wall; her eyes stare into space.

Now I can't even call her any more; she listens for other voices, answers them from far away, from some muffled depth. Who has abducted my child? Who has confounded her reason, stolen her soul? Who was the bad fairy I forgot to invite for the christening? She visits me in my dream: *Love is what you wanted to give her? Do you even know what that is?* And while I fall into the shaft of time, my child stands there with the eyes of the lost. Destruction passed on, moving like an avalanche, has reached my child, tears her out of my arms. Who can help me rescue her?

She longs to die, and I am afraid for her life. She doesn't eat, and she hoards pills, which I secretly take away from her. "The gift of life," she says, laughing bitterly. She hatches new ways of dying and shrugs her shoulders when I am overcome with grief. I have given twelve years and all the strength I had, but it was not enough to bring happiness into her life. It was too easy, too bright, this happiness; it blinded me and flew away. And my child sits in the dark, in my brooding shadow, in the shadow of my avenging mother. Grandmother, mother, and child together in a dark room. Did the angel of death pass by? Whom will he take with him? No, it was not an angel; it was the thirteenth fairy, the one who was cheated out of her gift; she steals my daughter's reason and orders her to sleep. For a hundred years? Don't wait for the prince, child; he will leave you before he has kissed you awake. And waking will be more painful than this sleep!

I knock on her door; I knock on her window; softly I call out the names I have given her, all the tender names. But the name she now calls herself by is not among them; she does not answer. If she would let me in I would descend with her into any depth; I would dive in and rescue her soul at any price. Her silence splits my heart. My reason shatters under the loneliness into which she has cast me. I listen for her breathing on the other side of the wall that separates our hells. The circle I hoped to break free from is irrevocably closed; all proofs are in; everything could have been predicted. My mother has caught up with me; I have caught up with myself; we have caught up with each other and taken each other back. I am

kneeling before the altar of the gods I don't believe in and
offer myself as the sacrifice. *Please, please, just this one time*,
I plead, and then stop, confused: I have forgotten to whom
I'm praying, but already I cower before the inescapable blows.
Then the door opens; she stands behind me and says, "Mama."
And there is a reprieve, this one time.

It was almost a lovely time. A time in which fulfillment came
without effort, in which dreams came so close one could
almost take them for real. The dream of our own plot of land:
we had saved enough money; a reasonable lot was advertised
in the paper, but perhaps something even better would come
along. On Heidi's land the foundation for the house was in
place; the whole family had hauled cement all summer. The
dream of a weekend house in the country: if the old farmer
would fork over part of the land he had demanded as his
retirement settlement, if he felled a few trees and divided the
meadow, one could build a weekend house and wouldn't need
to bow and scrape for a pitcher of breakfast milk from the
Häusler relations. If only they would remember, at home on
the farm, that twenty years ago she had been packed off without
an inheritance, without a shilling, with nothing except some
cheap furniture—if she pointed out to them long enough how
she had been dismissed from her parental home after twenty
years of drudgery—she would surely be given the piece of
meadow and could use the accumulated money for building.
But on the farm they turned a deaf ear. Not that this stopped
Marie from dreaming. She egged on her sisters: "They owe
each one of us a parcel of land, or the value of a parcel, as
our inheritance." The more often she repeated it, the more
real the demand became, its fulfillment already within her
grasp.

The efforts of seventeen years were beginning to bear fruit.
The child was almost grown, the only one among the relatives

who would graduate from a *Gymnasium*. The strict upbring-ing, all the money, all the work, had been worth it. The child didn't have boys on her mind, didn't even dare to listen to the Hit Parade on the radio, didn't care about going out, discos, the Beatles, far-out clothes; she studied and studied, read and read. She no longer needed to associate with the children of doctors and architects in order to be socially acceptable; she had shown them—once you've passed the *Matura*, all doors are open to you. Uli Reisinger was pregnant. Pride goeth before a fall: she would have to get married and take herself out of the running. If you could force recognition from those who counted in this society, you didn't have to beg for it; this was better. We floated toward church with our heads held high.

It was almost as she had imagined it eighteen years ago, when she was pregnant, how the child would raise her up and lift her out of the working class, out of degradation. It was only a daughter, but these days a girl could make it, too, if you raised her right and showed her who was boss. "Vera will graduate with honors: my child, my life's work." The relatives were mute with respect before this young lady in her immac-ulate clothes, with her hair pulled back in a braid that was held in a velvet clasp; nothing about this young lady could be faulted—no creases in her stockings or dresses, no hair out of place, her walk measured, her face solemn and dignified. Nothing about this young lady was youthful.

Mother and daughter, looking almost the same age, but at Monika's wedding, in the background among the duly in-vited guests, the mother was somehow livelier, in spite of her suspicious eyes and tight lips, and in spite of her bulk somehow more youthful than the daughter. Monika was a radiant sev-enteen-year-old, five months pregnant. Marie was in a dark-blue suit; her hair, tinted a bit too dark this time, was no longer piled in a high topknot but was pulled back from her face by her heavy, pinned-up plaits; her face was large and round. She was so pale under her chestnut-brown hair, in her dark-blue suit, her face so tired, almost a little doughy in spite of the rich night cream for the skin, a sad smile around her bitter mouth. The smile was for the photographer and wasn't supposed to be sad: a wistful smile with a touch of irony around the corners of the mouth. She had round shoulders and grave, resigned eyes—the eyes did not smile for the photographer. Mama in the third row of the group picture; Aunt Rosi had it cropped and enlarged after her death: her last photograph, taken ten months before her death.

In the afternoon, after the wedding, there was dancing and she came to life; she loved to dance, always had. "Your mother is an excellent dancer," her partners said and asked her for another dance, while I sat among empty chairs again and watched. The father of the bride was the only one who danced with me, but not for long: no verve, no fire. Whereas my forty-year-old mother had plenty of fire, became young again when she danced, reminded of her whole wasted girlhood, her whole unlived life, briefly living it, enjoying it—Where, never; too late now. But the never-used fire still came through during waltzes and foxtrots in the arms of strange men. There had only been one man in her life and he couldn't dance; he couldn't awaken any fire in her, only hatred. I couldn't believe it: even my mother bested me in the competition on the dance floor; even my mother, twenty-six years older, snatched the men away from me.

Monika became a farm woman and a mother; I passed the *Matura* and the doors were open to me. Which doors? That was the point of debate. Mama would have liked to see me in the book trade; she made inquiries and contacted publishers. After all, I loved books, and it was a peaceful occupation, secure, respected, the pay not bad. But I didn't want to sell books; I wanted to read them, speak about them, discuss them, write books myself. I wanted to study at a university—who if not I, who had for years been the acknowledged genius in my class when it came to language, whose papers had been read aloud for years by the most sonorous voice in class. Everybody else was going to the university; how else should educated young women sit out the time until Mr. One-and-Only came along? Why should I, of all people, train to be a bookseller? I wanted to study psychology. "No," the counselor said, "too fragile emotionally." I wanted to study art, but the art professor said that students who could draw better than I were flunking out of the academy. I dreamed of interior design, but my math professor said I would have trouble because I was weak in geometry and not neat enough. Once, over supper, I casually mentioned my greatest, most secret dream, that of becoming a journalist. "In the name of heaven, out with a microphone at every accident, every on-the-scene report!" I didn't dare talk about it any more, say I wanted to do it anyway; I only dreamed about it, night after night, until the application deadline had passed. Write for a newspaper? That was preferable: a cultural column, book and theater reviews. But how could one get in there, a working-class girl without connections? Maybe later.

"Yes, but you've got to do something after the *Matura*!" "I'm going to the university." Stated categorically, incontrovertibly, with finality. A big sigh: more money, support for four years, leaving home. "Does it have to be?" "I am going to the university, period; that's all there is to it." Where did I get the courage? "Well, if it has to be." "The *Gymnasium* was her idea, too," my father pointed out; I had persisted in it, and it had not turned out to be a bad idea. I could become a middle-school teacher; that would be something better than being a lower-school teacher. "And you always wanted to teach anyway." Really? I said nothing and thought, *The first thing is to get away.*

"And where are you going to study?" Cautiously they suggested the town, fortified themselves with arguments against my resistance—it's not so anonymous there as in the capital and not so far away from home, a train ride of less than two hours. Away, I don't care where; let them have this small triumph. "If you leave me, I won't survive," Mama said, with her chin trembling, wiping the tears from her averted face. "How can I live without you, when I'll have nothing, absolutely nothing, only him around me the whole time?" With whom would she go into town on Sundays, for whom cook lunch punctually at one-thirty, for whom exert herself every day shopping, cleaning, ironing, washing? The house would be empty and silent, her life empty and silent, the nest empty, and she suddenly thrown back on the man with whom she had not really lived for sixteen years, whom she merely permitted to live beside her because of his monthly salary.

For me there was fulfillment, undimmed happiness. *Matura* with honors. A trip with other graduates to the land from which my great-grandfather had emigrated; an opening into life, into the future; my first independent steps; a trip to the city where I would live alone, stand on my own two feet. True, I would be under the supervision of German nuns—my parents' wish—but I was used to smiling at and deceiving nuns; it was a small price to pay for freedom. To inspect the university, I was accompanied by my father—you couldn't let the child travel all that way by herself.

Dreams. I'm walking along the riverbank with the man of my life, holding his hand; the man I would meet, was bound to meet, in this city—where, if not here? Reading all night; no more seven o'clock bedtimes, eight o'clock at the latest. Dreams of freedom. I was gradually becoming aware of the restraints on me, but they would soon be over; the time at home would be only a brief transition, while everything was already flowing into the distance.

Mama next to me in the streetcar: why did her teeth sometimes chatter now? It was embarrassing for me. "Why do your teeth chatter, are you cold?" "What do you mean? My teeth aren't chattering. I just happen to be nervous lately; there's been so much going on, the *Matura*, all the excitement, and that you want to leave me, that you can't be satisfied at home any more—I can tell, and it hurts me!" So it was my fault that her teeth chattered. I passed the *Matura* with honors just to please her, and how did she thank me? She made me feel guilty. Let her teeth chatter. A brief sidelong glance; my mother looked old.

For graduation she came to school for the first time in seven years, stood in the large festive room, and wept, no doubt with emotion, when her daughter curtsied before the director and received an art book in recognition of her excellent achievement. Later she went up to her daughter's classroom teacher and German professor, a woman who had supported me with her interest and encouragement, and asked shyly, "May Vera write to you from the university, if she has questions concerning her studies?" She stood humbly before this teacher, who was a person her own age but occupied a pedestal she could never aspire to, a woman with a Ph.D., living in a more exalted world. The professor stared at the unlikely couple and almost forgot to answer and be gracious. So this was the mother of the colorless model student, a dark earth mother; there was a subterranean, almost volcanic force in this woman; she might have been a figure from Nordic mythology, a Norn, punishing and powerful. And next to her the father, small and puny, hung on her massive arm, uninterested, looking off into some undefined distance, squashed by the Valkyrie. You didn't need to know the background to understand this; you could see it with the naked, innocent eye. So these were the parents, and here was the source of the preoccupation with death and the wallowing in loneliness that appeared in their daughter's school essays, the intimate knowledge of suffering, the permanent sadness inside this precocious child. "You know, Vera," she said to me later in a Hungarian tavern, "it will take you ten

years to shake all this off, before you can really be yourself."
And Vera smoked her first cigarette, drank her first wine, and
wanted to become herself immediately, without delay, by
drinking herself senseless and unconscious. Instead, she felt
terribly sick on the sobering ride home the following day. But
for the first time in her life she was wearing her hair loose; it
hung over her face, over her shoulders in the thin nightgown;
her eyes were foggy with wine, her black-rimmed glasses missing, the model student unrecognizable, because what gleamed
behind her loose hair and black lashes was untamed, the part
that had eluded eighteen years of exemplary training.

During this long, triumphant summer, this high point with
its laurels and expectations of freedom, what was it that kept
ruining the mood, that made the air tremble with unspoken
bitterness, irritability, disappointment, and accusations on both
sides? The shared Sunday walks, the evening Masses in the
cathedral, the trips to the sulphur spa, the week in my grandmother's retirement cabin—all this remained as before, but
something had come between us. "What's wrong now?" A
reproachful look: Ungrateful brat. "What have I done?" Inconsiderate and selfish; the thanks for a life sacrificed for her.
"But I only want some peace." "Yes, just like your father; you
want your peace and let yourself be waited on hand and foot!"
When she used a wide-toothed comb on her hair, it came out
in bunches, curled in the washbasin and on the floor. "Look
how much hair you're losing; that isn't normal!" "Thank God—
all that red hair, I don't know what to do with it. Good thing
it's falling out; that way I can control it better." She mixed
the tinting solution in a pan; there were more and more gray,
even white, hairs along the temples. "Perhaps they're the result
of tinting, but at forty-four I don't want to go gray for quite a
while." And then there was this trembling, which made me
nervous because it was supposed to be my fault, stemming
from my lack of consideration and gratitude.

My girlfriend's graduation present was a two-week trip to

Italy—only five hundred shillings, a special travel-club offer. "Come with me," she insisted. "Only five hundred shillings for two weeks," I begged shyly. "Judith is getting a car, and Eva gets to go to a resort in Yugoslavia. I'm the only one to sit around home all summer." The choice was up to me. Which was more important: two weeks in Italy or two weeks in the hospital? And since I was always obedient and did what was in my best interest, I opted for the hospital. Italy would have been pure luxury, without any residual benefit, but the stay in the hospital meant the future; it could be the decisive factor as far as my life's happiness was concerned. Not that there was anything wrong with me, but she had been bothered for two years by my excess hair: long black hair on my legs and arms and especially on my face, on my chin, along the jaw to the hairline, and also on the upper lip. The child was growing a beard, had been since she was sixteen, since around the time of the dancing lessons; suddenly the concerned mother had noticed it. She hadn't said anything in the beginning, only watched and worried whether the growth was getting denser, the hair coarser, and once when we sat side by side on the bus she had noticed a woman squinting at me with fascination: a young girl with a beard. And the hair *was* coming in thicker and darker; we would have to start thinking about a coiffure that would conceal the cheek hair, since no loose strands were allowed. The beard became the topic of conversation at the table; somehow it was my father's fault, since his sisters were hirsute. "Racy," they used to call it, but this unwanted hair wasn't racy, it was creepy.

Now I knew how to interpret the disapproving looks: I, too, was somehow at fault, caused her worry, brought her distress, because I couldn't be like other girls. Look at the other girls with their smooth, delicate, hairless skin. I didn't need to look; I was painfully aware of the discrepancy, even in my sleep. Not only was I guilty, but something had evidently gone haywire. No time to waste: everybody was staring; an eye-catcher, stuck to my face; a disgrace, wherever I went; everyone looking at the unnatural growth, which was discussed, talked to death, among the relatives and presented to the family physician. The waiting room was full of sick people, but I knew that if I had had the courage to raise my eyes I would have found them all staring fixedly at my beard, my full beard. "Come on, a little bit of down; lots of people have that," a well-meaning teacher said when, in my panic, I confided in her. "Hair on your face?" asked my girlfriend, who would be going to Italy without me. "Where? Oh, there; I wouldn't even have noticed if you hadn't mentioned it." They wanted to make me feel better, bolster my self-confidence; they were just being nice to me because they felt sorry for me. "Possibly too many male hormones, not enough female ones," the doctor said and suggested a series of hormone tests. A sex change— my God, what ignominy! What is the masculine form of Vera? Now, do you want to go to Italy for two weeks and live with this shame, or undergo the test series in the hospital, which will only be partly covered by insurance? For the sake of becoming a real woman?

I would have done anything for the sake of becoming a real woman. Two weeks in the hospital were not too high a price—daily examinations; pills every hour until I hallucinated; balloon enemas; daily X-rays; more pills; no food until noon; who knows what's coming up next; nothing pleasant, that's for sure. Two weeks of fear, two weeks of degradation. The chief of staff enters my hospital room, a second-class room, which requires that my parents subsidize the insurance by a considerable amount; another sacrifice. The chief of staff is followed by the assistant chief of staff, the attending physician, the resident, the interns—all men. They stand over my bed, looking at my naked body; they have no diagnosis, since all my organs are functioning normally; they have only to

answer the question Woman or nonwoman or half-woman?—
from the perspective of doctors or of men? Exposed after so
many years of chastity.

Mama visited me every day, but how could I complain to
her when two weeks in the hospital were necessary and as
expensive as two weeks in Italy? She saw that I was afraid; she
held the pan into which I vomited after twenty-five pills every
two hours, pills whose names and purpose were kept from us;
she waited with me in the hallways and saw that I was getting
weaker and weaker. Finally I developed a fever and was released
from the hospital, sick. Why didn't she ask any questions; why
didn't she put a stop to the daily gawking at my body, which
she had trained to be chaste? She did not object and told me
to pull myself together; then at home she pampered me.

Weeks went by, and months, without a report. In fact, we
never received a report: the whole two weeks had been for
nothing. What had they done with me? My parents had asked
no questions, had allowed me to be used as a guinea pig for
a series of hormone tests, and had taken me home sick without
even questioning our family physician, who had arranged to
have me admitted, much less uttering a reproach, asking for
test results, or demanding an explanation. Were they afraid of
the authority of an M.D., or were they afraid of the impenetrable hospital apparatus, the hospital bureaucracy? Or did
they have such total confidence in the machinations of med-
icine? Was this the silence of a whole generation, when
animal experiments gave way to experiments on human
beings?

Since the two weeks in the hospital had resulted in nothing
except a waste of money, it was decided that I should go to a
dermatologist for hair removal. More money—four sessions at
five hundred shillings each, plus the cost of travel to another
city. The flaw had been removed, become invisible, gone
inward, turned into the conviction that I was not a real woman,

diagnostic height.

☐

Was this the end of my upbringing? For the time being. The
work complete, the last stone put into the mosaic, the walls
of the fortress solid, the embrasures covered. A proud piece
of work. Eighteen years of building this tower, hardening the
clay, putting stone on stone. Now the tower could stand by
itself, a landmark attraction, and no assault would cause it to
founder. The master builder can retire, put down his tools
without a qualm; the jailer can lie down for a long sleep after
his hard work. The tower would stand watch as it had been
ordered to do. Within, the painstaking orderliness of books
and thoughts piled high, layer upon layer, up to the ceiling.
There is a human being somewhere beneath the spiral staircase, but the weak light falling on her desk illuminates only
what she has written. The immense sadness that comes out
of books mixes with the stale air of exhaled breathing; there is
no window, no crack for air or light. No nourishment, no
fragrances. But nothing is built to last forever. The walls begin
to flake; dust settles in layers on the tops of books and moves
elsewhere. The human being beneath the spiral staircase lifts
her head; there's a crack in the ceiling above her; a streak of
black lightning shoots through the stone vaulting. The walls
lean; the books plummet so quickly that there's no time to
decide if the sense of breathless terror was mixed with joy when
sunlight invaded the destruction.

This was the beginning—a birth twenty years too late. Learning
to walk, to see, to speak, on the crutches of a careless love,
which broke before my legs were ready to carry me. The
miracle of liberation was an illusory fairy tale, but the tower
had become uninhabitable, a dismal pile of ruins. What good

was all my talking if my words never touched my own reality, had not even a remote connection with the thought-shattering experiences I had known? What good was a vision when sadness and doubt blackened the sun for me? "Fight to free yourself," a man called to me when we parted and took my trust along as sustenance for his journey. Now I was free, an outlaw. At this point my life began, a great game of roulette. I took chances on whatever the wind blew in my path and threw it back into the wind the next morning, whether crying or laughing. Many things happened to me; I moved through the countries and seasons of love. In winter my heart froze in the snow; I didn't even notice. At night I heard it ringing like a distant bell: *Still there? What do you want?* The desert sun melted my reason; who needs reason in a madhouse? To be like the others—I almost made it. To be a real woman, at any price. The price paid not once, but daily and hourly. A child beside me, a twenty-times-mended heart, a mind that refuses to live in the real world. I think I have made it. No tower could have protected me from myself now.

□

The summer vacation came to an end. The three of us went shopping for luggage; the three of us went to the train station together; but I left alone. At home, when we were ready to leave, my mother had as usual drawn the sign of the cross on my forehead in God's name, her fingers wet with holy water, and then she had turned away and tried but failed to hide her tears. "When you leave, that will kill me": she didn't repeat it, didn't need to; I felt guilty enough as it was. "It's going to be empty here," she said, standing on the platform. "Be good, and eat properly." "But I'll come home at least every two weeks," I said, trying to calm her, but she was turning away again, and then the train left.

And what happened after that? When they stood facing

each other as a couple, a couple again after eighteen years, though they called each other Mama and Papa? Did they link arms as they went home? Did they go home together, talk to each other—was there anything left that they could have talked about? My bed next to hers against the slanting wall remained empty, waited, freshly made up, for my weekend visit. How did they fill the empty house, their lives? What did they do in the evenings, every other weekend? What did they talk about at the table? "Either they'll find each other, or they'll finally separate," said—who did say that? Were there any initiates? Or was it one of my own know-it-all sentences? They didn't find each other; their silences passed by one another; his was indifferent, hers bitter, full of hatred. When I came home I could tell by the atmosphere, which was pregnant with disaster, that the scenes between them had become uglier after I left. Her letters were written in a meticulously drawn Latin script, which she had never really learned (she wrote to her sisters in German cursive script); loneliness, clumsily expressed, screamed from them. Even though there were only eleven days between my departures and arrivals, she sent me two food packages a week—*Gugelhupf*, pie, rolled ham—and I ran a race against spoilage as I ate in my refrigeratorless room.

How did she kill time on those endless afternoons, when the dishes were done and the laundry clean, the beds made, the furniture dusted, and you could hear the silence and there was no need to go into town in any weather? You could write letters; you could fix up packages, but not every day. You could pay visits, or receive them, but to whom, from whom? The Kovacs daughters were grandmothers by now and busy with their grandchildren. "It's OK if they come over," she said, "but without their brood; they get everything messy with their sticky fingers and run in and out of the house, carry in dirt. Keep those kids out of my hair! Nobody knows how to bring up kids these days anyway, not the way I brought up mine, teaching her to sit still and not talk when grownups talked. Grandma Franz, her old friend, was occupied with a great-grandchild and too happy to remember Mrs. Kovacs, who was longing for a visit from her at the other end of town. She was not interested in new acquaintances, new friends; people only wanted to find out things about you and use you; no one did anything without an ulterior motive, and you ended up as the dummy, the fall guy. Even Rosi had a child, born quite late in her life. "You can't go there, either," Mama complained. "Everything revolves around that child; you can't say ten sensible words the whole afternoon."

She went home more often, to the country, the farm, went there alone for the first time in eighteen years. Was there any feeling of relief, of ease, the delayed animation of recaptured youth? She stayed two days, helped to harvest potatoes, mowed grass, but it was all so tiring; she wasn't a spring chicken any more and had to lie down for a bit after work, to catch her breath. She became irritable and began to talk about the inheritance for which she had been waiting for twenty-one years. There were arguments, and the farmer, of all people, the one who had married into the family, the stranger, showed her the door; here in her own parental home, where she had slaved for thirty years, she was shown the door by a stranger who himself had every reason to be glad to be here. She was waiting for the bus at the stop in front of the tavern—the last house in the village, at the lower end, ten houses from her home. It was cool, a cool morning at the beginning of October; there was a nip of frost in the air, a trace of hoarfrost on the grass; it was only five-thirty in the morning. The bus was due at ten past six; she was wearing the short-sleeved lime-green suit and a sleeveless chiffon blouse; the afternoons were still hot, but the nights were already cold. The bus was an hour late; she began to shiver, but wild horses couldn't drag her back to the farm—they could all go jump in the lake. How cold October could be: her teeth chattered, and her feet in their cork-soled sandals were like ice. Finally the bus came, and once she got on the train she slowly got warm. Two days later she was sick, of course: you could catch your death; fever, cough, especially this cough, as if everything inside was blocked, walled up; this terrible fighting for breath.

After dinner she said, "I have to lie down; I'm still not all together." She was so exhausted that she didn't feel like talking, just lay there with her eyes closed, a slack hand resting on her stomach. "I'm all in." She kept on coughing, was coughing every weekend I came home, and would have to lie down and rest for a while; she was so tired, so dead tired, after cooking and washing the dishes, sometimes even in the morning after making the beds. "That's what happens when you go somewhere, when you imagine that there's a place where you are welcome." It wasn't easy to get along with her; she was impatient and irritable. "Why don't you help me out a little? Can't you see that the housework wears me out?" But I had never helped her; of course I wanted to, but she immediately yanked the broom, the dishes, the laundry away from me: "Don't act so stupid, as if you had two left hands. Here, let me have it, I'll do it myself. Talk about clumsy."

I had borrowed a book from the library in town, but it was closed on weekends and I urgently needed another book, a drama anthology, for a seminar. Surely she could get this for me within the next two weeks; surely that wasn't asking too much, since she always did everything for me. Three days later, an outraged letter: "There was writing in the book, in the margins, in your hand; I was wishing the earth would swallow me up; I had to pay a five-shilling fine, and the way they looked at me, with such distaste—me being the mother of someone like that. With such a daughter I don't know if they'll trust me with the valuable book anthology. Your disappointed Mama." Yes, in reading *Steppenwolf* I had been taken over by the book and had marked certain passages and penciled in exclamation marks, and after excerpting I had forgotten to erase them. I came across books like that all the time, with marginal comments by others, sometimes several stacked on top of one another; annoying, yes, but was it worth such excitement?

Her reproaches continued on Sunday, the next time I came home. She never would have dreamed that she had raised someone like that—such disgrace!—and why should a right-thinking woman like her be saddled with the disgrace of such a daughter, accept blame for the shameful offenses of a daughter who willfully damages property that doesn't belong to her? To have to stand there covered with shame before the librarian, and have her look at you like that because you are the mother—and publicly, in front of other people! And then she had to lie down again; she was all in from this excitement. The next morning she vomited, and again after lunch, and fought for air and couldn't make the beds until afternoon. That was how much my father and I plagued her, how we were destroying her; we drained from her body what strength she had left, and her head was roaring and hammering like mad. "You bastard," she screamed at her husband, "you would let me die like a dog and you would do it with a laughing face!" But then she had to cough and fight for air and rush to the toilet. It was especially bad in the morning. Toward evening she would feel better, except that she was always so exhausted in the afternoon.

Didn't anybody tell her to go see a doctor? Didn't anyone see how rapidly she was losing weight? Every week her clothes hung on her more loosely, but she was glad to reduce: perhaps it would ease her breathing. The persistent cough, the fatigue, the vomiting every morning? "You should go to the doctor," her husband finally said, but she fixed him with a hate-filled stare. "Yes, that would suit you, to slough off responsibility.

It's you, you're the one who's made me like this, all the misery $\qquad$
you cause me. You weigh on me like a ton of bricks. I don't
need a doctor—I need love." Her outbursts were briefer now;
she lacked the strength for night-long abuse.

But it wasn't only her husband who plagued her, causing
nausea and breathing spasms. I had been invited out for dinner—
the first invitation in my life—dinner at the home of my
German teacher. We drank wine, we smoked, we talked, and
when I looked at my watch it was eleven-thirty. "For heaven's
sake, I must go!" A taxi was summoned; the hostess put me
inside and gave the driver my address. Mama was standing in
front of the door, a mad look in her eyes, keys in her hand,
her coat on over her nightgown. She was just about to go to
the police and have them search for her daughter. What a
disgrace! And then she comes home in a taxi. Such a waste
of money, an exploitation of parents who were sweating out
the money for her university education with their hearts' blood—
the young lady took a taxi and rode right over her parents'
martyred bodies. No, there was no explanation for this; I could
save myself the trouble of making excuses. First I didn't come
home, putting my mother through hours of mortal fear, mortal
distress, fighting for air, and then I showed up in a taxi. There
was no excuse for this; it was the end, the last straw—this was
what she had raised.

I tried to bribe her with grades. "Imagine, another A
on a test, and here at the university, where I'm competing
with the elite; I've had nothing but A's." "I'm glad," she would
say, but without enthusiasm, as if she no longer was really involved in any of this. She stopped asking questions about my
new surroundings, the university, the dorm, the other students; she listened to my reports dutifully, without interest,
often with her eyes closed. "Go ahead and talk; I can hear
you. I just need to rest a little, take it easy for a bit; in a minute I'll . . ."

She couldn't sleep on her back any more, since she had a painful boil there. "Did you bump yourself?" No, the boil kept getting larger instead of smaller, and it wasn't blue; it was slightly raised and located between her shoulder blades, which stood out more and more. Her bra was too loose on her, and her garter belt slipped down over her hips; no wonder, since she threw up almost everything.

The November fog made the cough and breathing spasms even worse; the cough started up anew, a new cold before the old one was gone. "It's all closed up inside," she complained. "Probably the old goiter heart." When she spat into a handkerchief, the handkerchief was bright red. At first she was frightened to be spitting blood, but then she found an explanation: probably a vein had burst because of all the coughing. She had learned to live with the cough, but to have to throw up whatever she ate—there was certainly something very wrong there.

She went to the doctor, the same company doctor who had grinned when she had explained the source of her headaches, and this was followed by a series of interminable periods in the waiting rooms of an internist, a radiologist, a lung specialist: Breathe deep, don't breathe, all right; don't cough, for God's sake, you can cough later; breathe deep once more, don't breathe. Nothing by mouth before the examination; drink the opaque fluid. What, you brought it up? Come back tomorrow, on an empty stomach, be sure to remember. Pull yourself together—you can vomit as much as you like later. The long march through the waiting rooms, and no doctor ever blinked, not one explained what was happening to her, to her body; she dared to ask questions only with her eyes, and they met impenetrable faces, indifferent faces. She went to the famous doctor who had saved her father's life ten years ago, the most esteemed surgeon in town; surely he would help, would know. He took only private patients; no government insurance here. "I never treated myself to anything in my life; now I'll treat myself to something, to a surgeon who will cure me; he saved my father's life and he'll save mine." The surgeon looked at the results, lit up the X-rays. "Gallstones," he said, "gallstones the size of pigeon eggs." "Can they be operated on?" she asked shyly. "Well, yes, that might possibly prolong your life," he said vaguely. "Next, please." What did he mean by "prolong your life," she wondered. If the gallstones come out I should be well again, shouldn't I? "Doctors always say things like that," her husband said soothingly.

She was to be admitted to the hospital at which the surgeon practiced on January 2—no earlier, because there would be the holidays, when the child would be at home and she would have to be available. The child couldn't manage the household by herself; the child wouldn't know what to do at all; no, January 2 was the earliest date possible, she said, and no one suggested that there was any hurry.

"Dear Sister," she wrote in her stiff German script, "I have to go into the hospital. I have gallstones the size of pigeon eggs. The surgeon who operated on our father will operate on me. Thank heaven there's nothing wrong with my stomach—that's because I always took care of myself and never drank ice-cold beer. I always treated myself well. The doctor talks about prolonging my life; I don't know what he means by that. But you must promise me that Vera won't find out about that. Your sister Marie." A gall-bladder removal isn't as bad as an appendectomy, reported acquaintances and relatives who had had acquaintances and relatives with gall-bladder operations.

"Mama, your face is all yellow!" "That's from the bile I throw up every morning; that's the bile of forty years of grief, worry, frustration, and lovelessness; that's the bile that comes up every time I see *him*." *Him*, that was her husband; in May they had had their twenty-second wedding anniversary. He had completely forgotten it, and she had showered him with bitter, hate-filled reproaches, to which he had not replied. Who was standing by her during this December, while she spat blood and, worn out from the housework, fell on the sofa, though not into bed. It wasn't as bad as all that yet; to go to bed is to admit that you are sick. Was she in pain? The boil on her back woke her, bathed in sweat, every time she landed in the wrong position in her sleep. The cough hurt; her whole body hurt when she knelt at the toilet bowl and the bile came up. Her head hurt with the well-known throbbing pain.

"Bathed in sweat, you say? The pillow wet, the sheet, your nightgown? We learned in biology that night sweat is a symptom of TB." Were we really so stupid as to think the gall bladder was the problem and that nothing else was wrong? But who stood by her in her fear that it might not be all, that this might be the end? She did not speak to anyone about it. "You don't look well, Mrs. Kovacs," her neighbor said. "Oh, I'm glad I lost a few pounds," she said casually. But who tells the reserved, distant Mrs. Kovacs to her face that she looks like someone who is critically ill? The man to whom she had been married for twenty-two years had withdrawn, was out of reach; too much had been said, he had had to swallow too much in silence, and now her illness was supposed to be his fault. Gall-bladder disease is psychosomatic, said the know-it-all daughter, and he was responsible for the upheaval of her psyche, he, of course! So he said nothing and looked away from her and shrugged his shoulders in indifference or helplessness; perhaps he was simply helpless, because she was out of reach for him, too, by now, responding to every gesture, every word from him with an indignant cry. So she knelt alone before the toilet bowl at five o'clock in the morning, while her husband and daughter were still asleep, and what was the point in daily reports like "Today the vomiting was really bad," if she was only to see the horror in her daughter's eyes? If only the Christmas vacation was over.

Christmas Eve was to be as always, a day without quarreling: "Please pull yourselves together and keep peace, at least on Christmas Eve!" I had bought her some silver spoons and had had a drawing of mine framed, one that she liked, of a young woman in half profile, looking longingly through lancet arches into an open evening landscape. With that I had run out of money; I had no present for my father. I was careful with her, the way one is careful with the sick, but she wouldn't let me take over the smallest household chore. Or was I actually thinking of helping? I let myself be waited on; after all, I was on vacation and a student, a future Ph.D.

She didn't let down; the food was as good and plentiful as always, three courses at noon, but she no longer joined us in the meal. There was no point in it, since she couldn't keep anything down. Veal sausage was the only thing she could eat now; half a pound would last her two days. "Better to go hungry than to keep throwing good food into the toilet." "But you must eat so you'll get strong again." That wasn't concern; it was panic, and we both knew it. Something was happening before our eyes that we didn't want to see. We confirmed each other in the lie: "Once the gall bladder is all right again . . ." "But on Christmas Eve you've got to eat—frankfurters with mustard, Christmas beer and layer cakes; you can't dishonor this day by eating veal sausage right out of the butcher's paper!" She ate and threw up and had to lie down.

They kept their word: there were no arguments. But she made up for it on Christmas Day; there were limits to her self-control; there still were many scores to settle, and time was short. The hospitalization at the end of the holidays was never mentioned. Grandma Franz came to visit, and when she left my mother hung on to her hand and cried. She would never have done that in earlier years, would never have lost control like that—why, just because a visitor was leaving? Then I knew whatever was to be known, though my reason refused to take it in.

On New Year's Eve, when she went shopping, and on

New Year's Day after church, she waited breathlessly: would someone wish her good health in the coming year? As if some innocent, well-meaning New Year's wish could avert disaster. The grocery clerk casually expressed such a wish as she weighed half a pound of veal sausage. I left the next day, and her rescue was scheduled for that afternoon. She did not start putting her nightgown, underwear, toiletries into her tote bag until after I had gone. It was the second time in her life that she was getting ready to go to the hospital, but this time there was no hope for a blessed event.

She lay in a white room, in a white hospital bed, and could finally give in to her exhaustion, stop pretending that it would be over in a minute, capitulate to her body. A long tube in her respiratory tract, a biopsy, X-rays, radiation. In the beginning, during the first few days, the chief surgeon still seemed interested. "When will you operate, doctor?" "Soon, soon, but first we have to fatten you up a little, make you strong enough for the operation." She had to get stronger; the surgeon was expensive, and every day in the hospital cost money; the insurance paid for most but not all of it, because she was in second-class. And when would she finally get the result of the painful biopsy she told everyone about? They had taken tissue from her lungs without an anesthetic! The result was not forthcoming. The surgeon no longer stopped by her bed, but merely gave her a quick glance, unable to withstand her pleading, hollow-eyed look. "Soon, Mrs. Kovacs; we can't operate on you in this condition."

Her husband visited every day right after work, wearing his work uniform, which irritated her. He brought her veal sausage, which she ate right away, her only sustenance for weeks. Then he sat down on the visitor's chair next to her bed. "Say something," she screamed at him, pleading with him, threatening him with her remaining strength. "I've got to go now," he said, bending over her; she pushed him away, hit him in the chest with her fist, though not hard; she didn't have much strength left. He left without saying good-bye, then went to see the surgeon and asked humbly, his conductor's cap in his hand, "Doctor, is it possible that she has cancer? In her family, you know . . ." "Out of the question," the surgeon said and turned away brusquely. The chief of the unit, a resident, and the head nurse surrounded him and left the bus conductor standing there with his cap in his hand.

The relatives came, put biscuits on the table beside her bed, brought iron tonic and flowers. "You might as well take that back with you," she said weakly. They made small talk, bedside talk, embarrassed, easily disturbed. When they were out in the hall, they took a deep breath, looked at each other meaningfully: She's not going to make it, looks like a corpse already.

Then she couldn't keep the veal sausage down, either. When I visited her for the first time the IV pole stood next to her; her arm lay next to her as if it were no longer a part of her body: a long needle in her arm, a regular drip, artificial feeding. "At least you won't have to vomit any more," I said comfortingly, and she smiled weakly. It was snowing outside; the regular dripping, the regular falling of snowflakes, the sunken white face on the pillow, the matted red hair, the pleading eyes, large, horrified—what did those eyes want from me; what was she keeping from me? I didn't know what to say; I began to cry, though I wanted to be brave. I had only half an hour until train time and I wanted to discuss something important, say something encouraging; instead I was crying. The nurse came with a bath; she lifted the emaciated body from the pillows, slipped the nightgown from her shoulders, baring a skeleton: slack, shriveled breasts, yellowish skin. I stared in horror: this couldn't be her body, this loose skin all over. I saw the look she gave the nurse, an equal mixture of gratitude and shame, the burning look of someone who is dying. "Better to die young than to have others carrying a bedpan for you," she had always said. Fear of being dependent, of being obligated to others, of having to be grateful, this fear in her eyes, this shame—I fled from this look and sat on the train crying, with two curious Federal Army soldiers eying me. I couldn't have cared less: I cried uncontrollably all the way back.

"Look at him," she shouted, her free hand pointing to her stung, silent husband. "He sits there and says nothing; for twenty years he has said nothing; for twenty years he has destroyed me with his silence; not one loving word, no love for twenty years. Look, all of you," she shouted, "there he sits, the criminal, the murderer, the bastard!" It was during visiting hours; the visitors around the other beds stared at her: She's flipped her lid, she's off her rocker. The relatives all talked at once, trying to calm her down. "Hush, Marie, you're not supposed to get excited. You should be ashamed of yourself; you aren't the only one in this room!" He said nothing. "I'm going to have him declared incompetent; he has no right to be the head of a family, no right to be a man; as soon as I get out of here I'm going to have him declared incompetent!" The nurse came in. "Calm down, now, Mrs. Kovacs, or I'll have to give you another injection; you aren't the only patient here!"

After twenty years of silence, after twenty years of asserting *We have a good marriage; we are a model family*, the façade caved in. After a whole life of reserved, suspicious civility, she had become indifferent toward everybody; they all left her cold; it was OK for all of them to hear this. She had lied enough in her life; now it was time for the truth, her truth. Her father sent his regards and asked to be excused, her sister said at her bedside: he found the trip too inconvenient. "Too inconvenient!" she shouted. "I visited him every day for six months when he was in this hospital; that was inconvenient, too! And anyway, you can tell him I'm cursing him for having beaten me for twenty years. No love. None from my mother, either, not one iota of love. I'm cursing her in her grave. And then kicked out of my home without an inheritance, with that lousy dowry! You all let me starve; and someone like that claims to be a father, such a bastard, such an epitome of cruelty. May he get it back a thousand times, a thousand times, that's what I wish him!" God knows where she got the strength for such outbursts now that she was mere skin and bones, yellowish skin stretched over cheekbones, burning eyes, and the arm with the infusion immobile on the blanket. The relatives crept out of the room, avoiding the inquisitive, titillated stares of the other patients, who knew a nurse would soon appear with a tranquilizing injection. She had stopped speaking in the cultivated, lightly accented manner of the townspeople; she cursed and shouted in the broad, guttural country dialect of her youth. Who could want to visit her, now that every visit brought on such rage?

The nurse couldn't find any more veins in her arm; even her hands were yellow and blue from the needles. "What happens when they run out of veins? Am I going to starve to death?" she asked fearfully. Three weeks of intravenous feedings by now, four weeks in the hospital. Once, during the second week, she tried to get up in order to escape the humiliation of the bedpan, but at the door she fainted. Was she in pain? Not a great deal; she was on morphine and dozed most of the time. What was she thinking about all that time, or could she still think?

The break between semesters began. I visited her every other day, looked into her yellowish face—her eyes with their black circles—and started to cry as I stroked her pierced yellow-and-green hands. "Look outside, how nice the weather is, almost springlike; this spring, when you are home again and the sun is shining . . ." "Don't talk nonsense," she interrupted me. "We have important things to discuss, and time is short. Don't cry; time is too precious, and we have lots to discuss." But we didn't discuss anything; I cried and said I would stop in a minute and cried even more audibly; she was silent. I told her hurriedly about my grades, my successes; "Yes, yes," she said, no longer feigning interest. "The surgeon doesn't even stop at my bed any more," she complained, "but that doesn't mean we won't have to pay him."

Was she still waiting for surgery, or did she know she was dying? She spoke to my father about the funeral clothes he should buy for me: a black blouse and a black pleated skirt, preferably made of a ribbed material, and she wanted to be buried in the parish cemetery at home and have a proper funeral, with all the relatives present. "I didn't have a proper wedding and I haven't had a good life; you owe me a fine funeral." And they say she had no inkling? "Don't talk like that," her husband said. "And just so you know, I'm never moving back into that shitty little house where I've worked my fingers to the bone, never back to that piece of shit!" "And where are you going to go when you leave the hospital?" She said nothing. "Her mind has been affected," he said. "Ten years of headaches—I bet she has a brain tumor; she belongs in an asylum." He dreaded the visits to the hospital, her outbursts, her hatred, seeing the blind fury of her martyrdom; he was glad when she was in a morphine doze. They mentioned divorce, but how? How? She didn't care how any more, just so she could get away from the house on the hill, from him, from life; why was it taking so long?

The first Sunday on which I would go to evening Mass in the cathedral by myself. Just before, a brief visit to the hospital. My stomach turned queasy as I walked down the halls. It was snowing outside and her room was dark, though it was only four o'clock. She lay in bed motionless, her hair fiery red, sweaty and matted; she hardly moved her lips when she greeted me. Her hands, with their yellow and green marks, were stretched out on the blanket, fleshless, the hands that once had been so firm. She had never had delicate hands, always tough farmer's hands; now they were delicate, almost transparent. A nurse came in and posted the latest blood count above her bed; I pulled it down; I remembered the averages from my biology course. "She has leukemia," I shouted at the nurse. The nurse was not authorized to discuss the matter, so I went to find the surgeon and frantically shouted the figures at him. "My dear child," he said, "leave these things to me. White blood cells indicate antibodies." "But we were taught . . ." "I have to leave now," and he was gone. I went back to her room; she had gone to sleep. I looked back once more from the door: like a corpse, I thought, frightened. *Dear God*, I prayed, kneeling in the cathedral, *I'll give you everything, anything; you can give me a life without happiness, only leave me Mama; don't let her die.* I made a pact and was determined to keep it, convinced that God would have to keep it, too. I believed in justice and in keeping one's word.

A splendid February morning. I was sitting at my new typewriter, thinking Mama will be proud of me. A strange woman came to the door. "Is this where Mrs. Marie Kovacs used to live?" "She's in the hospital; shall I give her a message?" She was terribly sorry; after all, she didn't know us, just happened to have the next house number on the opposite side of the street. The hospital had just called; Mrs. Kovacs died last night. "No," I said, "no, that's not true." I had made a pact. "No, no, no, that's not true," I said again, quite calmly, while my father began to cry: "What now, what are we going to do?"

We went to the hospital; her bed was outside the room, empty. For the first time in six weeks we were received by her doctor. He recited the phases of metastasis and threw medical jargon at us; cause of death an embolism of the lungs. No, he was sorry, but we couldn't see her; we would receive his bill in the mail. The hospital chaplain had comforting words on ice: "She received extreme unction; God's will be done; whom God loves . . ." and so on.

We bought the black blouse and skirt in the shop she had designated; we took care of the formalities: death certificate, funeral director; arrangements for her grave in her childhood village. She had her fine funeral, was laid out in the village chapel for three days, until she started to smell. We went to visit her every day in the chapel because we had not visited her enough in the hospital. For three evenings the mourning women came together in the big room; they were drinking schnapps and mumbling the rosary endlessly. Then the funeral procession from the village to the church, and the entrance of the funeral guests when the death bell rang, with the casket already waiting. The priest was on the spot; he had not known the woman, who had left home some twenty years ago. He stirred around in the native soil, stirred the funeral guests to tears: a faithful wife, a selfless mother, a caring housewife. What else? A loving daughter, a religious woman, no doubt sainted by now, devout, humble, and gentle. What did he know about her? A brave woman, a role model—what more could he say? The mourners were sobbing; he had fulfilled his purpose; forever and ever amen, nearer, my God, to Thee. Then the funeral procession from the church to the cemetery. All the relatives had come for the festivities; they threw earth into the open grave, their stomachs growling as they looked forward to the funeral feast. They were in high spirits over their beers; the men belched, then went on to schnapps, and weaved down the road toward home when the tavern closed. A fine funeral, a festival for the survivors.

People talked about the departed—not disrespectfully, of course, but that she had been a difficult person and had had a hard life, that she and Friedl weren't suited to each other; she should have had a husband who showed her who was boss, someone who would have given her a good licking now and then. She did everything for her daughter, they said, and did I still have this bug about getting a university education? Unfortunately she had taught me nothing about keeping house and now it was too late; how would the poor, abandoned orphan manage now, when she didn't even know how to wash dishes and iron men's shirts? The aunts shook their heads worriedly when I wiped my nose on my sleeve: "She's still a regular child."

Then we went home and sat down to eat, Papa doing the cooking. We were silent, two strangers. When was the last time we had had a conversation? I couldn't remember. We talked about her timidly; we approached each other timidly.

Spring came; the wreaths on her grave faded and were taken away; we planted flowers on the dug-up hill. Night after night I dreamed about the body below, seeing it decay; I lost my excess weight, and my hair came out in bunches. I became her inheritor in the black clothes she had chosen for me from her hospital bed, with the hairdo she had approved, not a hair out of place. I became pious, severe, unapproachable, suspicious, and ambitious. I was brilliant in my seminars, and bit into my pillow to muffle my cries of loneliness. My father married within the year and became happy. Finally he could let himself express his hatred, distance himself from the humiliation of twenty years; it had become a chapter in his past. I loved her and wanted to be like her, until I turned into her opposite and hated her.

For sixteen years I buried her over and over, but she always rose and followed me. She caught up with me long ago. She looks at me with the eyes of my child; she observes me from the mirror when I think I'm unobserved; I meet her in my lovers, and I run her off with her own arguments. Then she punishes me with loneliness, and I try to win her back through achievement, brilliant achievement, the epitome of achievement. I never please her. I married her and then divorced her, but she transformed herself and lay in wait for me. Her embrace, granted so hesitantly and only in exchange for perfect behavior, always turns into a grip in which I suffocate. I push her away and feel pushed away. I am her and say, *You are worth nothing*, and sink into grief for my loss, my loss of I, my loss of Thou, the loss of all the love in the world. Because there are only the two of us. She is everything that is outside, night and the sun, sleep and the rain, love and hate and every person who crosses and darkens my life, and most of all myself. She has transformed herself into me; she created me and slipped inside me; when I died sixteen years ago, when she beat me to death thirty years ago, she took my body, appropriated my ideas, usurped my feelings.

She rules and I serve her, and when I gather all my courage and offer resistance she always wins, in the name of obedience, reason, and fear.